She c... when she recognised Max Trevellyan approaching her.

Their eyes met and locked for a moment. ...hen Marietta's opened wider and wider as s... experienced astonishment and incredulity b... e brusquely recollecting herself. He was dressed in a well-worn tweed jacket and the pale sunlight fell across him, touching his thick dark hair. His silver-grey eyes were clear a... ...

F... ... dreadful moment she panicked, fe... an urgent desire to turn and run. For h... ...'s sake—she was Marietta Westwood, a... of nothing and no one. She almost did tu... d run, but the fierce resolve with which sh... d been born and which had developed ins... her since she was a child kept her ro... to the spot.

'It's ...ou,' she said frostily, on a calmer no...e—...hough her heart, for some bewildering reaso... was beating quickly.

AUTHOR NOTE

I loved writing WHEN MARRYING A DUKE..., detailing the trials and tribulations of my heroine, creating a larger than life hero and the woman who loves him. It is a love story, and the hard and fast rule of a romance writer—which is carved in stone—is that there must be a happy ending.

Reading is a tremendous joy to me—I read anything from historical romance and family sagas to thrillers and fantasy. I love to absorb myself in the stories, and feel a real sense of discovery with each new book. Foreign shores rarely feature in any of my books, so using Hong Kong as the location in the opening chapters of WHEN MARRYING A DUKE… was an unlikely setting for me to choose. I enjoyed researching this fascinating island.

While the setting of Hong Kong and the issues of the time are real, my characters are entirely fictitious.

WHEN MARRYING
A DUKE...

Helen Dickson

First published in Great Britain 2012
by Mills & Boon, an imprint of Harlequin (UK) Limited.
Harlequin (UK) Limited, Eton House, 18-24 Paradise Road,
Richmond, Surrey TW9 1SR

© Helen Dickson 2012

ISBN: 978 0 263 89272 7

Harlequin (UK) policy is to use papers that are natural, renewable and recyclable products and made from wood grown in sustainable forests. The logging and manufacturing process conform to the legal environmental regulations of the country of origin.

Printed and bound in Spain
by Blackprint CPI, Barcelona

Helen Dickson was born and lives in South Yorkshire, with her retired farm manager husband. Having moved out of the busy farmhouse where she raised their two sons, she has more time to indulge in her favourite pastimes. She enjoys being outdoors, travelling, reading and music. An incurable romantic, she writes for pleasure. It was a love of history that drove her to writing historical fiction.

Previous novels by Helen Dickson:

THE DEFIANT DEBUTANTE
ROGUE'S WIDOW, GENTLEMAN'S WIFE
TRAITOR OR TEMPTRESS
WICKED PLEASURES
  (part of *Christmas By Candlelight*)
A SCOUNDREL OF CONSEQUENCE
FORBIDDEN LORD
SCANDALOUS SECRET, DEFIANT BRIDE
FROM GOVERNESS TO SOCIETY BRIDE
MISTRESS BELOW DECK
THE BRIDE WORE SCANDAL
DESTITUTE ON HIS DOORSTEP
SEDUCING MISS LOCKWOOD
MARRYING MISS MONKTON
BEAUTY IN BREECHES
MISS CAMERON'S FALL FROM GRACE
THE HOUSEMAID'S SCANDALOUS SECRET*

*Castonbury Park Regency mini-series

And in Mills & Boon® Historical *Undone!* eBooks:

ONE RECKLESS NIGHT

Prologue

Waking shortly after midnight and unable to go back to sleep, thinking a glass of milk might help to settle her, Marietta padded from her room. Yang Ling, her Chinese nurse, was asleep in a nearby bedroom, dreaming of the Chinese New Year that was upon them, and the visit she would make to her family to wish them well and good fortune in the year to come.

The night was moonless, a black quilt shrouding the hills of Hong Kong, but by the nuances and textures of the dark the girl was drawn towards the stairs. She moved quietly so as not to wake her parents, for she was ever conscious that her mother needed her rest. Ever since she had miscarried yet another child— three in total—her parents had slept in separate rooms, so Marietta was surprised to hear muffled voices coming from her mother's bedroom. Something had changed. Marietta sensed it and shivered. Concerned because her mother was sobbing, thinking she might be ill, she paused, straining her ears to listen.

'Leave me be, Monty,' she wept. 'You promised me there would be no more children.'

'Don't deny me, Amelia,' her father's pleading voice said. 'Not now—not again. I can't stand it.'

'No, Monty. Don't ask me to go through it again. When our last baby was born dead you gave me your word…that you wouldn't…'

Her mother's frantic pleas must have fallen on deaf ears because, apart from the creaking of the bed, there was silence. There was no one to see the swift shadow dart along the landing, the agile shape that fled silently back to her room. Scrambling into bed, Marietta pulled the covers up over her head to shut out any sounds she might hear. Confused by what she had heard and at nine years old still too innocent to understand what went on between a husband and his wife—only that whatever it was they did resulted in pain and suffering for her mother and another dead baby—afraid for her mother and desperately sorry for her father, she wept.

* * *

At breakfast the following morning, Monty Westwood experienced a sudden feeling of unease as his eyes met the steady gold-tinted green eyes of his young daughter sitting as still as a statue across from him. For one discomfiting moment it seemed that she was staring into the very heart of him, noting his faults and failings and measuring his guilt. Shifting uncomfortably in his seat, he reached for some toast, glancing down to spread it with butter. But he could not control the flush that rose to his cheeks, nor the slight trembling of the hand holding the knife. He was like a man caught red-handed in a felonious act.

Monty adored his daughter. She was vibrant and spirited, but now her eyes had a cold and knowing glint as she stared steadily back at him. She was accusing him without opening her mouth. She knew he had spent the night in her mama's bed. She knew, even at her age, what might follow as a consequence of his lust for his wife—for any woman who was willing to accommodate him.

Five months after that night and pregnant yet again, Marietta's mother went into labour. Everyone was too occupied to notice Marietta peering tentatively round the partly open door of her mother's room. What she saw caused her heart to sink and her stomach to convulse. The bed was soaked with a quantity of blood around her mother's body. Marietta knew she was dead. She was motionless, her face ashen, her eyes fixed for ever in a state of death.

Marietta took a backward step, her face blanching, her hand to her mouth, faltering so that she almost tripped over her own feet. Then she turned and fled the scene. Her mind had closed up, shutting itself against the sight of her mother. Her face was as blank as an unwritten page, all emotion having been driven deep within her, where it would fester for a long time to come.

Chapter One

With the sun shining out of a sky as blue as blue could be, a small, isolated knot of boisterous young people gathered to enjoy themselves at the horse racing at Happy Valley on the island of Hong Kong, which was a major trading post of the British empire. They were the sons and daughters of businessmen, merchants and bankers, all enjoying the freedom and entertainments to be had on this tiny island, the Sovereign British Territory off the Chinese coast populated by Westerners and Chinese immigrants.

'I honestly swear that if I have to sit and talk to those frumpish old tabbies I shall die of boredom,' Marietta declared sharply, observing the group of stiff-backed ladies all sporting a colourful array of flowered and feathered hats and bonnets on their coiffed heads seated on a veranda overlooking the racecourse. Young married women who no longer mixed with their unmarried friends, being excluded from the excitement and demure flirtation, were seated in chairs beneath the shade of the trees. 'Promise me, Oliver, that if such a thing should occur, you will have the goodness to rescue me.' Smoothing her skirts, she sighed in a way that displayed a very fetching dimple. 'I beg of you if you value our friendship.'

Glancing down into Marietta's wide olive-green eyes flecked with golden lights, Oliver Schofield would have forfeited both his feet to do her bidding. 'I give you my word,' he replied adoringly. 'You know perfectly well I would do anything you asked me to do, Marietta.'

Oliver Schofield was a good-looking young man, just one of several who hung around the group of pretty girls. They were like a cloud of bright butterflies beneath light and colourful parasols. Their fashionable wide skirts of palest pink, light-blue, lemon and creamy white, pleated and flounced in delicate tulle and chiffon and muslin, swung and swayed and dipped to reveal their shoes and the lower part of their white stockinged legs.

With a gay and uncritical nature, Marietta Westwood outshone all the other girls and was the most sought after among these bright young things. Having spent a great deal of her time with her father and allowed to do very much as she pleased, at seventeen she possessed an active mind, a lively wit and an amazing tendency to think for herself.

As a child, as soon as she had stepped off the ship she had been enchanted with the tiny island of Hong Kong. She loved life in the colony—the picnics, regattas and parties, where she waltzed and polkaed the night away. She was just one of a civilised society, if one could ignore the heat and humidity of the South China seas and the suffocating stuffiness of the Europeans. Sporting their beards and whiskers and top hats and waistcoats and woollen suits as if they were in London, they would never dream of succumbing to the natural elements of the colony—unlike her father, who favoured wide-brimmed hats and cool linen suits, which gave him a crumpled air.

Marietta moved towards Oliver with the lightness of step of a fawn. She was naturally cautious, like one who suspects there is a delightful danger ahead, but is prepared nevertheless to enjoy it. She smiled at him beautifully.

'I know I can rely on you, Oliver—always the gallant one and so sweet, that's what you are.' Taking his arm, she drew him to one side, leaning forwards so that only he could hear what she said. 'You haven't forgotten our outing tomorrow, have you? You said you would take me with you to the native quarter.'

His face fell. 'No, Marietta, I can't.'

'But you promised!'

'I've changed my mind.'

Her lips forming a petulant pout, Marietta gave an indignant toss of her head. 'Then I'll never speak to you again. I swear I won't.'

'It's not that I don't wish to take you with me,' Oliver said, goaded, 'but the native quarter is not a fit place for a young English girl to visit. It's not safe. Besides, your father would never consent to it.'

'He won't be here. He's leaving for Kowloon tonight and won't be back until the day after tomorrow. Besides, what possible harm can come to me in your company?' she added mischievously.

Oliver shrugged. 'I warn you, Marietta, it can be awfully dull. There can be little of interest for you there.'

Marietta lifted her chin. 'I will be the judge of that. But since you seem to be averse to my company, I shall not trouble you nor hold you to your promise. Perhaps some other gentleman will be more willing to accompany me instead.'

'Come, Marietta, you need not take that attitude with me,' Oliver said in a more conciliatory manner. 'The fact is you misunderstand my reluctance to take you with me.' He hesitated, then went on in a low voice, 'I would not wish it to reach your father's ears that I have taken his daughter to purchase opium supplies—on behalf of a friend of mine, you understand, who is unable to go himself. I have the address of a merchant and I plan to visit him tomorrow.'

She stared at him. It all seemed so terribly exciting. 'Are you afraid you can't trust me? Is that why you won't take me? I promise I will be all discretion if that's what worries you.'

Oliver shrugged. 'I see I am outwitted and shall have to give in to your wishes. But you must promise not to tell anyone, Marietta.'

With a sense of adventure and eager to explore Hong Kong's China Town, Marietta's eagerness increased. 'Of course you may trust me,' she exclaimed. 'Though you really need not fear my father's disapproval, for he has told me himself that he has the greatest faith in opium as a medicinal cure for everything from the most serious illness to toothache. I do know some people abuse it, but one has to be sensible about these things. I am already a convert to it since it was opium that Yang Ling gave me in the posset to cure a fever I had last month.'

Privately Oliver doubted if Marietta's father would approve of the use he planned to make for the drug, but he wouldn't express his doubts to Marietta. He wished he'd been firmer with his refusal to take her, but when Marietta turned her big, dark green eyes on him, resolutions were apt to vanish. He was happy enough to have her smiling at him again and told her he hadn't doubted her for a moment. Some people had prejudices and misconceptions about opium smoking, but since she wasn't one of these kill-joys, he would be happy to take her to the native quarter.

Thanking him prettily and arranging to meet him the following morning, Marietta turned her attention to Julian Fielding, who was holding the reins of Oliver's horse and seated atop his own. Suddenly she had what she considered to be a brilliant idea to spark up the afternoon. Spinning on her heel, she sprinted towards Oliver's horse and with a fluency that caught the eye, she hoisted herself up into the saddle, her legs astride the huge gelding.

Emma, a petite brunette and Marietta's best

friend, in a flurry of pink taffeta and bouncing ringlets, moved to stand beside Oliver. 'Oh dear! Whatever do you think Marietta is planning to do now?' she enquired, knowing that whatever it was, her friend was about to make a freak of herself cavorting on the back of Oliver's horse.

Oliver sighed, resigned as always to Marietta's reckless escapades. 'She will do whatever she wants to do—which is what she always does, Emma.'

'Come along, Julian,' Marietta urged with a shout of laughter, hearing the smattering of giggles as the group looked on and encouraged by it. 'Let's you and me have a little race of our own. To that post at the end of the green and back—and I bet I win.'

With a gentle kick at the horse's flanks with her heels and firing an amused glance over her shoulder at her friends, while feeling the force of the ancient ladies' unwavering scandalised cold stares, their faces taut with disapproval on the veranda, with her skirts ballooning behind her she was off, with Julian, always game for anything, tearing after her.

Their horses' hooves thundered over the hard green turf. All the way to the post they were neck and neck, and not until they turned for home did Marietta pull ahead, finishing a length ahead of Julian. Unfortunately her horse was going so fast she had to pull up sharply, causing the animal to stumble on a raised hillock and tossing her over its head. After flying through the air, in a tangle of flounces and frills and furbelows as her skirts were upflung, she landed on the ground. Unhurt and laughing happily despite the loss of her dignity—for she was the victor after all—she scrambled to her feet.

'Dear God in heaven,' she heard someone exclaim in a furious voice, his temper roused, not at all pleased at being almost knocked off his feet. 'Why don't you look where you're going, you stupid girl? You might have caused a serious accident.'

Marietta hadn't seen him at first. She was too busy trying to regain her balance, but she did feel a crackle in the air and perceived the unnatural silence when it fell among her chirruping friends. As she stood, with her nerves jangling like wind chimes in a typhoon, her heart began to beat unaccountably faster when she found herself confronted by the formidable Lord Trevellyan and his beautiful wife, Nadine, who had been forced to halt when she tumbled right in front of them.

Marietta was for once speechless. He was surely the finest man that ever was. Meeting his silver-grey eyes, she felt herself instantly redden with pleasure.

'What the hell do you think you are doing?' Lord Trevellyan demanded, his voice about as friendly as cold steel, not quite done with chastising her.

The icy tone of his voice checked any wayward thoughts Marietta might have concerning Lord Trevellyan. Having halted in a small puddle left over from the previous day's rain, she saw that Oliver's horse had splashed mud on to Lord Trevellyan's shiny black shoes.

'Oh dear!' she put in hastily. Able to see the funny side of the incident, she tried to stifle her mirth, but on seeing the look of unconcealed displeasure on Lord Trevellyan's face as he looked down at his shoes, her mirth threatened to erupt into hilarity. 'It really was an accident,' she began defensively, 'but I fear I've made rather a mess of your shoes...'

Lord Trevellyan's voice stopped her in midsentence. 'Never mind my shoes. My advice to you, Miss Westwood, is that you learn to ride a horse of that size before getting on to its back.'

Lord Trevellyan was at his most forbidding following yet another bitter altercation with his beautiful wife. The mocking smile on his lips did nothing to make Marietta feel better, although, had she but known, it was himself he was mocking, for Miss Westwood was renowned for her outrageous antics and having witnessed her unblushing display of riding a horse that would have horrified every strait-laced lady who'd borne witness, he grudgingly conceded that she was a refreshing sight in the circumstances.

From a distance he had watched her galloping at breakneck pace with the daredevil recklessness of youth. With her face pressed close to the horse's mane, a jubilation, there was a simplicity in the way she rode, as if she were one with her mount, confident, trusting and elated. At a glance she was one of the most fearless, skilled riders he'd ever seen mounted—man or woman—and he would love to see her over jumps. Her legs had been displayed to almost immoral advantage by the lifting of her skirts as she had ridden the gelding, golden ribbons around her slender waist that would require no subterfuge to make it appear smaller, flying jauntily behind her. Not until she was almost on top of him had she hauled the horse to a smart stop, and at the same time the horse had tossed her over his head.

Marietta looked at him with eyes that seemed to change through all the shades of green beneath the fringe of long, sooty lashes. Her hair—piles of shining rich mahogany-brown hair—had come loose of its pins during her reckless ride to beat her opponent. Drawing herself up, she set her bonnet at a ridiculous angle atop curls as undisciplined as she was, the ribbon streamers dancing this way and that. Immediately she launched into an apology.

Unimpressed, Max listened to her. The fact that this dratted girl had disrupted his day annoyed him intensely. It was not the first time they had met. He had noticed her vaguely at several events. All the other girls of her age were demure and for the most part kept their eyes cast down, whereas Miss Westwood always stared directly at those she was speaking to, looking about her with a keen and lively interest, her eyes bright with expectancy.

She showed none of the restraint impressed into young girls of good family. It would seem that when Miss Westwood conjured up some new escapade, she set about it with the determination and tactical brilliance of a female Napoleon Bonaparte. The ladies of the island heaped the blame for her undisciplined behaviour on Monty Westwood, of course, for allowing his daughter too much freedom to do as she liked. Max was apt to agree with them.

Based on that sweet pleading look she was giving him, she was apparently hoping he'd be as stupidly susceptible to her appeal as everyone else. Instead, Lord Trevellyan raked her with an insultingly condescending glance from the top of her gloriously tousled hair to the tips of her feet.

'Of all the brazen, outrageous stunts I have ever seen, yours, Miss Westwood, beats the lot. Didn't anyone ever teach you how to behave?' he asked contemptuously. He saw her flinch, but he went on, his voice penetrating. 'I believe you have been in the colony long enough to know its protocol and that young ladies do not go around flaunting themselves as you have just done. Have you lost all sense of propriety?'

Marietta hesitated. Thinking he would accept her explanation ceased to be tenable. She knew that Lord Trevellyan was a man who was used to giving orders, but she too had learned something, which was not to look abashed when she felt it. Her mirth having disappeared, she threw back her shoulders, lifted her head and met his eyes with a fiercely direct stare, unafraid and absolutely uncowed, the action telling him quite clearly that she was neither sorry nor ashamed of her behaviour.

'I was not flaunting myself, Lord Trevellyan. I was doing no wrong. I took a tumble, that is all.'

'And almost knocked my wife and myself to the ground in the process.'

'I have said I am sorry, I can do no more than that.' She looked into his wife's exquisite face. 'Lady Trevellyan, may I offer my sincere apologies for my clumsiness and for speaking so impulsively?'

'Yes, you may and apology accepted. Everyone who rides comes off at some time—why, even my husband has been known to take the odd tumble,' Nadine said, casting a cynical eye at the darkly scowling face of her husband before looking again at Marietta. 'You're not injured, I hope?'

'No—thank you for asking,' Marietta replied, her lips curving into a bright smile. 'I bounce pretty well.'

'Next time be sure to keep hold of the reins,' Lord Trevellyan snapped.

Marietta's smiled vanished. 'Can I help it if the horse was fresh and I could not hold him?' she countered.

Lord Trevellyan's brows snapped together

over dangerously irritable eyes as he stared down at the rebellious girl. 'You've a sharp tongue, Miss Westwood,' he said, his voice silky, but his eyes narrowed in the menacing fashion over which he appeared to have no control, 'and you are also an impertinent, spoilt, undisciplined child. Your father would have done us all a service—including yourself—if he'd turned you over his knee when you were of an age for him to do so.'

Stung, Marietta fumed, her green eyes almost black with temper. 'And by the tone of your voice, my lord, I imagine that you would gain immense pleasure in delivering the punishment yourself.'

'What a delightful idea,' he replied grimly.

Lord Trevellyan's rebuke was so unexpected, so public, so intense as to be offensive. He didn't even have the good manners to help her to her feet or enquire if she was hurt, unlike his wife. Marietta's face went scarlet and her precarious control snapped. 'How dare you say that to me? Is this how you talk when you are bullying the people you do business with?' She was tempted to include his long-suffering wife, but thought she'd better not.

Glancing at the blonde-haired woman by his side, not for the first time she thought how enchanting she was. She was so beautiful Marietta always found it difficult to tear her gaze from her. Dressed in the height of fashion, she had a slender body and the magnetism of a woman who is confident of her own beauty without being obsessed by it. Her poise was to be admired as she stood serenely by her husband's side. Acutely aware of her own dishevelled appearance, Marietta pushed her hair back from her face and brushed the dust from her skirt. She returned her gaze to Lord Trevellyan, her anger not appeased.

'And how dare you call me a spoilt child?' she retorted indignantly. 'As well you know, I am the daughter of a gentleman of some note on the island and you should treat me with more respect.'

Lord Trevellyan scowled gravely, though Marietta suspected him of a strong desire to laugh at her, to mock her.

'Respect is something that must be earned, Miss Westwood, and from what I have just witnessed, you have a long way to go before you can do so.'

In his mind this could also be applied to her father, for there were many on the island who would dispute his daughter's use of the word gentleman where Monty Westwood was concerned. It would never occur to her that her father and his partner were two of several traders in the colony whose shady endeavours were of professional interest. But he would not sully the sensitive ears of a seventeen-year-old girl with the disgusting truth about her adored father's illicit dealings in the opium trade.

The Chinese had banned opium from its territories, but it was smuggled into Hong Kong from India covertly, increasing the addiction of the Chinese to the drug. He was convinced that Miss Westwood's knowledge about the drug went no further than it being a very effective medicine. And, he thought, when he considered the misery it caused, long may she continue to do so.

'You don't know me, Lord Trevellyan, so you have no right to say that. And I have apologised to you—and your wife—which you would have heard had you taken the wool out of your ears.'

Max wasn't accustomed to being answered back and was taken aback at her remark. One dark brow lifted over an amused silver-grey eye, before he checked himself and his lips curled scornfully across his even white teeth. 'It sounded more like an excuse than an apology to me,' he replied crisply, wondering what the hell he was doing arguing with her. Hearing the sound of youthful laughter, he glanced beyond her, noting the boisterousness of her group. 'It's certainly a wayward bunch you are with.'

'These are my friends, actually,' Marietta snapped defensively.

'I think everybody would be obliged if they'd restrain their enthusiasm,' he remarked, glowering beneath ferociously dipping eyebrows.

'Why? We are just having some perfectly harmless fun.' Snatching her bonnet off her head, she assumed an appearance of remote indifference as she turned her back on Lord Trevellyan and his wife and haughtily flounced back to her friends.

'I say, Marietta!' Oliver remarked, astounded and full of admiration for the way she had stood up to the formidable Lord Trevellyan. 'You gave him what for.'

'He deserved it,' she remarked haughtily. 'The man is arrogant, high-handed and quite despicable.' Every word she uttered she believed was true, but if so, why was she drowning in an ocean of mortification? Why couldn't she have walked away instead of arguing with Lord Trevellyan, which was what any well brought-up, self-respecting young lady would have done.

Marietta had first seen Lord Trevellyan at a musical tea party being held at a prominent merchant's house. Her eyes had been caught by the handsome man who was a stranger in their midst. In contrast to the bored languor of other gentlemen present, he moved with an easy grace that expressed confidence, which sat on him lightly but with a strength of steel. His manner was authoritative, his tall frame positively radiating raw power and the kind of unleashed sensuality her best friend Emma was always talking about.

His charm was evident in his lazy white smile and there was an aura about him of danger and excitement that stirred her young and impressionable heart. Marietta thought it was an aura that women would find exciting and which would add tremendously to his attraction—indeed, every woman present seemed to be aware of his presence. But he appeared not to notice the smiles showered on him. His eyes looked cool and restless, his expression restrained and guarded. It was as if he were fed up with the whole occasion, which made Marietta suspect that he would very much like to be somewhere else.

As she'd continued to look at him she'd only become more aware of him as a man. She was motionless. There seemed to be a warmth, a hidden fervour of feeling, as if her whole being had been stirred and some change were taking place in its very depths. All at once she wanted desperately to make this fine gentleman notice her, to dazzle him with her wit and brilliance, while he had probably seen her merely as some silly schoolgirl.

Her eyes had continued to follow him until, unable to stand the suspense of not knowing who he was any longer, she asked her father.

'Who is that man, Papa—the tall man with the black hair? I can't say that I've seen him before.'

'That—Oh! Max Trevellyan—Lord Trevellyan. He's also a member of the British aristocracy—a duke, no less, but when he's in Hong Kong he prefers to leave his title at home in England. That's his wife, Nadine, a nice young woman and very beautiful, as you can see.'

'Wife? Oh, I see.' And Marietta did see. She'd been swamped with disappointment. Lady Trevellyan was perhaps the loveliest woman she had ever seen as she'd watched her walk across the room to her husband's side. Her hair was blonde, her face exquisite, and she was poised, her slender figure swaying beneath the silk and lace of her dress when she moved. When she looked at her husband her lips were smiling, her eyes half-closed. Marietta recog-

nised something in the charm of her attitude
that caused a strange disquiet to fall on her.

After that occasion, even though her eyes
sought Lord Trevellyan out, she always remained at a distance. Once they were introduced, but he took no more notice of her than
he would any seventeen-year-old girl.

Marietta's home was a substantial mansion
high up on the Peak, which, overlooking the
busy harbour and Kowloon, attracted prominent European residents because of its temper-
ate climate compared to the subtropical heat in
the rest of Hong Kong.

She had been born in England. Her father
had come to Hong Kong after the Charter Act
had opened the China trade to independent en-
terprise. Before that, taking advantage of the
fashion craze for Kashmir shawls, which were a
prized possession for any woman who could afford to buy them, and aware of the commercial
opportunity, he'd made his fortune importing
shiploads from India to Europe and America.
Before long he was trading in other commodities from India—sumptuous goods, luxurious
and exotic. It was in India that he'd met Teddy
and they'd formed a partnership.

Arriving at the house, Marietta encountered

Teddy on the veranda—the debonair Teddy Longford, a lady's man who oozed charm and flattery. He was sitting in a bamboo chair with a cigar in one hand and a brandy in the other, his long legs stretched out in front of him. On seeing her he smiled a welcome.

'Ah, here you are. Your father was wondering where you'd got to. I feel I must warn you that he's not in the best of moods, having heard of your escapade at Happy Valley.'

'Oh dear,' Marietta said ruefully. 'I was hoping he wouldn't have found out about it. I thought I'd see you there.'

'Not today. I had other fish to fry.' A warm gleam lit up his brown eyes.

Marietta laughed, giving him a knowing look. 'You're looking very pleased with yourself, Teddy. Do I know the lady?' she said teasingly.

He lifted a dark, winged brow, his lips twitching with humour. 'I very much doubt it—but she's a looker all right.' Taking a long draw on his cigar, he squinted at her through the smoke. 'Are you looking forward to the New Year celebrations?' he asked, referring to the forthcoming event to be held at Government House.

'Very much. What about you, Teddy? Will you be there?'

'Naturally. Your father and I have a very important lady to escort.'

'Then how could I resist two such handsome escorts?' Marietta laughed, dancing off to placate her father.

Lord Trevellyan's rebuke for her inappropriate behaviour had done nothing but inflame Marietta's smouldering resentment towards him, but when confronted by her father's state of agitation over her escapade, she felt a deep remorse for causing him such anxiety. Her first idea of slipping to her room to change her clothes was instantly discarded when she saw how pale he was.

Upright and decisive, Monty Westwood was a tall man with thinning fair hair and mutton-chop whiskers. His olive-green eyes were flecked with gold—a feature his daughter had inherited. He was a handsome man, though his flesh wasn't as firm as it had once been, but he'd lost none of his ability to charm the ladies, although of late Marietta had noticed he'd lost weight and his tan had become an unhealthy yellow.

For a long time now Marietta had begun to suspect he wasn't well—although if he wasn't he would never talk to her about it. He did not burden his daughter with his own worries, for there were some things he might have talked about, but didn't. His eyes held a faraway look and his pupils were often dilated. Of course he drank too much, but then everyone in Hong Kong drank too much and many suffered from damaged livers.

Marietta loved her father passionately. He was the only person in the world she did love— the only person she had loved since the death of her mother.

'Please don't worry about me, Papa. Here I am, safe and sound. I am sorry to have caused a fuss and I hope you are not too cross with me. I'm sorry. I know my behaviour doesn't reflect well on you.'

Relief at seeing his daughter unharmed following her tumble caused the blood to return to Monty's cheeks and he gave rein to his feelings. 'You naughty child, Marietta! What have you been doing? Ever since Mrs Schofield called I have been so anxious.'

Marietta grimaced. 'Oliver's mother! I might have known she would seek you out to inform you of my latest misdemeanour. She hates it that Oliver and I are such good friends.'

Having stopped off at his club for a reviving

drink after extensive negotiations with business associates at his office, which had taken up most of the day, Monty had arrived home to find Mrs Schofield—a tiresome busybody who minded everyone's business but her own—waiting in the hall to relate his daughter's latest escapade. She had gone on to list all of Marietta's shortcomings and insisted that he kept stricter control on her at all times.

It was one of those occasions when Monty felt a twinge of guilt over not having remarried, because it meant that Marietta had been left to the care of her amah, Yang Ling. Yang Ling was like all Chinese, industrious and cheerful, and Marietta was extremely fond of her. She acted as her companion and personal maid and accompanied his fun-loving daughter everywhere.

'I thought you must have been injured,' he went on. 'As for Julian Fielding—it is singularly tiresome of him to cause so much trouble. I shall speak to his parents. He should not have ridden off with you like that. It was totally irresponsible—of you both,' he added as an afterthought.

'Julian isn't to blame. It isn't his fault,' Marietta said defensively. 'It was my idea to race. I took a tumble on Oliver's mount, that is all. I didn't mean to make a scene and it was nothing serious. Unfortunately I happened to land at Lord Trevellyan's feet and he was none too pleased.'

Monty glanced at her sharply, his interest peaked. Lord Trevellyan never failed to make a big impression on those he came into contact with. He had a clever financial brain and was possessed of one of the finest business minds he knew. As with everything in his life his business affairs were conducted like a well-oiled machine. Those he dealt with were in awe of him, regarding this cold, frighteningly unapproachable deity whom, because of his wealth and the benefits of being associated with such a clever, powerful man, they strove desperately to please.

'So you have spoken to the formidable Lord Trevellyan.'

'Yes—although what he had to say wasn't at all pleasing. What does he do? Is he very rich?'

'I've made a lot of money, Marietta—I won't go into the intricacies of it because you wouldn't understand—but the days of the small shipping businesses are over. This time belongs to financial wizards with money, power and authority—men like Lord Trevellyan with grand ambitions. It's about economics and insurance

and industrial development. What did he say
to you?'

'He gave me a dressing down for muddying
his shoes.'

'Then I can only assume that coming from
Lord Trevellyan it was well deserved.'

'I suppose it was. I tried to apologise. His
wife was more forgiving, though. How does she
put up with him? She has my sympathy. She's
very lovely, isn't she, Papa?'

'Yes, she is. But—things aren't always what
they appear to be on the surface.'

Marietta looked at him with sudden interest.
'Why, what do you mean?'

'Never mind,' he said airily.

She didn't ask him to explain, but it left her
wondering.

Arriving at Marietta's house the following morning, Oliver didn't recognise the girl
dressed in loose black trousers and a long-
sleeved, green-and-yellow-patterned tunic,
round-toed slippers and one thick pigtail hanging down her back waiting at the gate. She had
pencilled thin kohl lines around her eyes to alter
their shape. It took him a moment to realise it
was Marietta, waiting for him to take her to the
native quarter. He was about to walk past her

and, seeing his intent, she broke out into peals of laughter. Failing to see what was so entertaining, Oliver turned and looked at her stiffly.

'I had you there, Oliver. Did you not know me?'

'Marietta!' Oliver was deeply shocked. 'Why are you dressed like that? And whose clothes are they?'

'I've borrowed them from Yang Ling. You said yourself that the native quarter is not a fit place for an English girl to visit, which is why I've adopted this garb. It's going to be such fun. No one will recognise me.'

'Yang Ling? You have told Yang Ling?' He sincerely hoped she hadn't.

'Of course not,' Marietta laughed. 'I wouldn't dare. She is convinced that Europeans lose face by visiting the native quarter and she would have a fit if she were to find out. Now come along! We are wasting time and if we loiter any longer someone may see us and ask questions.'

Oliver wasn't enthusiastic about taking Marietta in disguise to the native quarter, but saw no way of making this plain to her without throwing her into a tantrum which would draw unwelcome attention to them. So without another word, they set off on his proposed tour in a light carriage driven by a coolie and drawn by a skinny horse, instead of the more common mode of transport of sedan chairs, which were carried up and down the steep roads of the island. Neither the grilling heat, which beat down on her little flat hat with relentless force, nor Oliver's attempts to tell her how she should behave when they reached the native quarter and that she must remain silent could dim her enthusiasm.

Their conveyance made good speed, eventually entering the seedy area of China Town, an area where not many respectable Westerners ventured. The streets were lined with shabby establishments with palm-leaf walls and thatched roofs. Bamboo curtains hung in doorways and Chinese writing was on boards dangling above buildings. The streets were narrow, steep and densely packed. The strong smell of hot oil mingled with spice, garlic and incense wafted above the general odours of dirt and decay. Washing was draped like bunting across the streets and heavily laden donkeys trundled along while barefoot children played.

At last the vehicle stopped in front of a large framed house with an open veranda. Marietta followed Oliver inside. The air was oppressive. Several men were taking their ease—Chinese and European—stretched out or sitting cross-legged on heaps of cushions with long pipes before them. The room into which they entered was dimly lit. Marietta's eyes opened wide when from behind a beaded curtain two girls glided forwards. One had blue-black hair that was drawn back from a face that was pearl-like in its perfection and colour, with large slanting eyes. Her gown of crimson silk clung to her curves. The other girl was almost identical except that she was dressed in yellow. They stood in front of Oliver like dolls. They smiled with perfect teeth between plump red lips.

'Who are they?' Marietta whispered, never having seen Chinese women who looked like these.

'The entertainment,' Oliver replied, leaving it at that, not wishing to shock Marietta's sensibilities by telling her the nature of the entertainment they performed.

Looking around the room lit by oil lamps, Marietta saw there were more girls, some so scantily clad as to be indecent. The crimson-clad woman sidled up to Oliver.

'You likee me?' she said, playing coy.

'Yes, but not now.'

A portly middle-aged Chinese man with long moustaches drooping on either side of his small, fleshy mouth seemed to appear from nowhere, his hands tucked into his sleeves. He bowed respectfully.

'May I present Tiger Lily and Jasmine. They are offering you their services with the magic of their exquisite bodies. They are skilful and will soothe your aches in some infinitesimal degree, but if their clumsiness is offensive, you should beat them for their correction and your pleasure.'

'No,' Oliver said. 'I have not come for the girls, Mr Chang.'

Mr Chang accepted this and clapping his hands sharply, the girls melted into the background. He paid small interest to Marietta, who had her eyes cast down. Facing Oliver, he bowed in greeting while Marietta felt inordinately pleased with herself when his eyes passed over her without suspicion.

'It is good to see you again, Mr Schofield,' he said in silky tones as well as perfect English. 'Will you honour me by accepting refreshment?'

'I should be glad to, Mr Chang.' Turning to Marietta, he said in quiet but firm tones, 'Wait for me in the carriage. I'll just be a few moments, but on no account wander off.'

Resentful at being so casually dismissed, but knowing better than to argue, Marietta returned to the carriage, expelling a sigh of exasperation on seeing the driver with his head bowed taking a nap. As time passed and Oliver did not return she became annoyed. The shadows were lengthening and the native quarter was beginning to wake from its afternoon torpor. Deciding she'd had enough, she stood up, then climbed down from the carriage and went back into the building to look for Oliver.

Like a moth blundering in the lamplight she stumbled over the cushions littering the floor. Eventually she saw Oliver. She was disappointed to find he had given in to the temptation to sample the wares. He was reclining on a pile of cushions with a pipe in his mouth, sucking in the vapour from a bowl held over the flame of a lamp, holding it in as long as possible, then slowly letting it out through his mouth. He was already on the blessed edges of oblivion, the strong narcotic having dulled his senses to forgetfulness and Marietta's presence.

Angry that he could be so irresponsible, forgetful of her disguise, before he could take another pull from the pipe she snatched it from him and, placing her hands on his shoulders, shook him hard.

'Oliver, wake up. Please pull yourself together.'

When he opened his eyes they were unfocused, his pupils just pinpricks in the centres of his irises.

'Do not be alarmed.' Mr Chang suddenly appeared silently behind her. 'Your companion will wake soon and be none the worse for smoking the pipe.' Turning his glittering black eyes on Marietta, he saw her more clearly. He opened his slit eyes a fraction wider. 'Ah, you are English missee.'

'Yes, I am English missee,' she repeated crossly.

He moved closer and brushed her cheek. 'And with skin like a peach. A treasure beyond price. You stay here, English missee. There are many who would pay handsomely for your company.'

Not so naïve that she didn't know what he implied, she gasped. 'How dare you? Despite what I look like, I am a respectable English girl and my father counts for something on the island. Be good enough to wake Mr Schofield and we will leave.'

Ignoring her, Mr Chang took her arm. 'Not so hasty now, English missee.'

Beginning to get alarmed and feeling a sudden chill when she became aware of furtive figures lurking in the shadows, Marietta shook her arm free. 'Do not touch me. I warn you that the British Consul knows of our whereabouts and you will be in serious trouble if you try to keep me here.' Looking at Oliver, she saw him stir. 'Oliver, wake up,' she said sharply. 'You must take me home at once.'

Seeming to remember where he was, Oliver thrust the pipe away. Shaking his head, he staggered to his feet, struggling to fight the opium fumes that fogged his brain. 'Marietta! Oh God—forgive me—I quite forgot.'

'Clearly.' She raised a knowing eyebrow. 'What a complete idiot I have been. I thought you had come to buy the drug for an acquaintance when all the time you wanted it for yourself.'

Swaying slightly, Oliver regarded her for a moment with a closed expression, then leaned in with a confidential whisper. 'There you have me, Marietta. I will confess that I am here to purchase the narcotic for my own use. As you have witnessed yourself, I am rather fond of the odd pipe. It's quite common, you know.'

'I don't dispute that, but how could you, Oliver?' Marietta found the idea of smoking opium frightening. Her imagination was already vibrant. She was aware of what happened to people who took mind-altering substances, that it ruled its addicts with its weapons of need and distrust. Once in its grip, there was no escape. She sincerely hoped that, where Oliver was concerned, his indulgence in this particular vice was a passing phase. 'Now pull yourself together for I think there is some villainy afoot. I think your Mr Chang wants to keep me here.'

Taking his arm, with great difficulty she managed get him on to the veranda, relieved when no one tried to stop them and ignoring the pipe smokers who rose and drifted away into the shadows.

'Devil take it,' Oliver mumbled, stumbling to his knees and grabbing at a post to keep himself from falling flat on his face. 'I'm all at sea.'

'It jolly well serves you right,' Marietta scolded.

Suddenly a tall, lithe black-haired man materialised from across the street. 'Get up, man,' he retorted as he hoisted Oliver to his feet.

'Thank you,' Oliver muttered. 'I am much obliged.'

Marietta's head spun round on hearing the strong authoritative tones. Suddenly she wished the ground would open and swallow her up. She lowered her head to hide her face, for there was no one in the whole world she would so much dislike to discover her in this disguise as Lord Trevellyan.

'What the hell are you doing here?' Max demanded of Oliver.

Oliver's eyes darted about, but he saw there was no escaping Lord Trevellyan's interrogation. 'I—came on behalf of a friend to collect a package, and before I knew...'

'Like hell you did,' Max ground out. 'You knew what kind of establishment this is—that not only is it a house of ill repute, but that Chang deals in narcotics. If you are hell-bent on self-destruction, young man, you are going the right way about it.'

Marietta was about to move behind Oliver when a warm hand on her shoulder pulled her back and spun her round to face him.

'Wait. Are you with him?'

Knowing there was no escape, Marietta raised her head and met his gaze, her eyes wide with horrified embarrassment. She saw astonished recognition in his eyes and tried to shrink away, but he held on to her shoulder, his fingers digging into her soft flesh.

'Miss Westwood. Just as one might have expected. What an absolutely tiresome girl you are.' She flinched before the exasperation in his voice. 'I might have known—although I didn't expect to meet you engaged in yet another mad escapade quite so soon. It leaves me wondering what the devil you'll get up to next.' He rounded angrily on Oliver. 'Have you no sense? You must have known it was the height of danger-ous folly to bring a young girl to a place such as this. Not only does Chang deal in opium, but slaves are his speciality—the younger the bet-ter, and the fairer the skin the higher the price.'

'I hadn't meant to bring her, but...'

'She insisted.' Max fixed his fierce gaze on Marietta. 'Do you go out of your way to court danger and excitement? I suppose it's pointless me asking if your father knows you are here?'

Marietta shook her head.

'Then he should.' He looked at Oliver with severe approbation. 'It would be advisable for you to leave now, Mr Schofield. I'll escort Miss Westwood home.'

Eager to be gone, Oliver didn't raise any ob-jections as he was hoisted up into the rickety carriage. Turning his attention to Marietta, Max took her arm and almost dragged her across the street to a waiting sedan chair.

'Kindly take your hands off me,' she snapped, angry and resentful of his interference. 'I don't want to go anywhere with you.'

'That's too bad. Get in.'

'I most certainly will not.'

'Shut up,' he hissed, his voice like acid.

As he shoved her inside without gentleness, her ill-fitting shoe came off and dropped into the street. Cursing softly, he picked it up and thrust it into her hands. In a silky, dangerous voice, he said, 'Be still. I am averse to leaving you to the mercy of an opium-soaked idiot.'

Clutching her shoe, taking judicious note of the taut set of his jaw and feeling the first tendril of fear coil in the pit of her stomach, Marietta did as she was told. She didn't think she could escape and, anyway, she would only enrage him further. Besides, if she didn't let him vent his wrath now, he would undoubtedly tell her father—which he would probably do anyway. She shot him a mutinous, measuring look. He looked dangerous and invincible. She already knew he had a vile temper. She judged from the ominous look in his silver-grey eyes that he was even now considering shaking her for her idiocy. Rather than give him the satisfaction, she sat frigidly in the sedan while he walked briskly along side.

Steeling herself to endure the journey home, she sat in angry silence all the way, relieved when the coolies carrying the sedan halted out-side the gate. She scrambled out, impatient to be rid of her persecutor.

Chapter Two

Instructing the coolies to wait, Max looked down at Marietta, his face hard. 'I'll have a word with your father before I go.'

'He isn't at home.'

'Then I'll catch up with him later. He should know what his daughter gets up to in his absence—for your own good, you understand.'

'No, I do not understand,' she flared. 'Tell me, Lord Trevellyan, are you really as heartless and unfeeling as you sound right now?'

'Absolutely.'

'You're a monster. Why are you talking to me like this?'

'Someone has to.'

'What I do has got nothing whatsoever to do with you. I would be obliged if you would mind your own business.'

'When I find a girl of your age in one of the most notorious opium dens in Hong Kong, I make it my business.'

'It's also a place where brothels and gambling dens thrive,' she flared, 'which leads me to question the purpose of your own visit to the native quarter, Lord Trevellyan.'

He raised one sleek, questioning brow. 'And you know what a brothel is, do you, Miss Westwood?'

Her face turned scarlet with embarrassment and she found she couldn't look at him. 'Yes—at least—I think so.'

Max was shocked, for such things were never discussed with an innocent girl. 'Damn it, there are some things a girl of your age shouldn't know about.'

Marietta didn't, not really. One day she had asked Oliver to explain what a brothel was, having overheard some young men making ribald remarks among themselves about such establishments. In a roundabout way Oliver had told her what a brothel was, firmly stating that, of course, *he* never visited them. She had always taken everything Oliver said as the gospel truth—but today had changed all that.

'I can't see why not. I'm seventeen, Lord Trevellyan, not six, and I cannot for the life of me understand why a man would want to visit such places if he is in love with his wife.'

'Brothels are full of married men, Miss Westwood,' he replied drily. 'When you are older you will no doubt realise that. Why did you go there? What made you want to?'

She shrugged. 'It was the adventure, I suppose, the excitement of doing something different.'

'Something wrong, more like. Just what did you think you were playing at, doing something as lunatic as going to a place like that? Have you no brains at all?'

'Don't speak to me like that. I won't listen.' Her hands were trembling now, and her legs felt weak beneath her. *I'm usually so strong*, she thought. *Why do I feel like a child?* She knew why it was. She was in the wrong. In a fit of pique, Marietta threw her shoe at Lord Trevellyan, almost hitting him in the face, before turning on her heel and flouncing off.

'Miss Westwood.'

Marietta paused and scowled back at him. She beheld a face of such dark, menacing rage that she shuddered. 'What?'

'That's a nasty temper you have there. You could have taken my eye out.'

'I'm only sorry I didn't take your head off.' On that note she left him and stalked away.

Max watched her disappear down the drive, her ridiculous fat plait bouncing against her back and her shins exposed like a couple of white sticks beneath her wide trouser bottoms and wearing only one shoe. Although he was accustomed to being assaulted, it was usually by someone of his own age and sex, not an angry young woman. Tiresome though Miss Westwood was, she didn't lack personality, perhaps to be expected of Monty Westwood's daughter. He was a man fond of breaking regulations, who believed his nefarious dealings in Hong Kong were a well-kept secret—it was hardly surprising that he had fathered such a little firebrand.

Marietta was full of self-recrimination. 'Oh, my goodness,' she whispered as she walked away in belated shame. The silent punishment she was heaping on herself for throwing a tantrum, as well as her shoe, at Lord Trevellyan was reinforced by her childish reply. It was all she could do not to turn back and explain that she had never intended to hurt him. Never had she felt so obnoxious or so miserable. How she hated herself for lapsing into the silly tempers she'd indulged in as a child.

After several moments of self-recrimination, she wondered how she could possibly atone for this calamity, for her father, always malleable in her hands and ready to forgive her any misdemeanour, would never forgive her for her actions today. Going to the native quarter disguised as a Chinese girl and visiting an opium den was bad enough, but she could imagine his righteous wrath when he found out she had physically assaulted Lord Trevellyan. What she had done could not be kept from him. Lord Trevellyan had said he would tell him and there was nothing she could do about that.

Instead of going into the house she went into the garden. Beneath the largest tree a circular bench had been constructed to fit around the trunk. This was where she sat looking down at the jumble of rooftops that tumbled down the hill to the harbour. Her unhappy reflections were disturbed when she heard someone approaching from behind. The next thing she knew, her lost shoe appeared on the bench beside her. It was him. For a split second she was tempted to flee, but checked herself. She would remain here and face him and admit her fault.

'Well? What have you to say for yourself, Miss Westwood?'

Marietta realised he was waiting for her to

apologise. Without turning to look at him she said, 'If you must know, I'm not nearly so angry with you as I am with myself for what I did. I never meant to hit you. It was irresponsible and dangerous—and—and childish.'

'I agree, it was. But thank you for apologising.' Picking up her shoe, he sat beside her, admiring her honesty and candour and her ability to admit her mistakes.

His closeness brought to Marietta a warm waft of his cologne. It was a fresh, clean scent, but with a masculine undertone, a spicy blend of citrus and sandalwood.

His gaze slid over her, his expression neutral. 'You look ridiculous, by the way.'

'I know I do, but for obvious reasons I had to disguise myself. Are you really going to tell my father?'

'I should. Have you any idea what might have happened to you today? Young Schofield should have known better than to take you there and he deserves to be horsewhipped for becoming intoxicated while he was supposed to be taking care of you.'

'I made him take me,' Marietta said in Oliver's defence.

'Then he should have known better than to agree.'

'Please don't tell my father,' she whispered. 'He—he isn't well—in fact, of late I have seen a deterioration in his health. The last thing he needs is to worry about me.'

'Then you should try harder to behave yourself.'

'You're right, but I seem to have a habit of always doing the wrong thing, no matter how hard I try not to.'

'And your father will do anything to make his little girl happy and not give you the punishment you deserve.'

'Please don't say that,' Marietta said quietly, unable to conceal the hurt his off-the-cuff remark caused her. 'It's isn't like that. Since my mother's death I've spent my life trying to fill the void in my father's heart with the love her death took from him.'

'Trying to be the antidote to his grief.' Max regretted his remark about her when he saw how much it pained her.

She smiled wanly. 'Something like that.'

To Max it sounded more like she needed her father to fill the void in her own heart, that she needed to be needed. 'You are obviously concerned about him.'

'He is my father. Of course I'm concerned. He may not be the perfect father, but he is the only one I have and I love him dearly. For a long time we've only had each other and I cannot think what my life would be like without him.'

'I think I have the picture,' Max said. And he did. Miss Westwood was young, a brave, proud, spirited girl who was trying to make the best of things in a world she wasn't equipped to face on her own. In retrospect, she did seem rather like a vulnerable child.

'Please don't tell my father,' she pleaded, tears not far away, and completely unaware that she was a vision with dark-lashed, olive-green eyes and a face too lovely to be real.

'That depends.'

'On what?'

'You must promise me there will be no repeat of today.'

'There won't be. I promise, and I am so sorry to have interrupted your day.' Something which resembled a smile crossed Lord Trevellyan's face.

'You did not disturb anything,' he replied briefly. 'Consider it forgotten. However, a look of contrition sits charmingly on such a pretty face.'

It was not a compliment so much as a calm and sincere statement of fact.

'You are most generous. Thank you.' He

was obviously trying to reassure her and she thanked him with a pale ghost of a smile, embarrassed by his attentiveness. She experienced an unfamiliar twist to her heart when she met his understanding gaze—an addictive mixture of pleasure and discomfort. 'I seem to be making a habit of apologising to you of late.'

'I have noticed,' he replied, meeting her gaze.

Tilting her head to one side, she asked, 'Are you really a duke? My father says you are.'

He gazed down at her searching green eyes. 'Absolutely. Although I prefer to play down my rank here in Hong Kong. Why do you ask?'

'I'm curious. I've never met a duke before. You're not in the least like what I imagined a duke should look like.'

'And how do you imagine a duke should look?'

'Old, stout and gouty with a quizzing glass.'

The image her description conjured up brought a smile to his lips. 'Good Lord, what a fertile imagination you've got, Miss Westwood. But even dukes have to be young at some time during their lives.'

'Yes, I suppose they must,' she said with a laughing look.

For a moment Max's gaze lingered on the rosy perfection of her face, then settled on her entrancing green eyes. He stood up. 'I must go,' he said abruptly. 'I have things to do. Will you be all right?'

Marietta stood and faced him. 'Yes—and thank you.'

'It was my pleasure, Miss Westwood.'

As she watched him walk away, she thought how nice he had been. He had treated her better than he had at Happy Valley. And he really was very handsome, she smiled to herself. He was an intimidating man, but his eyes had been kind and warm when he'd looked at her, and his mouth… She checked herself. It's not right, she thought. Lord Trevellyan was a gentleman with a wife. He was only being friendly. *Don't be so foolish*. But she did think of him and when she did there was a small spring of joy which kept bubbling up, no matter how hard she pushed it down.

Marietta was in high spirits as she prepared for the New Year festivities. She had spent three days behaving in an impeccably ladylike fashion in order to reassure her father that her lapse from grace at Happy Valley had been an isolated incident, and that there was no need to revert to the strict surveillance that Mrs Schofield had recommended. She was thankful that Lord

Trevellyan had kept his word and not told him of her visit to the native quarter.

Despite not having a mother to exercise a restraining influence, Marietta was attired in a sensible dress that made every concession to the modesty of a seventeen-year-old girl. She accompanied her father to the Chinese New Year party being held at Government House. It was eighteen eighty, the year of the dragon. The Chinese were on holiday. It was a time for celebrating, for colour, noise, processions and dancing dragons.

Yang Ling was taking time off to pay ceremonial calls to relatives and friends, to wish them well and a prosperous New Year, which was the custom on the first day of the Chinese New Year. In the native quarter the celebrations, which had only just begun, would go on for days. The junks and sampans cramming the harbour were all illuminated, as were the streets, through which a tidal wave of multicoloured paper lanterns, gaudy banners, dancing dragons and flower girls filed.

At Government House there was to be dancing and feasting and fireworks throughout the night. Marietta had been looking forward to it for ages and as she was being transported from her home in a sedan chair, she was incandescent

with excitement. Already the air was thick with
sulphur from the fireworks, drowning out the
strong night scents of jasmine and all the other
exotic flowers that grew on Hong Kong. Every
so often salvos of firecrackers ricocheted from
street to street. The night held every promise of
being a truly splendid affair.

On arrival at the flower-decked lantern
blazing Government House, along with Hong
Kong's most illustrious, languid and sophisticated personages, Marietta stood beside her
father, looking a picture of scrubbed and shining innocence with her rich chestnut-coloured
hair tied back with a bright yellow ribbon, pink
cheeks and olive-green eyes above the full-
skirted yellow dress with its puffed shoulders
and long sleeves. It was the opinion of everyone who saw her that she was an exceedingly
pretty girl and in another year or so would be
a ravishing beauty.

In no time at all she was whisked away
by her excited group of friends. Julian and
Oliver were just two of her personal entourage
of admirers and she listened patiently as they
lavishly complimented her with passionate
pledges of undying devotion, smiling at each
one sweetly. They all vied with each other to
dance the waltz, the quadrille, the schottische

and the polka with her, while she happily scribbled their names in her gilt-edged programme. Oliver complained bitterly to find she had his name down only once, especially since he had something of extreme importance to tell her—as did Julian.

'I'm sorry to disappoint you, Oliver,' she said without the slightest remorse, 'but you're not the only one to be disappointed. The ball would have to last all night and all day tomorrow for all of my suitors to be satisfied. I hope you suffered no ill effects from our outing the other day.'

Oliver coloured pink to the gills and he was right out of countenance for once. 'I say, I'm sorry about that, Marietta. There was the devil to pay when Father found out.'

'Why? Did you tell him?'

'Not me. Lord Trevellyan. Why did the man have to interfere? As a result I am being sent to England—Oxford, to be precise—where I'm to read history for the next three years. How appalling is that?—although I suppose the fact that Julian is to come with me will alleviate the misery,' he said miserably.

Marietta stared at him in disbelief. Knowing she was to lose two of her best friends was devastating. As if that wasn't bad enough, she already knew her friend Emma was to leave for Europe, to be finished off at some school or other. To lose all three would bring such a big change to her life that she couldn't bear to think about it.

'Surely not! I'm sorry, Oliver. I shall miss you—both of you—and Emma. Things won't be the same without you.'

'Did Lord Trevellyan tell your father about— you know?'

'No. He threatened to, but I'm relieved he didn't.'

Their conversation was observed by Oliver's mother, whose whole life had been scrupulously and religiously dedicated to the precepts of convention and keeping up position, and maintaining her dignity. She was shocked by Marietta's behaviour and the unacceptable influence she had on Oliver, which was one of the reasons why she had persuaded her husband to send their son to England.

'I have to say, Mildred, that that young lady's manners are an outrage, her conduct reprehensible. She is a wilful hoyden who must be the despair of her father and an embarrassment.'

'Be that as it may, but it is just high spirits and she has such a sweet disposition,' said fair-minded Mrs Mildred Beaumont, 'and that dress is exceedingly becoming on such a young girl.'

'Handsome is as handsome does,' snorted Mrs Schofield, her displeasure concerning Marietta deepening when she saw her practically dragging Oliver on to the dance floor where they proceeded to dance a lively polka. She was also annoyed that her good friend did not appear to agree with her over Marietta's shocking conduct. 'Do you know what my maid told me tonight as I was dressing? She told me that Monty Westwood is thinking of engaging a teacher to instruct his daughter to speak Chinese. Did you ever hear of such a thing?'

Mrs Beaumont was startled out of her customary calm. She said incredulously, 'Learn Chinese? You must be mistaken. No lady would do such a thing. Besides, I doubt Mr Westwood will be able to find anyone to teach her since the Chinese consider us all barbarians.'

'I assure you it is true.' Mrs Schofield's attention was diverted from this fascinating topic by the arrival of Lord Trevellyan and his charming wife.

Marietta's attention was also captured by the arrival of Lord Trevellyan and his wife. Observing them enter the room as she was being spun around at a maddening pace by her partner, forgetting to hop when she should have, she gazed with something like awe at Lady Trevellyan. Wearing a shadowy smile, tall and slender in woven green silk, her gown decorated with silver thread and seed pearls, she really did look quite splendid and Marietta's wasn't the only gaze that was drawn to her.

As her husband escorted her into the centre of the room, she did not glance to left or right. Her figure swayed as if the very air that surrounded her set it in motion. Her hands were gloved in dove grey, her grave, charming face held to one side. There was warmth, but little colour, in her cheeks and her eyes, large dark eyes, were soft, her lips sensitive and sweet. There was something inexplicably dainty and fragile about her and the look on her face was as though she had come into contact with a force too strong for her—her husband, perhaps? Marietta wondered cynically. She watched Nadine say something quietly to her husband. Whatever it was she said, his long mouth curled with derision.

With the festivities in full flow and the reception rooms full to overflowing, Marietta danced with her friends and dashing young officers until her feet ached and smiled so much she thought her face would crack. Feeling somewhat downhearted that she was about to be deserted by her three closest friends, she headed for a door that led to a veranda where, hopefully, she could be by herself to collect her thoughts.

She smiled to herself as she watched her father socialising. It wasn't too long ago when he had been invited everywhere and treated as someone of importance, but things had changed. Now the gentlemen conversed and laughed with him, but of late she'd noted a hint of reserve in their manner towards him. Perhaps she was imagining it, but for some unknown reason she didn't think so and it was beginning to worry her. She was also concerned because he didn't look too well tonight. He looked tired, his face was flushed and his eyes over-bright. She hoped the evening wouldn't be too taxing for him.

Lady Trevellyan was in deep conversation with Teddy by the door, talking low-voiced. The lace on her white shoulders stirred with the soft rise and fall of her bosom. While they were smiling at one another, Lord Trevellyan suddenly appeared behind his wife and said something, at which Teddy stepped out of the room.

Thinking nothing of it, Marietta slipped out on to the veranda. The sky was bright with flares and rockets and Catherine wheels. She was relieved to find she was the only one there, but her solitude was to be short lived.

Minutes later, stepping out on to the veranda, Lord Trevellyan strolled towards the young woman leaning on the balustrade with her small chin propped upon her palms, gazing at the harbour lights and the rockets soaring into the night sky leaving a blaze of colourful sparks in their wake. The moon shone and the sea shimmered—there couldn't have been a more romantic setting.

Hearing a step behind her, Marietta turned and looked at Lord Trevellyan, unable to explain why her heart suddenly did a somersault at the sight of him. 'Oh, it's you,' she said, turning back to the wonderful panoramic view spread out before her.

'So this is where you're hiding. I was beginning to think a dragon had carried you off.'

Marietta's heart skipped another beat. 'Why? Were you looking for me?' she asked, hoping this was so.

'No, but I did see you leave the party and thought you might have gone home when you didn't return.'

'I'm amazed that you thought of me at all, and I'm not hiding. It was so stifling inside. I wanted some air.'

'I couldn't agree more. Would you mind if I stayed out here with you a while?' he asked, perching his hip on the balustrade and looking down at her, with none of the anger of their recent encounters. She wore her hair loose, the weight of it rippling about her shoulders like a rich silken cloud. She really was quite refreshing, not at all overawed as many of the women were when he spoke to them.

Marietta's senses went into instant overload at his nearness. His voice sounded as dark and sultry as the night. With a faint scent of his familiar cologne wafting over her, he loomed tall, as indomitable as the hills on which Hong Kong was built.

'No, of course not,' she said in answer to his request. 'The veranda's for everyone and the view is quite splendid, don't you think? It's also the perfect spot from which to watch the fireworks.'

'It certainly is. It's a rare display.'

'I cannot understand why, when the Chinese are so thrifty, they spend a tremendous amount of money on something that is so short lived and soon forgotten.'

'Ah, but they will be remembered by many—along with the noise they make. Some of them are quite deafening. This night, the first of the year of the dragon, will be remembered for its festivities. Without the fireworks and the cymbals and the gongs to frighten away evil spirits, it would not be the same. And what has caught your interest?' he asked as she leaned forwards and looked down.

'If you must know, a rather long orange-and-purple caterpillar that's just crawled along the street below. It had huge blue eyes and wobbly feelers with knobs on the end. I was wondering...' she sighed almost wistfully '...how many people were inside it and if they talk to each other as they go along.'

'I imagine they do. So tell me, why the long face?'

'I wasn't aware that I had one.'

'Take it from me, you have. Has someone upset you?'

'No—at least...' She sighed. Nothing seemed to escape those penetrating silver-grey eyes of his.

'I hope I'm not the cause and that you're not bearing a grudge over our little altercation when I forcibly made you leave the native quarter.'

'No. I don't bear grudges—even if you do think I'm a flighty, fluff-headed socialite who only cares about enjoying herself,' she said with a puckish smile curving her lips. 'I said I was sorry and I meant it. I hope you will accept my thanks for not telling my father. I'm grateful to you for that. And I was quite obnoxious on our encounter in Happy Valley, wasn't I?'

'Yes, you were, but I don't bear grudges either.' He grinned, his eyes dancing with humour. 'It's not every day a pretty young lady throws herself at my feet,' he teased lightly.

'Not intentionally. I'm glad I didn't land on you or your wife. I should hate to have hurt her, or you for that matter.'

'Thank you. I appreciate your concern. But you might have hurt yourself. So—why the long face?'

'Oliver and Julian are going to Europe to further their education. I've only just found out.'

'I see. And you'll miss them, naturally.'

'Yes, of course I will. Emma, my closest friend, is also leaving the island. Her parents are sending her to be finished off somewhere in Europe.'

'And that bothers you?'

'It felt like having a bucket of cold water poured over my head. If it weren't for you telling Oliver's father about his visit to China Town, he wouldn't be leaving. Do you make a habit of interfering in other people's lives, Lord Trevellyan?'

'Only when I deem it necessary,' he replied coolly. 'I'd like to think I've done young Schofield a favour.'

'But his father is sending him to England.'

'It's the best thing for him, if you ask me.'

'I wasn't, and that is your opinion.'

'Which I trust.'

'But to see my three best friends leave the island! We've been together for a long time. I can't bear to think of the group being broken up. Nothing will be the same any more. Life will be so boring.'

'Oh, I think you're still young enough to change all that.'

'I doubt it,' she admitted bluntly. 'To be honest, I don't know if I would want to.'

'So a betrothal to the opium-smoking young man I found you with in the native quarter the other day is not to be considered?'

'Oh, no,' she replied. A frown marred her

smooth forehead at the idea that she and Oliver might be linked together. 'Even though my father is unaware of Oliver's partiality for a particular narcotic, he would not encourage a match between us.'

'He doesn't like Mr Schofield?'

'Oh, no, that isn't the reason. In fact, Father would have no reservations about Oliver making me an excellent husband. It's just that he would have serious reservations about my life with my prospective mother-in-law.'

Max chuckled softly. 'Having encountered Mrs Schofield on several occasions, I can see his point. She's a tiresome busybody and worse than a washerwoman for the pleasure she takes in idle gossip and malicious talk.'

'Exactly. Besides, I believe she thinks I have a disruptive influence on her precious Oliver.'

He arched a brow. 'And have you?'

'I don't think so, but perhaps the fact that I love having fun and don't always listen to the dictates of my father has crystallised all my sins in her mind.'

At the tragic note in her voice, humour softened Max's features and his firm, sensual lips quirked in a smile. 'Poor you. What a truly miserable time you are having, Miss Westwood.

Still, I applaud your honesty. It's a rare virtue in one so young.'

'My father says I'm unconventional and I suppose I am, which is why all the old tabbies on the island are always complaining to him about me and giving him advice on the best way to deal with a wayward daughter. But he likes me the way I am and wouldn't like it if I were to change.'

'Your father is quite right. You are what you are. You can't please everybody. One's true character springs from the heart and dwells in the eyes. Unconventionality is an invitation to disaster in the world we inhabit.'

She stared at him. 'My word, how very profound.'

Gazing into his unfathomable eyes, she saw cynicism lurking in their depths. There was something primitive and dangerous about Lord Trevellyan. She had the uneasy feeling that his elegant attire and indolent stance were nothing but disguises meant to lull the unwary into believing he was civilised, when he wasn't civilised at all. He looked like the sort of man who had seen and done all sorts of things, terrible and forbidden things, things that had hardened him and made him cold. A chill crept up her spine as she wondered what dark secrets lay hidden in his past. Surely there must be many to have made him so cynical and unapproachable.

'I don't mean to pry, but are you happy, Lord Trevellyan? What I mean is, do you get the very best out of your life?'

He looked irritated by her question, but he answered it. 'I don't suppose so, but then, who does?'

'There you are, you see.' She lifted her face up to the star-strewn sky, her entire being radiant with optimism, innocence and hope. 'I love life, even when things happen to me and my friends are deserting me. I can't *stop* loving life.'

Transfixed, Max stared at her. Marietta Westwood was unspoiled, without artifice or pretence, young and naïve and realistic. Her irresistible smile doused his momentary irritation and brought an answering smile to his lips. 'Long may you continue to do so.'

Marietta turned and looked at him. In his late twenties, Lord Trevellyan's potent attraction to women was a topic of much scintillating feminine gossip among the ladies, young and old, in the colony, and as Marietta gazed into those cynical grey eyes, she suddenly felt herself drawn to him as if by some overwhelming magnetic force. Understanding was in his eyes, along with a touch of humour. It was these things, as well as his dark good looks and blatant virility, that impelled women towards him, even though their attentions went unrewarded, for he ignored them all. He was so worldly, so experienced, that he clearly understood them. He understood her, and although it was obvious he didn't approve of her, he accepted her for what she was, with all her faults.

'Are you going to return to your wife?' she asked. 'She might want you to dance with her.' A strange expression crossed his face, as if he were struggling to master some emotion—anger, she thought.

'Not yet.'

'Why not?'

'Because, Miss Inquisitive Westwood, she's dancing with someone else.'

'I know—Teddy—my father's business partner.'

His smile disappeared and his face darkened. 'I am aware of that.'

Marietta tilted her head to one side and considered him quizzically. 'Do you mind?'

'Should I mind?'

'Since it's the custom to dance with different

partners when one attends a ball, then I don't think you should.'

'Then I don't.'

Unaware of his sudden change in attitude, Marietta proceeded to delight Lord Trevellyan with a wickedly humorous description of some of the events she'd attended on the island and some funny stories acquainted with the people she knew. She told him of how, on one of her trips to Kowloon on one of her father's boats, Teddy, who was leaning comfortably against the side of the boat and made soporific by the warmth of the sun and the lulling of the waves, had fallen into a doze and slipped overboard.

'You managed to pull him back aboard, I see,' Lord Trevellyan remarked somewhat drily.

'But of course. He was most indignant about it and was sure someone must have pushed him in.'

Inexperienced and unsophisticated as she was, Max was fascinated by her clever tongue, by her sharp mind and the fount of knowledge she stored about others as she went on to relate other tales, her olive-green eyes shining into his.

Marietta smiled at him impudently, surprising him with her next question. 'Why don't you want to dance with your wife?'

He drew back. 'Because I'm not in the mood.'

They both turned to look at the dancers twirling around the polished dance floor. As if on cue and within three yards of the darkening veranda, his wife and Teddy waltzed by. Lady Trevellyan's eyes were raised to his, as though answering some question he had asked, and he was gazing at her intently. She wore a white gardenia in her hair and from where they stood Max and Marietta could almost smell its perfume. Her every movement was feline, containing the same elastic mixture of confidence and sophistication that masked an underlying interest in her partner. They saw the rise and fall of her bosom and the languor in her eyes, her parted lips and a look on her face Marietta thought quite strange, for it was a look a woman usually bestowed on her husband.

Lady Trevellyan peered over Teddy's shoulder before they disappeared from view. There was a sudden glint in her eyes now as she fixed them on her husband, a glint in which there was no sympathy at all, but only pleasure sharpened with a trace of something very much like spite. There was no perceptible movement of muscle or vein, no change in colour, but it was impossible to mistake that Lord Trevellyan had moved straight from condescension into cold rage.

'Teddy is always a popular figure at dances,' Marietta told Lord Trevellyan quietly, wondering why she felt a sudden need to defend her father's business partner. 'He dances so well that all the ladies are eager to have his name on their dance card.'

'So it would seem,' Max murmured drily, turning his back on his wife.

Marietta saw the cynical curl to his lips and observed the way his shoulders tensed, but she didn't comment on it. Perhaps matters weren't as they should be between Lord Trevellyan and his wife, but he was far too English and private a person to talk openly about it, and it was not for her to ask.

'If you're not in the mood to dance with your wife, then dance with someone else.'

One dark brow lifted over an amused silver-grey eye. 'Are you asking, Miss Westwood?'

Her answering laughter tinkled like bells, filling the air around them with its gaiety. 'Heavens, no! My friends wouldn't let me live it down—dancing with a man much older than myself.'

He leaned back and gave her a look of mock offence. 'I'm not so long in the tooth. How old do you think I am?'

After giving his question a moment's thought, she said, 'About thirty?'

'Wrong. Nowhere near.'

'Then how old are you?'

'That's for me to know and you to find out, Miss Westwood.'

Tilting her head to one side, she gazed up into his mesmerising grey eyes. Standing so close to him, she was unable to think clearly. She wasn't certain anything mattered at that moment except the sound of his deep, compelling voice. The piercing sweetness of the music drifting through the open doors wrapped itself round her. How she wished the man beside her would smile and take her in his arms and dance with her, despite what she had just said, that he would place his lips against her cheek and... She checked herself. She wished so many impossible things.

'I hope you weren't offended when I said I wouldn't dance with you. Of course,' she said, lowering her eyes, her cheeks suddenly warm with embarrassment and anticipation, 'if you were to ask me, I wouldn't dream of refusing your offer. I would be happy to dance with you.'

Slowly she raised her eyes to his and Max noted the unconcealed admiration lighting her lovely young face. She didn't know how explicit her expression was—like an open book, exposing what was in her heart. Max saw it and was immediately wary. He had schooled his face over the years to show nothing that he did not want it to show. He was therefore perfectly able to disguise his exasperation with himself for having misjudged things. He should have realised she was of an age to have a school-girl crush.

The lines of his face were angular and hard, and behind the cold glitter of his grey eyes lay a fathomless stillness. Marietta watched his firmly moulded lips for his answer.

'That won't happen,' he said flatly, gentling his voice, while knowing he was being deliberately cruel, but it was necessary.

Marietta was mortified and shocked by his refusal, but she was more shocked by her nerve for having the audacity to ask him. 'No, of course not,' she said in a shaky, breathless voice. 'I should have known better than to suggest such a thing.'

Max didn't like having to wound her sensibilities, but it couldn't be helped. His voice was condescendingly amused as he tried not to look too deeply into her hurt eyes, eloquent in their hurt, which remained fixed on his face. 'Think nothing of it. And I wasn't offended.'

'Oh—well, that's all right then. You don't have a very high opinion of women, do you, Lord Trevellyan?' she said, unable to stop herself from asking.

'Should I?'

'Yes, when you have such a beautiful wife.'

'You've noticed,' he remarked drily.

'I would have to be wearing blinkers not to.'

'Do you have a beau, Miss Westwood?'

'No, not as such.'

'Some day you'll have to marry in order to have children.'

She glanced at him sharply. 'Oh, no, Lord Trevellyan. If I marry, it won't be to have children.'

'Don't you like children?'

'Yes, of course.'

'But you don't want children of your own?'

'No, and if I have to pledge my hand in order to produce an heir, then I might very well remain a spinster.'

'That's a very decisive statement for a seventeen-year-old girl to make.'

'I'm sure you must think so, but seventeen or sixty, I won't change my mind.'

Marietta meant what she said. She would never forget what her mother had gone through to try to produce another living child, or the pain and the terrible grief that came afterwards. Yang Ling had told her that daughters often took after their mothers and the thought of childbearing preyed dreadfully on her nerves. She went cold every time she thought of it— what might be the sequel to making love, when past dangers and future fear might become utterly submerged.

'You're still very young, Miss Westwood, with time to change your mind. Tell me, am I really all those unflattering things you called me at Happy Valley? Arrogant, high-handed and despicable, I believe you said.'

'Oh, yes,' she said. 'I haven't changed my mind about that. I'm only sorry that you heard me say them.' She was laughing and he smiled at her, his teeth flashing against his tanned skin. He looked all formal in his evening attire—a figure of authority, assured, cynical and formidable. But having spent the last few minutes with him, he suddenly seemed a hundred times more rakish and with hidden depths. Without thinking, she said, 'You also look like a pirate—not the kind they have in the China Seas, but one of Caribbean kind—a buccaneer that carries beautiful ladies off to his lair on some island known only to him.'

That made him laugh and, in the shimmering light from a thousand lanterns, he saw her flawless young face and the brilliance of her long-lashed eyes and generous mouth. Abruptly he stood back. He stared down at her for a long, long moment, then, quietly serious, he said, 'Don't change, Miss Westwood. Don't ever grow up. Stay just exactly as you are.'

'That's impossible.' She cocked her head to one side and gave him a quizzical look. 'I thought you didn't like me.'

'What made you think that?'

'Because of what happened at Happy Valley—and then in China Town—you were awful to me.'

He grinned and with his finger and thumb tweaked her chin playfully. 'You deserved it.' Momentarily distracted when the music stopped playing, he glanced into the ballroom. 'Please excuse me. I think it's time I returned to my wife.'

Marietta didn't move as she watched him go, not realising that in years to come they would both have reason to think back on this short time they had spent together on the veranda at Government House, as flower girls, fire-breathing dragons and caterpillars snaked their way through the streets below.

* * *

The rest of the evening passed all too quickly for Marietta. Her father retired to a card room, there to join other merchants to drink some fine brandy and to discuss the previous year's profits and losses. Marietta returned to the dance floor where she was reunited with her friends. With her father out of the way she drank some champagne with Oliver and danced with some of the young officers in the colony, who exclaimed ingenuously about her looks and the way she danced, making her feel very grand and grown up. Would Lord Trevellyan ask her to dance? she wondered. She hoped so. Eagerly she looked for him, disappointed when she couldn't see him. Assuming he must have left with his wife, from that point her evening declined.

Later, when Marietta walked past the table where Lord and Lady Trevellyan had been sitting, she looked down and spotted a fan on the floor beside a chair. She recognised it as being Lady Trevellyan's. Retrieving it, she thought she would have one of the servants return it to her hotel, but as she was making her way to the ladies' rest room, she saw Lord and Lady Trevellyan standing alone close to the main entrance and assumed they were on the point of leaving and awaiting their transport.

She hurried towards them, but something she saw on Lord Trevellyan's face made her pause. Hidden by the fronds of a large potted plant, she saw that as Lord Trevellyan looked at his wife there was revulsion on his face, and above all contempt. Having no wish to intrude or to listen to what they were saying, Marietta stepped back, but if she were to move now they would see her and she had no wish to be accused of eavesdropping.

'Did you have to make a total spectacle of yourself, Nadine? Everybody was watching.' Max's mood was mocking, cruel and angry as he addressed his wife.

'Why should I care?' she asked.

'Why? Because it's embarrassing that's why. I'm your husband, in the same room, and you were making a degrading spectacle of yourself.'

His voice was sharp and Nadine recoiled from the coldness in him. He saw the tautness return to her face along with the ice-cold politeness, which was the sum and substance of their marriage.

'What's wrong, Max? Are you jealous?'

'Jealous? No. Just humiliated. What you do

in private is your business. What you do in public, when I'm present, involves me, too.'

'What about you?' Nadine asked quietly. 'What about what you get up to?'

'I don't embarrass you in public.'

'No? Then it's all right for you to spend almost the entire evening on a lantern-lit veranda alone with a woman?'

His look became one of scorn. 'Don't be ridiculous. If it is to Miss Westwood you are referring, she is seventeen—hardly out of the schoolroom—a juvenile. You've got a very suspicious nature, Nadine.'

'I'm your wife.'

'And I've heard it all before. You have a weakness. You can't help yourself.'

'What do you want, Max? Little did I know when I married you that the position I thought honourable would become my own special prison.'

Max paused a moment and gazed at her coldly. 'A prison of your own making, Nadine. You do well out of it. And you needn't worry about me in that respect. I won't be cutting off my nose to spite my face. You're only one woman among many, and for a man it's easy to find relief for his baser needs.'

'Nothing would please me more,' she replied, equally as cold.

'I'm sure that's true—but be warned. Don't tempt my temper too far. Tread carefully and perhaps you will survive.'

In the silence that followed, the conversation Marietta had overheard hung in the air like the acrid smell of smoke that lingered after a fire. Her cheeks burned with mortification as she stared at the open doorway through which they had just disappeared, her mind a blank. How could Lady Trevellyan think that she...and her husband! Oh, the very idea was too awful, too embarrassing to contemplate. The evening suddenly felt bleak and black and her earlier high spirits had been dented. Everything was well and truly ruined.

The following day Marietta's father became very ill, the worry of it driving all thoughts of returning Lady Trevellyan's fan from her mind. She had been in the breakfast room when Yang Ling came to tell her. Marietta sprang to her feet, her face blanching in sudden terror.

'It's your father, Miss Marietta. He's had some sort of attack. The doctor has been sent for.'

Her father was in bed propped up against the

pillows, the mosquito net having been turned back. Fighting for breath, he turned his eyes to his daughter as she stumbled across the bedroom.

'Father—what—what has happened?'

She sank to her knees beside the bed and took hold of one of his hands, which rested on the snow-white sheet, and into her head came the fragmented thought that this was the first time she had seen her father ill in bed. Despite her worries concerning his health of late, he had always been about his business. The thought that he might die terrified her and she clung to him as a child clings to its mother in a childish nightmare.

'What is it, Father? Tell me? Oh dear, where is the doctor?'

'Calm down, Marietta. It's only a bit of a turn.' His voice was a thread, but his blue-tinted lips turned up in a small smile.

'I know, I know, but we can't be too careful.'

The doctor came—old Dr White, who attended her father on a regular basis. He was a tall, angular man, dressed from head to toe in black except for a stiff white collar trapped beneath his jawbone. He took his patient's wrist and placed his ear to his chest and whispered to Marietta that he didn't like the sound of it, but to keep him warm and feed him nourishing broth and custard.

'Give him this draught to help him sleep and I'll call again tomorrow.' It was laudanum. 'If you should need me, Miss Westwood, send one of the servants and I will come at once.'

Chapter Three

After days of watching her father's health deteriorate and becoming extremely despondent, Marietta went into the garden to collect her thoughts, sitting on the circular bench beneath the tree. She felt as if the peace and security of her world was somehow threatened by her father's illness, as if she were being plunged from the secure haven of childhood into a cold and terrifying reality.

A shadow fell over her. Resentful of the intrusion, she continued to stare straight ahead.

'I thought I would find you here,' Teddy said softly, moving to stand beside her. 'You're upset about your father, I can see.'

'Yes, it—it's just so sudden, that's all.' She cast him a sideways glance. He was smoking a cigarette and she couldn't be sure, but she thought he was slightly drunk. 'He's been ill for a long time and I should have expected this—only I—I suppose I didn't want to face it.'

'Of course you didn't. Neither did he, but it had to come. You have always been his main concern. He didn't want to worry you. When the time comes, nothing will be able to alleviate the pain of losing him. It's a deprivation which cannot but raise compassion in any person of feeling. But as some small consolation to your grief, I humbly offer my best services I can provide.'

'Thank you, Teddy. Like you say—when anything happens... All my father's things, the house—what am I to do with them?'

'I'll take care of everything. Anything you wish to keep, set aside.'

'Where the business is concerned, as you know I know very little about that side of things. I do know that the trade in tea and cotton is not what it was, but apart from that I am quite ignorant. Of course when Father—' She bit her lip, finding it extremely hard to contemplate being without him. 'When anything happens, I think I would like to learn more about the business.'

Something of her desperation communicated

itself to Teddy. Although he sympathised, when Monty died it would not be conducive to him for Marietta to suddenly show an interest in the business and he would do his utmost to keep her out of it.

'It's true that business isn't what it was, but we do well enough. If it's agreeable to you, Marietta, I will continue to manage the business as before—which I know is what your father wants me to do.'

'Yes, yes, that's true, and I can't tell you what a relief it is to me. You have always been amazingly good at it so I will be quite happy to leave you to run things as before for the time being.'

'Of course, if you find it all too much, I am willing to buy your share of the business. As you know your father and I are equal partners. We could get the lawyers to draw up a settlement.'

Marietta stared at him, unable to comprehend his meaning at first, then it hit home. 'Sell the business? Oh, no, Teddy. The business will be all that I have left of my father.'

'Why not? It's a sensible proposition.'

'You mean to own the company outright?'

'That is what I mean.'

She frowned. 'It's an interesting proposition,' she said slowly, 'but of course I'm in no position to decide such a major issue without speaking to Father's lawyers. It would have to be considered very carefully, although I'm not sure that I shall want to sell it. I might even wish to become involved myself eventually.'

'I'm not trying to push you into anything. It was simply an idle thought. There is another way. You are no longer a child, Marietta.' He turned and faced her. 'The time is fast approaching when you will have to think of marrying.'

'I suppose it is natural in all young women to think of marriage. But I have no doubt that any who asked for my hand in marriage might well have his thoughts on my inheritance. I do know that my father is a very rich man.'

'All the more reason to consider marrying someone you know, someone you can trust.'

She looked at him, a little smile of amusement playing on her lips. 'Teddy, are you by any chance proposing?'

'I am. If you consent, you will make me the happiest of men. You are a woman already. You should not delay your enjoyment of womanhood. Do not reject me without consideration, Marietta. I do believe most sincerely that it is what your father wants. He would not object to a union between us. I know that he wants to see you under the protection of one he can trust—and who better than his friend and business partner? For these are troublesome times in which we live.'

'But—marriage! My father is not even dead, yet you are already making plans. If I were to become your wife, then you would have it all since a woman's property becomes her husband's when they marry.' He looked at her, smiling, but Marietta knew she had put into words the idea fermenting in his head. Perhaps Teddy was like the jackal who was biding his time, waiting for the moment when he could come in for the kill. 'You are an ambitious man, Teddy. I always thought so.'

'Ambitious men frequently get what they set their hearts on.'

'In business maybe. No one can ever achieve the impossible.'

Marietta had risen. Teddy was a clever man and an asset to the business, but he somehow repelled her. Her heart was pounding and she felt afraid—and she could not tell why the sudden desire to run should have come to her. She was in the peaceful garden with a man she had known all her life, a man who was like family to her, a man her father thought highly of, yet she experienced a sudden revulsion.

Teddy's eyes were warm, alert and golden-brown and his hair had a reddish tinge. His face was quite handsome and when he leaned close and the lines seen so close, she thought it resembled a wolf's mask. She knew in that moment that she was afraid.

'When my father dies I shall make my own choices, Teddy, and be advised by my father's lawyers. But whatever happens, I will not marry you. Now please excuse me. I have been away from my father's bedside too long.' She turned and left him, glad to get out of the garden.

Over the following days Marietta stayed close by her father's side. When he fell into a coma Dr White told her he could do no more. He might survive the week, but he doubted it. She sat in the chair beside his bed, holding his hand, willing her own tenacious strength into his body. The days came and went.

Emma sent her a note reminding her of a forthcoming picnic. She didn't feel much like socialising, but she had promised Emma she would go and she didn't want to disappoint her. Besides, Emma was to leave Hong Kong for England shortly, on the same vessel as Oliver and Julian, and it would be the last time the four of them would be together.

Relieved to be away from the confines of the sickroom for however short a time, Marietta joined the picnic party. Ahead of her a colourful spectacle of people were being carried up the steep path of the Peak in chairs by coolies, along with large hampers of food, while some of the fitter younger members of the group preferred to walk. Marietta was one of them. In no hurry she kept stopping to take a look at the view of the busy harbour below and the surrounding hills, breathing deep of the air, fresh and fragrant with the scents of jasmine and eucalyptus.

'Come along, slowcoach. You're lagging,' Emma called as she tried to keep up with Julian's long strides.

'You go on,' Marietta called to her. 'I'll catch you up.'

She paused to take an appreciative look at the magnificent scenery spread out before her, the warm breeze caressing her face. Her gaze spanned the Kowloon Peninsula, the vast country of China and the South China Sea dotted with islands. The harbour was a scene of great activity. Junks and sampans and sailing ships were all crowded together, bobbing and shifting on the water as if they were moving to some music only they could hear. Shining from a clear blue sky, the sun was strong and diamonds of light played upon the surface of the sea.

All thoughts of her father's sickroom were swept from her mind in the pleasure of the moment. She pushed her bonnet to the back of her head, allowing it to fall down her back between her shoulder blades on its ribbons. The sun lit her freshly washed hair to the warm polished sheen of mahogany and put a light in her eyes. Her pleasure was painted in a rosy hue on her cheeks.

Aware of someone coming to stand beside her, she whirled sharply, her heart tripping a beat when she found herself looking into a pair of silver-grey eyes.

'Impressive, isn't it?' Max said quietly, his gaze doing a slow sweep of the panoramic view.

'I think so.' He was lost in the view so Marietta took the opportunity to study him. She thought he looked very handsome, his cool linen suit setting off his dark skin, which emphasised his silver-grey eyes. In a relaxed pose with his hands behind his back, his hair, stirred by the breeze, dipped over his brow. She saw how the sunlight turned it to polished ebony. She saw the way his smile softened the hard planes of his face and turned his eyes to liquid silver. 'I love to come up here. It's a hard climb, but the invigorating air and the view are well worth the effort.'

'Not forgetting the monkeys and the snakes,' he teased, tearing his gaze from the view and settling on her upturned face.

'The monkeys I don't mind so much, but I have an aversion to the snakes. But on a day such as this, I am prepared to put up with them. I often come up here to pick small flowers— such beautiful flowers—especially the orchids, which I press in my scrapbook to carry forwards into another time and place. Wherever I am in the world I will cherish the memory of Hong Kong.' She smiled up at him. 'But all that is a long, long way away and I refuse to think of it on such a lovely day as this. Are you going to the picnic?'

Thoroughly enchanted by her words, he shook his head. 'No. I'm merely out for the walk.'

'Lady Trevellyan is not with you? She is not ill, I hope.'

His eyes hardened and he averted his face. 'She is resting. Nadine is impatient to return to England. The heat of Hong Kong does not agree with her.'

'I see, although today the weather is delightful—perfect for a picnic. Which reminds me. Your wife left her fan at the New Year's Eve party. She must have dropped it when she left her table. I will see it is returned as soon as possible. How long do you expect to be in Hong Kong?'

'My business will keep me here for two more months, then we will go back to England. Tonight I leave for Macau for a few days for trade negotiations, which Nadine finds tedious, so she will remain here at the hotel.'

Marietta turned her face to the breeze blowing off the sea, which was as green as an emerald.

'How is your father?' Max asked, having heard that Monty Westwood was gravely ill.

'He's very sick. He—he's fallen into a coma. He's not expected to recover. He could go at any time.'

'I'm sorry. This can't be easy for you.'

'No—no, it isn't. I spend all my time with him. I know he doesn't know I'm there, but then again he might, and if so I hope he takes comfort from knowing I'm close. I didn't want to leave him, but Emma is going to England very soon, along with Oliver and Julian, and it will be the last time we can all be together.'

Max stared at her stricken face, wishing he

could say something that would ease her distress. He tried to think of the words to describe her. Brave, he decided, knowing she was on the picnic to please her friends and trying to keep her mind occupied rather than dwell on her grief. And compassionate, he thought, remembering how she had told him how she tried to console her sick father.

'What will you do?'

'I don't know. I have no idea what will become of me. Father has always refused to discuss it. He has told me that everything is in hand and he expects me to do as he has written down. With that I have to be content, but I sincerely hope I don't have to leave the island. I would like to become involved with the business in some way, but Father and Teddy are adamant that I do not.'

'And you don't understand why?'

'No, I don't. How is it that men think that women don't have the brains men have, that they must be treated like Venetian glass, and want to wrap them up in fine linen?' she demanded, her expression defiant. 'They truly believe that women are too unintelligent to deal with matters of business, implying that youth and inexperience are synonymous with stupidity.'

'That is an unfair assessment.'

Marietta looked at him with curiosity. 'Then you would value in a woman the capacity to form her own opinions and express them?'

'Of course, if they are well informed.'

'It's a pity more men don't think like that. As it is, women are taught how to run a house and manage household accounts, which on the whole they do admirably. I promise you, Lord Trevellyan, that any woman who can do that is quite capable of working in a man's world with the fortitude of a soldier.'

Max was surprised by the ferocity of her argument and conceded that she had a point. 'It's a fact that no one would take a woman seriously and the Chinese would refuse to deal with them in business matters. Convention would forbid a woman to have any direct contact with suppliers.'

'Where business is concerned there is a good deal about which I am ignorant, but I am sure I can learn.'

'I believe you would, and I am also certain you would make a formidable businesswoman, but here in Hong Kong the barriers are insurmountable. You would have more chance in England. Do you have relatives you can go to in Britain?'

'My maternal grandmother is my only living relative that I know of. She lives in England.'

'But you want to stay here.'

'Yes, although I have not always lived on Hong Kong. Before I came here I lived in England, in Eastbourne. Not wishing to leave me and my mother so far away, my father brought us here to live.' Casting her eyes down, hesitantly she stammered, 'T-Teddy wants to marry me.'

For a moment, Max was unable to absorb the full shock of that. He stared at her in disbelief, his reaction quite forceful, which surprised her. 'Marry? But you are just seventeen years old. He is old enough to be your father. It's insane.'

'What is?' She already sensed that Lord Trevellyan felt a certain amount of antipathy towards Teddy and had already deduced that it might be because Teddy spent too much time with his wife.

'Marrying a man like Teddy Longford. You're not considering it?'

She shook her head. 'No, I couldn't marry him—although I suppose if I did, I would be able to remain here.'

'You would be marrying a father figure.'

'But—wouldn't I learn to love him—as a wife, as my mother loved my father?'

He shook his head, his features tense. 'Love can't be forced. You can't *will* love to happen.' *If you could, Nadine and I wouldn't be where we are now*, he thought bitterly.

'But won't love come with marriage?' Marietta asked with the innocence of a seventeen-year-old girl who had been raised in a loving household with loving parents.

'Don't ever let anyone convince you that you can be happy with someone who doesn't love you, and don't ever love anyone more than he loves you. Don't allow yourself to do it.'

'I won't,' she whispered. 'When I marry, my husband must love me at least as much as I love him. I shall marry someone just like my father, and I won't marry until I know my own mind.' Suddenly the last image she had of her mother lying in her own blood raised the ugly thought of what she would have to endure as a wife and she shuddered.

Max noticed. 'Is something wrong?'

'No. Just a memory.'

'An unpleasant memory?'

'Yes.'

Max's mind flashed back to the conversation they had had on the veranda at Government House, when she had told him she didn't want babies. He thought that perhaps her memory might have something to do with that, but decided not to pursue it. Perhaps most young ladies had an aversion to giving birth, so she was no exception. He had no doubt that when she married all that would change.

Marietta raised her disconcertingly direct green gaze to his and quietly said, 'I suppose if I were to marry Teddy I would be doing so for no other reason than to stay on the island.'

Her blunt candour amazed Max, but he must make her see what a mistake it would be for her to marry a man as worthless as Teddy Longford. 'I sincerely hope you won't marry him for any reason. The man is not to be trusted and, with any luck, in time he will dig his own grave.'

'How can you say that? I may not like Teddy perhaps as well as I ought to, but he is my father's business partner and not a criminal, so please don't speak of him like that. You shouldn't.'

'Someone has to. Since your father is unable to and there is no one else, the task has fallen on me.'

'Why? You don't know me.'

'I know Teddy Longford and he is not—respectable.' What Max said was true.

'Not respectable? Why do you say that? It's clear you know something. I want some answers. Credit me with a little intelligence, please. I am only ever told what is fit for a female's understanding.' She was tense all over, waiting to hear what Lord Trevellyan had to say. 'Are you trying to tell me Teddy has been doing something illegal? Is that it? And please, I don't want you to mention my father in any of this. Not now. It would be disrespectful.' Marietta didn't want to know what her father did in his private time. She didn't want to think about it so she wouldn't. 'It would not be appropriate.'

Max drew a deep breath and returned her expectant gaze as steadily as he could, aware that she was awaiting his answer. There was every chance his next words might shatter any fondness she might have for Teddy Longford. Her feelings for her father were strong and constant. Max didn't want to say anything that would damage that and hurt her, but Longford was another matter.

But whatever shady deals Westwood and Longford were mixed up in, they were amazingly good at it, at making money. Monty Westwood had become wealthy in his own right from his trade in luxury goods in India before he'd met Longford, and on his death his daughter would become an extremely wealthy young woman and a target for fortune hunters. It was as well that she was forewarned what she would be up against when she found herself without her father.

'I understand, and the answer to your question is yes. Please understand that it gives me no pleasure to tell you what I must, but when your father dies and I have left Hong Kong, you will be better prepared to deal with any unpleasant situation which might arise. So listen to me and brace yourself, for what I am about to tell you is not pleasant. There is more to Teddy Longford than is allowed to meet the eye. He is involved in the shady business of opium smuggling and has been for years.' Max had her attention and he could see he was stirring up her resentment.

Marietta stared at him with disbelief. In a few harsh words Lord Trevellyan had already begun to turn her fears into huge black monsters. But despite her own growing dislike of Teddy, he was her father's partner and she felt a sense of loyalty. She knew that opium was as important to Hong Kong as its harbour and an aspect of the colony's prosperity. But after her visit to the native quarter with Oliver, and afraid of what it might do to her friend if he continued to take it, she considered it abhorrent that Teddy had no scruples about using it as an item of trade.

'That's a very serious thing to accuse him of. I find it difficult to believe it of Teddy.'

'If you doubt my word, a few enquiries in the Chinese quarter will tell you all you need to know about your father's partner. I am a businessman myself, having come here to make investments in what I consider to be profitable ventures. Through studying profit-and-loss accounts and meeting with other businessmen in the colony, I know which firms to trust and which to avoid. It's a fact that the island is awash with opium and there are several businesses in the colony of which the authorities are suspicious.

'I have to tell you that they've had their sights on your father's business partner for a long time. Longford is ambitious and greedy for money and too tough-minded to be frightened on to the straight and narrow by the threat of customs officers and having his ships set upon by pirates. When he has opium on board, rather than pay for an armed escort, as most legitimate merchants do to protect their ships against pirates, he avoids the treaty ports where customs duties are levied and actually pays the pirates well to leave the ships of Westwood and Longford alone.'

Max was brutal in his assessment of Teddy.

Marietta had said she didn't want to hear her father accused of any wrongdoing, but now she had to know. 'Since Teddy and my father are business partners, I suppose it would be naïve of me to believe my father is innocent in all of this.'

'Yes, I'm afraid it would,' he replied quietly but firmly. 'I'm sorry. I beg your pardon if what I have told you has upset and offended you, but you said you wanted to know.'

'Thank you. I am grateful to you for that at least.' Marietta bit her lip. She'd been expecting something like this, but it was dreadful to hear it out loud. She closed her eyes. It was too much to absorb all at once. The scale of what her father and Teddy were involved in shocked her. It made her feel angry, sick and utterly stupid for not having known. But how could she? Opium smuggling wasn't the sort of thing that was mentioned in female company and certainly not with girls of her age.

'Listen to me and take note of what I am telling you,' Max said. 'Be strong, because when anything happens to your father, you're going to need to be.'

'When my father dies and Teddy is arrested—for if the powers that be already suspect him of smuggling opium, he cannot continue doing so for much longer—does that mean that I, too, will have to pay for their crime?'

'No, it doesn't have to be that way.'

'Doesn't it? Are you saying I won't be ostracised by every decent family on the island—by people I have always thought of as friends? They will cease to look on me favourably as marriage material for any one of their precious sons lest I corrupt them.'

'That is nonsense. You are young and popular and exceedingly pretty. There must be a veritable army of young men on the island who would be more than happy to marry you.'

'No. I've only ever been close to Oliver and Julian—as friends you understand.'

'Then when anything happens to your father, go to England. That is where your friends will be, don't forget. Your father's lawyers will sort out the mess he and Longford have got themselves into.'

The softly spoken words had been filled with such quiet conviction that Marietta simply stared at him before she finally said, 'Yes, you are right. How clever you are to think of that.'

She smiled for the first time, a slow, enchanting smile that illuminated her face and melted Max's bones. She looked so lovely, so fresh and unspoiled that the armour of bitterness and cynicism that had surrounded him for more years than he could remember began to melt, leaving him suddenly lonely and empty.

Marietta was not yet awakened to the ways of men. She had young male friends and soaked up their admiration and flattery and knew, although she had no experience of it, the minds of men in love. Max recognised something in her expression as he looked at her, something joyous, yet reverent. Her gaze was warm and gentle, at the same time vivid and urgent. Her feelings shone luminously from her smiling face, and her mouth moved and lifted in its desire to be about something of which she was scarcely aware. But Max knew and his heart lurched with the pain of it.

Reaching out, he tilted her chin with the tip of his finger and reverently looked down into her eyes. 'I hope the man you eventually fall in love with is worthy of you,' he said gently. 'I hope he is a man who will have your head spinning and your legs turning to jelly.'

For an endless moment Marietta searched his features and suddenly her world seemed safe and secure again and warm. 'I think,' she whispered softly, 'that it will be more a question of whether I can be worthy of him, since everyone who knows me would tell you that

I am troublesome and opinionated. I've never talked to a man like this before. It's a pity you are married, Lord Trevellyan, for I am beginning to think you are different and the only man who would understand me and put up with me.'

Max stared down at her, then abruptly turned, staring down at the harbour, his hands shoved deep into his pockets. Uncertain of his mood, Marietta remained silent. His profile was harsh. He looked like a man in the throes of some deep, internal battle. A gentle breeze lifted her hair. Suddenly it seemed colder and she shivered.

'I suppose I should go and find the others,' she said when some time had passed and his silence had become unsettling. 'But—before I do, I would like to take the opportunity of saying thank you for taking the time to talk to me. I appreciate your kindness and your friendship.' She felt a wave of gratitude, and something else, too—a desire to show her appreciation.

Max turned and looked at her. 'It was my pleasure.' He meant what he said. Beneath the heavy fringe of her dark lashes, her eyes were amazing, mesmerising in their lack of guile.

'I…will never forget it,' she said softly, hesitantly, her words sincere and heartfelt. He was looking at her intently and suddenly, taking her courage in both hands, she raised herself on tip-toe and placed her mouth on his.

She felt his initial surprise, his shock, his withdrawal, but she kept her lips on his, feeling him respond and gently take her arms and draw her towards him. His lips began to move on hers. It was the most wonderful, warm feeling.

Max was a man used to taking what he wanted when it presented itself. He was also a man who had just left his wife after yet another blistering row and he wanted to forget it—and what better way than being with an innocent girl, pliant and sweet in his arms, seeming to welcome his embrace? He felt his own response, but his conscience chose that unlikely moment to suddenly assert itself.

Marietta pressed towards him, longing for him to kiss her more deeply, but urgently, almost violently, he pushed her back.

'No, Marietta. This has to stop. I deserve to be horsewhipped. For God's sake, you are a child still. I'm not in the habit of kissing innocents. Do you forget that I am a married man—that I have a *wife*?'

'No,' she said, her lovely face mirroring her bewilderment at his abrupt change of mood. He was angry, and why shouldn't he be? He saw her as a child, a stupid, pathetic child who had a lot of growing up to do. 'It is I who should be horsewhipped. It wasn't your fault. I made you do it.' She was engulfed with shame that she could so easily have put aside his marital state. She had not meant for this to happen—before God she had not, but it had and could not be undone.

Marietta saw his shoulders stiffen and he took a step back. She could see by his expression that she had gone too far. Reaching out, she placed a hand on his arm. The gesture was spontaneous, but one she immediately regretted, for Max drew back further, resisting her. She dropped her arm and he took another step back. His expression was a curious blend of withdrawal and derision.

'What exactly did you think you were doing?'

'I—I acted without thinking. I'll know better next time.'

Max's gaze narrowed on her face. 'Of course you will. But there won't be a next time.'

Marietta placed her hands to her burning cheeks in an attempt to fend off the hurt she had inflicted on her raw emotions. 'No, of course not. I'm so sorry. I've gone too far. I shouldn't have done that. It isn't what you want.' She widened the gap between them, almost tripping in her eagerness to get away from him. How he must despise her.

Their gazes linked and held, hers horrified by her actions, his a blend of seriousness and anger and frustration. She was the first to look away.

'No, it isn't, Marietta. Friendship is no basis for a love affair.'

'But I never meant—'

His voice cut across hers with the slashing force of a knife blade. 'Don't make the mistake of falling for me. That would be a foolish thing to do.'

'I won't, and why are you saying these things? You are heartless.'

'You're right,' he bit out, his voice all the more frightening because it was so low. 'I don't have a heart. Whatever sentiment I have created, you have deceived yourself. And don't kid yourself into believing that beneath my harsh exterior, I'm as tame as a lapdog. Many women have made that mistake and regretted it.' When she opened her mouth to speak, he said, 'Stop it, Marietta. You will oblige me by refraining to speak of this again.'

Flinching from the sting of his tone, Marietta looked at his hard, handsome face, at the cynicism that was a part of him. She swallowed convulsively. 'But—that isn't what I want—not what it meant,' she said in an attempt to relieve the tension vibrating in the air between them. She felt her control collapsing and there were tears in her eyes. 'I'm sorry if I offended you. I didn't mean to. Oh dear! I don't know what I was thinking of. I'm such an idiot. I'm stupid, embarrassingly naïve and gullible. I—I must go. There is nothing left to do or say—at least, nothing you want to hear.'

'No.' He stood still, taut, fierce tension marking his mouth.

Marietta heard the absolute finality of that word. She could no longer look at him. 'Please excuse me...'

Never in all her life had she felt so humiliated. The memory of what she had done was intolerable and she wished she were dead. She walked away from him on legs that shook, trying to retreat from a predicament into which she should never have put herself in the first place. Not until she was well away from Max did she dare to reflect on what had just happened. He had made her head spin and her legs go weak and set a fire burning in the pit of her stomach and her breasts to tingle. But what had she been thinking of? Lord Trevellyan wasn't a youth like Oliver and Julian, but a man. Yang Ling had often remarked that all men were boys at heart—but that certainly didn't apply to Lord Trevellyan.

He had a wife and she should not have kissed him—it had been sinful of her to do it. She chided herself as being stupid, for that was exactly what she was—seventeen years old and stupid. But ever since she had met Lord Trevellyan she had been struck by a tempest of emotions, which had led to the incredible realisation that what she felt for him was different to anything she had ever felt before.

But as her battered nerves cried out for relief, she remembered the cruelty with which he had rejected her kiss. Her eyes turned stormy with indignation. How could she have imagined they might be friends! He was cold and cynical and hard—and he had a vicious, unreliable temper. But why had he spoken to her so harshly, as if she were a mentally deficient schoolgirl, when all she had wanted to do was to thank him for his kindness? Had he deliberately wanted to hurt her?

Max watched Marietta run up the hill in search of her friends. He knew how upset she was and his conscience tore at him, but he would not go after her. His rejection had hurt her, but he'd done so because he had to, he reminded himself. He couldn't let her waste one moment of her precious life believing she was in love with him. Cursing softly, angry with himself, but none the less inclined to change nothing, he strode down the hill.

Two days later Monty's condition was unchanged. Feeling the need to get out of the sickroom, out of the house, remembering Lady Trevellyan's fan, Marietta went to the hotel. Initially she had intended sending one of the servants to return it, but in the light of the conversation she had overheard between Lord and Lady Trevellyan—and also swamped with guilt and misery following Lord Trevellyan's kiss, full of regret and extremely upset about it and not wishing to be the cause of any unpleasantness between Lord Trevellyan and his wife—she decided to return the fan herself, hoping to explain to Lady Trevellyan that she really had nothing to worry about.

After that there would be no further communication between her and Lord and Lady Trevellyan. Yet, despite her philosophical understanding of the situation, she sighed with a deep unfamiliar feeling of regret.

She arrived at the hotel just as afternoon tea

was being served in the dining room. Leaving Yang Ling in the foyer to wait for her, she went up the wide, curving staircase and along corridors, stopping outside a door. Next to it was a brass bracket with Lord and Lady Trevellyan written on the card. Her knock was not answered. Disappointed, she was about to turn away when she thought she heard a sound from within.

For some seconds she stood, not knowing what to do, then, her curiosity getting the better of her, she tried the knob. The door wasn't locked. Hesitantly she pushed it open and entered a small ante-room. Slowly she moved to one of the two bedrooms and went in. The curtains were half-drawn so that the room was dimmed. A queer smell hung in the air. It was a sour stench—blood, she thought. Her eyes were drawn to the bed, where Lady Trevellyan lay against the pillows, a brightly patterned Chinese robe draped on top of the bed covers. Her eyes were wide open and staring. Her skin was pasty and beaded with perspiration, her eyes fever bright and there was a desperate look about her.

Concerned, Marietta went to stand beside the bed, but the poor woman didn't acknowledge her presence. In her delirium she rambled and muttered softly. Marietta was both shocked and alarmed by her condition. She took a deep, controlling breath. Lady Trevellyan was obviously very ill and must have been like this for a long time. But where was her maid and why wasn't her husband with her? Taking her hand, Marietta squeezed it gently, leaning over to speak.

'Lady Trevellyan? It's Marietta Westwood. I—I've come to return your fan. I found it at the ball at Government House. I'm so sorry it's taken me so long.' Placing the fan on the bedside table, she gazed down at her. Her voice must have penetrated Lady Trevellyan's mind, for suddenly she clutched Marietta's hand. Her fingers were dry and hot, her breathing shallow.

'Marietta…? Oh, yes…I remember you— such a pretty little thing. You fell off your horse, didn't you? Max was so angry—and you were so very brave. I congratulate you,' she breathed softly. 'There are not many people who would dare face up to my husband's wrath head-on—especially a woman. Please don't go— don't leave me. I have been at my wit's end, not knowing what to do.'

'But you do look very ill. I think I should find someone…'

'No—no, you mustn't.' Closing her eyes, she took a moment to catch her breath, her weakness almost overpowering her. 'I need your

help. There is no one else. You must promise
to help me… He doesn't love me, you see,' she
uttered quickly, her eyes opening and fasten-
ing on Marietta's. 'He doesn't want me or our
baby. What kind of man is it that doesn't want
his own child?' she whispered wretchedly.

Marietta didn't want to listen to this. 'Please
let go of my hand. I must get someone to help…'

'No—no. Stay with me—you mustn't leave
me. Promise me you will help me.'

'But how can I help you if I don't know what
the problem is?' Marietta cautiously replied.
'You look very ill. How long have you been like
this? Have you seen a doctor? If not, I must get
one to come and see you.'

She became alarmed. 'No—no doctor.'

'Are you in pain?'

She shook her head, exhausted and perspir-
ing heavily. 'Not any more. I was—but it's over
now. No one must know what I've done.'

'What do you mean? What are you talking
about?' Marietta's heart began to pound and
she had an awful premonition that what Lady
Trevellyan was about to disclose would horrify
her. 'Lady Trevellyan—what have you done?'

'The baby—he didn't want it. I had to do
it. Please don't hate me. I had to get rid of the
baby, you see… It was the only way…' Calmer

now and beginning to float away into a dark oblivion, she looked at Marietta as if she saw her for the first time. 'How could he do this? He has ruined my life.' Closing her eyes, she whispered, 'Don't fall in love, Marietta. All it brings is pain and heartache.'

'But—your husband—he will support you.'

'My husband?' Her lips twisted with bitterness. 'My husband hates me.' She became still and closed her eyes. 'I—think I'm bleeding. Would you—look?'

After several deep breaths, Marietta turned back the covers, steeling herself to look at the sickening pool of blood Lady Trevellyan was lying in. Her stomach rolled. So much blood—Oh God, she had seen it all before. Memories, images of her mother—three babies—dead babies, two boys and one girl, two of them not quite right.

'Oh, my goodness—what shall I do?' Her face was frozen, but her eyes were enormous and there was disbelief in them. She looked at Lady Trevellyan, only to find she appeared to have slipped into unconsciousness.

There was the taste of bile in her mouth. Feeling sick and terribly light-headed, she darted through the open door of the adjoining dressing room and was sick into a bowl. Reluctant to go back into the room, she wiped her mouth and slowly went to the door at the same time that someone came into the room. Unable to make her escape as a visiting stranger should have done, Marietta stayed where she was, her hands shaking as she pulled the dressing-room door to, so that it was almost closed, hiding like some dispossessed ghost. She watched what whoever had come in was doing through the crack. It was Lord Trevellyan. Holding her breath hurt her chest and throat. She exhaled silently, not wishing to draw attention to herself.

Striding to the bed, he stood and looked down at his wife. His back was towards Marietta so she couldn't see his face, but she saw the tension in his shoulders as he pulled the covers up over his wife. Striding back to the door, he went out quickly.

Marietta emerged from the dressing room. Alone now, the silence settled around her like a shroud in the room with its elegant hangings and brooding pictures. Looking towards the bed where Lady Trevellyan lay so still, pity for the poor woman welled up within her. Not wishing to be found, she rationalised that it would be imprudent of her to stay.

So extreme were her thoughts that her brain retreated into some kind of limbo. She waited until her breathing was normal and the resolve to act like nothing untoward had occurred became cold and firm with her before she let herself out of the room, but she had no clear recollection of leaving the hotel, for the insensibility nature provides to protect the mind fell over her.

She thought she would wake any moment and find that it had all been a hideous nightmare, no more than that.

The next day when the sun came up over the harbour and the community was abuzz with Lady Trevellyan's sudden and unexplained death, Marietta realised it had all been real and the reality of what she had witnessed began to solidify in her mind.

Her feelings for Lord Trevellyan had always been nebulous. Now a part of her hated him because she judged him to be cold, heartless, cruel and the cause of his wife's death.

Monty Westwood's health declined steadily over the following days. Fearing the end could not be long, Marietta sent for Dr White. It was a joyless time for her. She waited, looking drawn and anxious, the handkerchief in her hand limp and damp with her tears.

'How is he?' she asked when a sombre-faced Dr White appeared. 'Is he worse?'

'I fear so. You must prepare yourself.'

Bright tears filled her eyes. She swallowed and held herself very erect. 'Then I will go to him.'

Because it was the height of summer the funeral was held without delay. Teddy took care of all the arrangements. After a brief ceremony Monty Westwood was laid to rest in the colonial cemetery on the island. Marietta held herself tightly in check as the coffin was lowered into the deep pit. The cleric intoned the final words of interment, reminding them all of where they had come from and where they would return to, then it was over.

It was a modest affair with few mourners, for even in her innocence and grief Marietta was not ignorant of the rumours concerning her father's questionable business affairs, which instigated cautious messages of sympathy.

From a discreet distance Max watched her. Even in the depths of his own misery, he could feel her despair. Her face was creased with pain and her eyes were lost and lonely, like those of a child who found itself among unfriendly strangers.

In a moment of weakness when Marietta felt that everything was just too much for her to bear, she swayed. Someone took her arm. She felt a chill touch her, and because there were some feelings too painful to hide, she spun round to find Lord Trevellyan by her side.

She was still in a state of devastation over the loss of her father and unable to shake off the appalling death of Lord Trevellyan's wife and what had transpired in that hotel room. It had been a constant wearing down of her strength, which was at its lowest ebb. Now she looked at this man who would give her comfort. Through her pain, wonderingly she saw compassion in his eyes, but she didn't want it. She didn't want anything from him.

Her eyes were ice-cold green, hard and merciless when she spoke coldly and quietly, for his ears alone. 'Please don't touch me. You're vile. I know about your wife. I know what she did—what you made her do. I had no idea you could be so brutal.'

Max stepped back. Her words cut him to the bone, sliced into his heart, but his face remained impassive. 'You are at liberty to think so, Miss Westwood.' He inclined his head stiffly. 'I bid you good day.'

* * *

Afterwards close friends and acquaintances gathered at the house to discuss with a great deal of interest what was to be done with Marietta. She would spend the next twelve months in mourning. There would be no outings, no parties, no nothing. It had all been too much of a strain, for Marietta was far too shocked and weary to be dragged into the argument of where she would live.

It was a relief to her that the scene in the garden when Teddy had proposed marriage was not repeated. No doubt he had taken her at her word and was prepared to leave it at that. Besides, it was all taken care of—her father had seen to that. She had inherited his half of the business. Since it was unacceptable for a woman to enter into the male domain of business affairs, his lawyer told her he would deal with everything and send her regular reports.

He was astonished when she instructed him to find a buyer for her share in the business, and that he should approach Teddy, since he had shown an interest. She didn't want it. She would not be party to anything that was illegal, that ruined people's lives and might result in her being arrested.

* * *

Marietta was to go to her grandmother in England, who would be her guardian until she married or reached twenty-one. But Marietta didn't want to go to England and live with some unknown old lady who would have charge of her. Even though Oliver and Julian had already left the island for England, she doubted that she would be allowed to see them. She wasn't ready to leave. She didn't *want* to leave Hong Kong. She didn't want to change her life. She liked things the way they had been before... But she had no choice in the matter.

The weeks of her father's illness and Lady Trevellyan's death had had a profound effect on her. It had also made her strong. She felt a cold, powerful determination to endure like nothing she had felt before and that made her able to face things she hadn't thought she could face.

On the long voyage to England, through the blistering heat of the Indian Ocean and the passage through the newly opened Suez Canal, which cut weeks off the voyage, as the knowledge of all that had happened surged through her veins, she had to stop and steady herself, to reassure herself that the years of carefree days, of laughter and dreaming, were behind her and, no matter what the future held, she must get on with it.

She was resolved to marry as soon as possible, because being a married woman would have its benefits. She would have more freedom, for it would liberate her from a good many restrictions—but no matter who she married, she was determined that there would be no children. Let other women bear them if they wished, but childbirth was not for her.

Chapter Four

The night was sultry, the sky a canopy of twinkling stars as the day slipped slowly by. Delicate lanterns suspended at intervals among the trees shone down on exquisitely manicured gardens, where the rich and privileged of London's society promenaded. They wandered between herbaceous borders, pausing to admire the elegant Grecian statues and Roman gods and cascading fountains. The splendour and grandeur of the scene—a shimmering sea of sweeping skirts, rustling silks and satins all the colours of nature, and delicate lace festooned with ruffles and bows, low-cut bodices, sparkling diamonds and softly glimmering pearls, jewel-encrusted headwear festooned with feathers, hair arranged in curls and ringlets adorned with ribbons and flowers—gave to the occasion an effect so unique, so fraught with grace and grandeur, that it seemed exquisite, sublime and joyous.

Green liveried footmen passed among the guests with salvers of champagne and exotic delicacies. Inside the house tables were laden with an amazing feast—a riot of plenty to be eaten off Sèvres plates and wine to be drunk out of Venetian glasses. Guests wandered into the ballroom through French windows opening on to the lawns. Here music played by an orchestra floated out on to the air.

The whole was an elaborate display, exquisitely beautiful, for this reception being given by the Dowager Lady Wingrove in her London house for the introduction of her granddaughter into London society. To be invited to such an important occasion was an honour and a privilege and a true mark of distinction, for Lady Wingrove was only ever seen in choicest circles and her friendship with prominent members of royalty meant that her invitations were not bestowed lightly.

The orchestra stopped playing and a lightning bolt of anticipation fell over the guests. Heads turned, champagne glasses halted halfway to lips, conversation ceased in mid-sentence and left behind a silence. All eyes gravitated to the terrace. They waited with baited breath for this, their first glimpse of the girl from Hong Kong, possibly the wealthiest young woman to leave the island.

Two young women got up from the bench in the rose garden where they sat drinking champagne and nibbling on delicious delicacies. Here the mood was relaxed, the night air filled with the fragrance of roses, sparkling with laughter and conversation spiced with the knowledge that all present were unquestioned elite. One of the ladies was Lady Claudia Murray, a stunning, fair-haired beauty dressed in a low-cut gown of shimmering apricot satin and swirling lace. Her husband, Lord George Murray, was a Member of Parliament, his country seat in Kent.

As curious as everyone else, the two ladies moved closer to the terrace, craning their necks for a better look.

'At last we are about to see the heiress for ourselves. Lady Wingrove has kept her under wraps for long enough. My dear husband George says he's heard that she's a stunning beauty,' Claudia said, trying not to sound too acid.

'I believe she is,' her friend Amelia replied. 'But what I don't understand is why everyone is making such a fuss.'

'Nor do I. George says she's been raised to believe that money will open any door to her, and, with both her parents dead, her grandmother, whose ambitions for her granddaughter are limitless apparently, has her down for a coronet at least.'

'I dare say that her kind of wealth can buy her pretty much any husband she chooses within the British aristocracy, but one cannot forget that her wealth stems from trade and if it's a prince she's after, then she'll have to go abroad, where royal titles are plentiful.'

'That is quite true, Amelia,' Claudia replied, working her fan vigorously, 'although there is more than one impecunious blue-blooded man here who would welcome a commoner as his bride if she's rich enough to enable him to rebuild and refurbish his crumbling estate.'

'If she proves to be the intelligent beauty everyone is talking about, then she might well wring an offer out of a duke.'

'Don't be ridiculous, Amelia. There isn't one duke I can think of without a wife.'

Amelia cast a smug look at her friend. 'You are mistaken, Claudia,' she said in a breathy voice. 'One particular duke does come to mind.'

'It does? Who?'

Amelia directed her gaze back to the terrace, a faint smile tugging her lips, for she knew perfectly well how her next words would upset Claudia. 'The Duke of Arden. If what everyone says about Lady Wingrove's granddaughter is true, then he might find her as irresistible as the rest. Have you ever seen him with a woman who wasn't a raving beauty on his arm? He's just come back from America, has he not? If anyone should know, it is you.'

Amelia's words hit their intended target. Claudia stiffened and her face turned ashen. 'He wouldn't,' she whispered hoarsely.

'And you are certain of that, are you, Claudia? You know how fond Lady Wingrove is of the Duke of Arden. It's quite possible she's paired him up with her granddaughter already.'

They fell silent as they fixed their eyes on the terrace. Two pairs of matching footmen stood on either side of the French doors, their faces impassive in the lantern light. The butler stood to one side, his back ramrod straight, and in stentorian tones announced Lady Wingrove and her granddaughter Miss Marietta Westwood.

Then on to the terrace stepped Lady Wingrove, majestic and elegant in saffron-coloured satin and a diamond necklace. With her white hair and the delicate lines on her face, she looked

every one of her sixty-five years, but with a
regal quality that made her transcend age.

But it was the young woman who was just
a step behind her that everyone's eyes were
focused on. Rumours were rife concerning
this lovely young woman, and word was out
that she was already being tipped as the next
Season's leading lady of society. Holding her
gloved hands loosely at her waist, the exotic
goddess with a face of unforgettable beauty
stood straight and slender with her head held
high. She stared out over the crowd, her slightly
slanting, lustrous olive-green eyes above high,
delicately moulded cheekbones opened wide.
Her reddish-brown shining hair was swept up
in a mass of curls about her head, while a fat
soft ringlet was draped over one bare shoulder.
Her lips were generous, her nose perfect, her
cream-coloured silk gown simple yet exquisite.
Made for her by one of London's finest couturi-
ers it skimmed every curve to the waist before
floating down in a full skirt. Over it the softest
net embroidered with hundreds of tiny crystals
sparkled and glinted as though the gown had
trapped a galaxy of stars.

The hush broke into a dozen whispered questions, which spread out in envious ripples. All
her senses finely tuned to the slightest variation

in the tone of the crowd before her, Marietta stared at them all—she could not afford to look at anyone in particular. She seemed in awe of the magnificence all around her, as if she had not yet grasped that all this fuss was for her. Then she smiled. Secure in herself, secure in certain victory, her confidence was to be admired. This was for her. She drank it all in with shining eyes. It really was quite astonishing.

When she had arrived in England her grandmother had taken it upon herself to help her become a part of this strange new world, full of so many unknown people who all knew how to behave in it and looked down their snooty, aristocratic noses at a foreign girl whose money was associated with trade. Not wishing to expose her too soon into society, her grandmother had whisked her off on an extended tour of Europe to acquire what she called 'polish'.

They had arrived back in London just two months ago, with enough time for Lady Wingrove to prepare her for her introduction into society before they journeyed north. Marietta had not yet seen Grafton le Willows, the Wingrove family mansion in the Border country, but she knew her grandmother was impatient to go there. Usually at this time of year—which she had told her ignorant granddaughter was the hunting and shooting season—she invited a party of friends from London to partake of her hospitality for one week.

Lady Wingrove had made her intentions clear to Marietta. She wished for her to make what she called a brilliant match, and to that end she had in mind a duke who was a widower with no children. He was the Duke of Arden, a neighbour of her grandmother's on the Borders. He had sailed for America several months ago, but was expected home at any time—hopefully in time for Marietta's début. Failing that, she would meet him at Grafton le Willows.

Pleading her case—and contrary to her decision to come to England to marry as soon as a suitable beau could be found because, having enjoyed her time in France, she was no longer impatient to wed—Marietta had told her grandmother that she was in no hurry to find a husband, that she wanted to enjoy her freedom a while longer, giving no indication to her grandmother that at the heart of her resistance lay the dread of bearing a child. She also told her grandmother that she might have an aversion to the duke she had selected for her and might not want to marry him, but the lady didn't seem to listen and had merely stared at her with an expression on her face that could best be described as blank.

Marietta had ceased to argue, but, having failed to make her understand, she resolved to take more drastic measures if she took a dislike to the duke when they met. In Paris she had loved attending the many social functions continually held in the nation's capital and had looked forward to enjoying the same in London, but her grandmother was impatient to take her to what was now her home in the north of England. This gave her even more reason to enjoy the party, to have the eyes of everyone upon her. She would revel in the admiration and the envy. The finery and the flattery would delight her and she would snap her fingers at those who showed their dislike of her.

She loved to dance and she did so with a natural grace which delighted her grandmother. She could sing and play the piano in a strange and untutored way which was somehow more effective than if she had been taught by a maestro.

Marietta was alluring and fiery and with an unshakeable sense of her own worth. Her moods were like quicksilver and unpredictable, but whether she was aloof and frosty or wickedly appealing, she drew men to her side almost without conscious effort. Those who fell victim to her potent magnetism soon learned to their cost that the fascinating Marietta Westwood had her heart set on a loftier destiny.

'So that's the famous heiress,' Claudia remarked, staring at her. 'She is beautiful, I grant her that. But she's nothing but a parvenu.' A pleased expression came over her face. 'I don't think any of the girls of our acquaintance has anything to worry about.'

Amelia wasn't too sure about that. Marietta Westwood was magnificent. She would give any of their friends a run for their money.

Max Trevellyan stood in the gathering dusk while the last of the sun pulled elongated shadows across the gardens. He was there only because to refuse would have offended Lady Wingrove. Such an invitation could hardly be ignored by anyone wishing to remain on the lady's very exclusive guest list. Having just returned to England after travelling extensively abroad and in no mood for socialising, he would have declined, for Lady Wingrove and his mother had been close friends and she was extremely fond of him and would forgive him anything. But the note she had enclosed telling him she had a matter of the utmost importance to put to him, had piqued his curiosity, which was why he had accepted her invitation.

He was wearing a finely tailored cutaway coat of deep-moss green, narrow fawn trousers and cream-coloured waistcoat. Conducting himself in that august society with the solemn dignity of his rank, his handsome, brooding good looks turned many heads and caused several young women to heave a quiet sigh. Overpoweringly masculine at well over six feet tall, with his thick black hair, piercing silver-grey eyes, his lips firm and sensually moulded with a cynical twist, wide shouldered and narrow hips, he stood out among his fellow men like a magnificent panther.

Above his white neckcloth his face was tanned to a warm brown by the sun, his grave expression relieved from time to time by the appearance of a dazzling white smile that lit his features, but failed to reach his eyes. The beauties whom he took to the balls and theatre—and bed—were in awe of him, for he treated them with little more genuine warmth than he did his servants But this did not deter them from eyeing him with unveiled longing wherever he went, for, despite his cynical attitude, there was an aura of virility about him that made their hearts flutter.

At present his face was a brooding mask. Motionless save for the steady movements of his breathing, the image of relaxed elegance, he stood with his shoulder resting against the statue of a naked Adonis, his hands hanging by their thumbs from his jacket pockets, his eyes resting with little interest on the figure of the young woman who stood by Lady Wingrove's side.

Suddenly he felt a stirring inside him, for there was something about her that was vaguely familiar and attracted his attention. He had the impression that he'd seen her before. She stood quite still—so still that in that moment he knew where he had seen her before. His face became grim and unsmiling, his silver eyes smouldering with emotions too long held in check. When he had last seen her she had been a young girl and she had stood in the same rigid attitude as she did now, when she had stood beside her father's grave in the colonial cemetery in Hong Kong.

When she had faltered and almost fallen, he had reached out with an attitude of benevolence to a grieving girl and she'd spurned him. At the time he had thought she would be grateful for the gesture, but when she turned and raised her eyes and looked straight at him, her face so very young and unguarded, hatred had filled her eyes, so much hatred that he had been puzzled by it. When she spoke her words had reviled him, then she had turned from him and moved on.

After much thought, he realised there were two reasons why she could have turned against him, the first being the sudden and unexplained death of his wife. At the time it had caused much gossip and speculation among Hong Kong society. Because Nadine had been found in her hotel bedroom covered in blood, when no explanation was forthcoming, it was rumoured that he'd somehow had a hand in it. If Marietta had believed the gossip, then she was not the girl he thought she was. But, if so, the fact remained that she had judged him and condemned him and left Hong Kong without giving him a hearing.

The second reason for her coldness to him might have been because of his harsh reaction to the impulsive kiss she had given him, and his words of recrimination afterwards. She had been just seventeen years old, a young, inexperienced and impressionable girl, and he a married man. In all moral decency he could not have acted in any other way.

After that there had not been enough liquor

in the whole of Hong Kong to wash away his self-loathing and to douse the wrath burning away inside him like an inferno. She was dead to him and he didn't give a damn what happened to her. Marietta Westwood had a way of surviving. She'd land on her feet whatever she did and wherever she went—and the very fact that she had turned up here, the granddaughter of Lady Wingrove, proved that.

As he continued to watch her, he wondered how it was that such complete immobility could manage to convey such a vivid and unmistakable impression of uninterest in what was going on around her. She was heartbreakingly beautiful. More beautiful than he remembered—a radiant sunburst in a world choked with darkness. Her face was just as he remembered—heart shaped, wider at the brow and pointed at the chin, with enormous eyes under delicately arched black brows—and though her mouth was too full to suit the accepted standards of beauty, it was a mouth to set a man's pulses beating. It was evident, too, that the gloved hands clasping the painted ivory fan at her waist were possessed of surprising strength.

Max didn't want anything to do with her. It would take an invitation from her—unmistakably and hopefully irresistible—to lure him to her again. But his decision to ignore her existence became harder to adhere to as the night wore on. He saw her hovering on the edge of his sights wherever he turned. The shock of seeing her again had fortified him for a while, but now he no longer had the advantage of that barrier.

Standing on one side, he watched her glide around the ballroom in the arms of first one gentleman and then another without being observed, while the memories of a laughing, adorable girl with shining hair that he couldn't seem to quell paraded across his mind. People turned to look at her and she ignored the stares, but he knew by the way she held her head and smiled secretly that she was aware of the effect she had and enjoyed it.

Meanwhile Lady Claudia Murray and her friend Amelia were taking a short respite from the dancing, the topic of conversation Lady Wingrove's granddaughter.

'Marietta! Who ever heard of such a name? Why—it is not a name that I've ever heard of!' Claudia said spitefully. 'She's quite the lady already—although she'll always be considered an upstart. Having been brought up among the native Chinese, she can hardly be classed as top drawer. Her manner tells me she is quite fearless.'

'That's just as well considering she has Lady Wingrove as her grandmother.' Amelia could see her friend was quite envious of the foreign girl, who was causing quite a sensation on the dance floor.

'That's true. And I hear she has brought a native of Hong Kong with her—Yang Ling! Would you believe? Whatever next? A Chinese coolie I expect. Having been in Paris for so long you'd have thought she'd have a fancy French *mam'selle* to wait on her, not a Chinese foundling. It would appear she has caused much talk among the servants—and those funny clothes she wears are quite outrageous.' She was sitting on the edge of a fountain, leaning over slightly and trailing her fingers on the surface of the water. 'It is clear that Marietta Westwood, or whatever her name is, thinks too highly of herself—but then I suppose we must make allowances for her since she's a foreigner.'

Suddenly she felt something hit her shoulder and then she was engulfed in a horrible sense of shock as she tumbled head first into the water, disappearing for several seconds before reappearing. Struggling to right herself, she spluttered and gasped, horrified as she realised what had happened and that her hair was drenched and her beautiful apricot gown soaked with slimy dark-green weeds clinging to the fine lace.

'What...' she spluttered, wiping the strands of hair from her face, 'what happened...?'

'Oh dear,' an unconvincing sympathetic voice purred. 'What an awful thing to happen. It was lucky for you the fountain isn't deep.'

Claudia blinked away drops of icy water and saw Marietta Westwood standing in front of her, her eyes sparkling with glee—and something akin to satisfaction. Everyone around them had paused to watch with barely restrained amusement as they took in the extent of her drenching. Amelia had one hand clamped to her mouth and her eyes were as big as saucers. Claudia was unable to take in what had happened. Never had she been so humiliated. It was like a nightmare, being at the centre of all these people while looking like a drowned rat, her beautifully coiffed fair hair straggling down her back.

Remembering the pressure she had felt on her shoulder prior to falling in, she turned her venom on Marietta. 'You! You pushed me!' she fumed, taking a hand proffered by a kindly gentleman and climbing out of the fountain, her wet gown and petticoats clinging to her legs.

Marietta's eyes were wide with mock innocence and incredulity. 'Pushed you? Now why on earth would I do that? I don't even know who you are. You simply leaned in too far and overbalanced. It could happen to anyone. If you make your way to the house, the servants will take care of you.'

Still laughing and shaking their heads, people began moving away as Claudia continued to glare at Marietta. 'Say what you like,' she hissed, 'but you *did* push me. I know you did.'

Marietta leaned her mouth close to Claudia's ear, smiling serenely, but when she spoke, quietly and for Claudia's ears alone, her voice was like steel. 'You say I pushed you. You are right. You see, I overheard the nasty and spiteful remarks you made about my maid. Do you think I would let you talk like that about someone who is worth a hundred of you and get away with it? She is Chinese—there is nothing wrong with that. You are mean and disgusting and if it were up to me I would see you marched off the premises without the courtesy of allowing you to clean yourself up. Say what you like about me, but if I ever hear you pour scorn on my maid again, you will know soon enough what my intentions are,' Marietta said cuttingly through her brilliant smile.

Claudia stiffened, shaking with anger, her eyes glittering with malice. 'How dare you speak to me in this manner? I will not take it from the likes of you.'

Marietta lifted one brow. 'Then you would be a very foolish woman. As I said, never speak of my maid like that again. You may be assured that for every insulting word you utter I will repay you tenfold.'

'How dare you threaten me,' Claudia hissed, struggling to maintain her composure despite the way she looked.

'Oh dear,' Marietta said sweetly, her face wearing the expression of a concerned friend. 'If you do not heed my words, you will find there is precious little I do *not* dare. And just to set the record straight. I am not a foreigner. I was born in England and partly raised in England. So, you see, I am as English as you.'

Marietta stood back as a gallant gentleman stepped forwards and draped his jacket about Claudia's trembling shoulders. She shook her head, spraying a shower of drops on anyone within reach. Then, too furious to utter another word and trying to remain impervious to the stares and amused comments, the drenched woman, accompanied by her friend, allowed the gentleman to lead her towards the house.

Marietta watched her go, her heart racing, still full of anger. Who the woman was she had no idea, but she really was the rudest person she had ever met. She turned and made her way round the fountain, only to find her path blocked by a man who was standing watching her.

'That was badly done, Marietta. Of all the brazen, outrageous things to do! I can see you haven't changed.'

Marietta looked up at him. His face was painted in harsh shadows from the flickering lights of the lanterns. At first she had thought he was a stranger, but his voice... How well she remembered that voice and those handsome tanned features. With her heart beating in deep, fierce thuds of disbelief, she stared at him, her eyes drawn to him of their own volition, thinking there must be some mistake, but he was there, his presence a certainty beyond proof of sight. But the expression in those eyes staring at her, those silver-grey eyes, was a mixture of reproach and accusation and he was unsmiling.

'Lord Trevellyan!' she gasped, telling herself to calm down, to control herself. 'What—what are you doing here? I—I never...'

'Never mind that.' He raked her with an insulting glance from the top of her shining head to the tips of her slippered feet. 'Didn't anyone ever teach you how to behave?' he asked contemptuously. He saw her flinch.

'You, more than anyone, know I have a habit of getting into scrapes,' she reminded him tightly, recalling the shame and the humiliation of their encounter on the Peak. Never would he know how deeply his rejection and his cruel words had hurt her that day.

'And I thought you would have grown out of it by now. I saw what you did. What did you think you were playing at? Lady Murray could have drowned. Did you not think about that when you decided to push her into the fountain?'

Marietta continued to stare into his eyes that were glittering liked shards of ice, unable to deny the truth of her actions to this man. 'She deserved it,' she said fiercely. 'If you'd heard what she said—'

'I didn't need to. Whatever was said, she did not deserve what you did to her.'

'I have never heard a woman talk so much and say so little. I have never been so insulted in my life and you take her side.'

'I don't take sides, Marietta,' he said coldly.

'You are in England now, not Hong Kong, and you have to learn to control your temper. You cannot go around shoving people into fountains just because they say things you don't like. That is not how adults do things. They are the actions of a spoiled child throwing a tantrum.'

Putting a hand on her hip, Marietta cocked her head at him, meeting his ruthless stare. 'Lady whatever-her-name-is asked for it,' she retorted tartly. 'She should not have said what she did about Yang Ling.'

He frowned down at her. 'You have brought Yang Ling with you to England?'

'Yes. I gave her the choice. She wanted to come, but I did not bring her here to be insulted by the likes of that—that woman.'

For a moment Max looked disappointed in her, then his expression turned grim. 'Nevertheless, you should be ashamed of yourself. That woman, as you call her, could do you a lot of harm if she has a mind. And you have given her plenty of ammunition. You've got to admit that what you did wasn't exactly a constructive way to settle a disagreement. I've been in a lot of tricky situations myself and I've generally found retaliating the way you did to be the least effective way of sorting them out. When you have climbed down from your high horse, do the decent thing and apologise—although you cannot blame her if she tells you to go to the devil. I cannot believe you didn't know who she was, that you have not been introduced.'

'She knows who I am,' Marietta retorted sullenly.

'There isn't a man or woman here tonight who doesn't know who you are,' he said coldly. 'This whole evening is all about your vanity, Marietta.'

'You're being extremely mean and most unfair! You don't understand...' Suddenly she wanted more than anything to convince him that she was indeed sorry for her actions.

But Max's face hardened again. One corner of his mouth curled and Marietta saw there was a mocking smile in his eyes. She could have wept then, because in that look she saw again the stranger she had seen in Hong Kong, when she was barely out of the schoolroom and he had caused havoc in her heart.

'I think I understand well enough. I recall on our last meeting you told me I was brutal, vile and not to touch you.'

'I remember and I meant every word.'

'I found your change of attitude curious after our previous encounters.'

Marietta blanched. The memory of the scene

flooded through her—as it often did when she thought of the years she had spent in Hong Kong and her meeting with Lord Trevellyan—and that dreadful, humiliating kiss. She flushed hotly, wishing he hadn't mentioned it. 'I'm afraid I was unseemingly forward when we met on the Peak that day. The memory is abhorrent to me. I should prefer to forget the whole unpleasant episode if you don't mind.'

Max's anger returned. He had presumed correctly that she was embarrassed about the kiss and held some resentment towards him for his harsh reaction to it. 'Why, Miss Westwood, what are you talking about?' he mocked, implying that the incident that had so shamed her had meant so little to him he had put it from his mind. 'What Peak? I should imagine we have travelled in different circles. My wife was still alive at the time, if you remember.'

Marietta blushed with an awkward mixture of embarrassment and anger. She had tried to apologise, only to have sarcasm flung back in her face. She felt Lord Trevellyan's penetrating eyes boring into her, eyes flashing with bold insolence. Drawing herself up to her full height, she stared back at him.

'I do not wish to hear about your wife. Your

marriage and her death are your affair and nothing to do with me.'

'Precisely,' he bit back. 'I do not wish to discuss it.'

'Believe me, Lord Trevellyan, neither do I. I'm sorry, but you'll have to excuse me,' Marietta managed in a breaking voice.

Stabbed to the bone by his cutting remarks, biting her lip, she turned on her heel, skirts swirling in a flurry of creamy hues, and headed back to the house. Her eyes misted with the tears his anger and harsh set down had induced. Suddenly she felt so very wretched and deeply regretted her actions. But it was too late now. What was done was done and whatever the consequence of her actions, she would just have to face it.

She had come upon the two women after stepping through the ballroom's French windows, the idea of taking a short stroll through the gardens in the cool evening air to catch her breath too tempting to resist. They hadn't heard her approach. She had remained quite still beneath a rose-covered arbour, breathing in the fragrant scents to clear her muddled head, becoming still as she listened to their exchange and their malicious comments, before realising they were talking about her.

Not particularly upset by this since she seemed to have developed the hide of a rhinoceros since leaving Hong Kong, she was about to turn away. But on hearing the insults directed at Yang Ling, she felt that familiar prickle inside her that would lead to the surge of anger which, before she had learned to control it, had got her into trouble in the past. At that moment it had deserted her. She forgot everything and, careless of flouting everything she had been taught, was eager to give that woman her comeuppance. It was a strange feeling, a certain knowledge that she was doing something very wrong, yet an inability to resist doing it.

Nearing the terrace she paused. The sound of the party drifted to her, filtering through the French windows. She stood alone as guests strolled beneath a sky as clear as a London sky could be in August, crowded with stars that disappeared near the horizon. The evening had started off as well as could be expected, and her grandmother had introduced her to the guests at the right moment so those inside and out could see her and managed to divert every eager male and jealous female eye in sight. Suddenly, with the arrival of Max Trevellyan, everything had gone badly wrong and in the midst of all these people Marietta felt confused and disorientated.

Hearing the orchestra playing a slow waltz, she went inside. It wasn't long before the storm broke. Her grandmother came up beside her, and, not wishing to give the impression that anything was wrong, with a smile on her lips she said, 'You will see me in the library, young lady. You will be there in five minutes and not a second later.'

With a sinking heart Marietta watched her walk away. Clearly the fountain incident had been related to her in every graphic detail. The storm would be violent but brief, she hoped.

In the library Marietta stood mute and un-moving before her grandmother's unwavering stare. Her face was stern, her lips compressed. She certainly looked fierce. They faced each other in timeless attitudes of belligerence until Marietta decided she might as well make the first move and start her off. The longer she waited the more the pressure would build and the more angry her grandmother would be.

'What is it you wish to speak to me about, Grandmother?'

'As if you didn't know. It concerns a certain incident that happened a short while ago in the garden. This is a very serious matter, Marietta. What were you thinking of? Have you any idea of the damage you have done to your reputation?'

'I'm sorry, Grandmother. Lady Murray was saying some terribly insulting things about Yang Ling. I've never heard such unmitigated gall. I was angry—no one speaks about Yang Ling like that.'

'So you pushed Lady Murray into the fountain, and in the process embarrassed everyone concerned. Lady Murray has been escorted from the party by her very irate husband—and he has every right to be angry. However, despite Lady Murray's anger and humiliation, I can only hope we can make amends.'

'Lady Murray told you that I pushed her into the fountain?'

'She did, and I am inclined to believe her. I truly thought that the time and expense of teaching you how to behave like a lady had paid off, Marietta. It would seem I failed. If you wish to be treated as a lady, you must behave as one. A lady does not go around pushing people into fountains.'

Marietta had the grace to look contrite. 'I'm sorry, Grandmother...'

'Of course, her story was confirmed by Lord Trevellyan. He witnessed the whole sorry incident.'

'Yes,' Marietta said tightly. 'He did, and you may rest assured that I have been severely chastened.'

Her grandmother looked at her expectantly. 'I have the impression that Lord Trevellyan did not make a favourable impression on you, Marietta.'

'I'm afraid not. It was one of the most unpleasant encounters of my life. The man is heartless and unfeeling, arrogant, rude and cold beyond words. In fact, I'm of the opinion that I should have dealt with him in the same manner as Lady Murray and shoved *him* into the fountain, too.'

Lady Wingrove smiled and lowered her face, as if she were hiding a secret. 'On the surface he may appear arrogant and cold, but that is only a shell—a thick one, I'll admit, but I have always suspected that the right woman could get past that and discover the gentleness inside him.'

Marietta's look was scathing. 'Not for a moment do I believe there is any gentleness inside Lord Trevellyan and, moreover, I want as little to do with him as possible.'

'Maybe if the two of you were to dance...'

Marietta was still stinging from Lord Trevellyan's cruel set down and, angry because

he had embarrassed her by hatefully report-
ing her altercation with Lady Murray to her
grandmother, her dislike turned into genuine loathing. 'I don't think so, Grandmother. I
doubt Lord Trevellyan would ask me to dance
if someone held a gun to his head.'

Lady Wingrove's brows rose in ironic amusement. 'Oh dear. That bad.'

'It's worse than you can imagine, Grandmother.
Much worse.'

Leaving the breakfast room the following
morning, Marietta was surprised when she saw
the tall, proud-looking Lord Trevellyan standing in the hall. What reason could he have to
be here at such an early hour? She had forced
him from her mind since their parting on Hong
Kong. His life did not impinge on hers. She had
tried to put the memory and the manner of his
wife's death from her, wanting to escape from
the nightmare which had sucked her into its
centre. But the unexpected meeting with him
at the party had badly upset her for some inexplicable reason.

Taking a deep breath, she walked towards
him. Her brows were raised in curiosity, her
small heart-shaped face mirroring her surprise.
She was determined not to be intimidated by

this man so, lifting up her chin, she clasped her hands firmly together. 'Good morning, Lord Trevellyan,' she said crisply, pushing back a stray lock of rich reddish-brown hair from her eyes—eyes that were always bright and enquiring. 'Forgive me if I appear surprised, but after your crushing set down last night you are the last person I expected to come calling—and at such an early hour. If you've come here to vent your spleen on me some more, you can leave.'

He held up a placatory hand. 'As far as I am concerned the incident is over—although it may linger for a long time to come for Lady Murray. I'm sure you must be feeling more angry with yourself this morning than anything she said.'

'Not at all. What are you doing here?'

'I have come to see Lady Wingrove,' he informed her.

'Really? And here was I thinking it was my own charming self you had come to see.'

His lips curled into a tight smile, her sarcasm not lost on him. 'Then I'm sorry to disappoint you.'

She shrugged. 'Please don't flatter yourself, Lord Trevellyan. I'm really rather relieved, but I'm sure my grandmother will be more than happy to see you.'

'I expect she will be. How are you liking England? Does it meet with your expectations?'

'Yes, I like it very well.'

'I am surprised you brought Yang Ling with you. I can imagine she must have raised a few eyebrows.'

'I'm glad she agreed to come with me. I couldn't bear leaving Hong Kong without her. Grandmother raised a disapproving eyebrow on seeing her, but apart from commenting that she appears to be a most efficient lady's maid, she has made no further comment. Yang Ling speaks very good, somewhat pidgin English— but it's flexible enough to meet the needs of those she comes into contact with and I can understand her perfectly, which is the main thing.'

'How does she get on with the other servants?'

'Initially she was a constant source of bewilderment. They didn't know what to make of her peculiar Chinese ways—the way she rearranged my room to make sure the furniture was all in the right place and didn't block any traditional paths used by dragons. Thankfully she managed to achieve the correct balance between the elements of nature and the forces of Yin and Yang, until she was satisfied its *feng shui* to be favourable.'

From his own experiences in Hong Kong, Max could well imagine the peculiar looks and comments Marietta's Chinese maid must have drawn from the other servants.

'Tell me, Marietta, have you seen the papers this morning?'

Taken off guard by his question, she stared at him and shook her head. 'I don't read the newspapers.'

'Then you should, although I must warn you that they don't make for satisfactory reading. Your actions of last night have not gone unrecorded.'

She felt a sense of foreboding as a cold chill trickled down her spine. 'Why, what do they say?'

'They highlight on Lady Murray's tumble into the fountain. The lady's husband claims you pushed her.' He chuckled softly. 'He said what a fine party it was—to be attacked by the hostess.'

Marietta stiffened, her eyes flashing angrily. 'My grandmother was the hostess, not me.'

He shrugged. 'No matter how you look at it, the party was given for your benefit.'

'How can Lord Murray possible say I pushed his wife into the fountain when he wasn't even there?' Marietta retorted crossly.

'Lord Murray believed what his wife has told him. He was none too pleased, apparently, at having to leave the party early last night— because his wife wasn't fit to be seen.' He smiled, delighting in her discomfiture and prepared to twist the knife a bit more. 'And that isn't all.'

'It isn't? Are you telling me there is more?'

'Much more. It would seem you have made a bad start to your stay in London, Marietta. The papers go on to list your other questionable activities, activities such as riding unaccompanied in Hyde Park, partaking in a mock duel in the aforesaid park with two young gentlemen before challenging them to a race.' Max went on to name several other escapades listed that were relatively harmless, but when catalogued in this way read like an indictment.

Furious, Marietta turned away from him, her hands clenched by her sides. 'How dare they? Why, the gossips here are no better than the ancient tabbies in Hong Kong.'

'But you're not in Hong Kong now, Marietta. You are in London and your grandmother's good name is being brought into disrepute by your outrageous activities. If she had been hoping for a dutiful, obedient, penitent granddaughter, I'm afraid she must be feeling sadly disappointed.'

Rage, full bodied and fortifying, brought Marietta round to face him. Never had she expected Max Trevellyan would have the gall to criticise her behaviour in London as he had in Hong Kong. Her misdemeanours compared to his were as nothing, when she recalled how he had treated his poor wife.

'Why, of all the hypocritical, arrogant—' she burst out, then, with a superhuman effort, she took control of her rampaging ire. Lifting her chin, she moved to stand in front of him, looked up into his enigmatic silver-grey eyes and declared, 'Yes, I admit it. I am guilty. I am guilty of everything I am accused of, and if I have brought disgrace upon my grandmother then I shall apologise to her. So there. Are you satisfied now? I consider I have been suitably chastised—although for the life of me I cannot think what any of it has to do with you. What is to be done about it, do you think?'

Max gazed at the tempestuous beauty standing before him, her eyes flashing like angry jewels. He moved his eyes up and down her slender body attired in a daffodil-yellow gown in undisguised familiarity. She had matured in the last two years and she moved with a natural grace and poise that evaded most of the women he knew. Her skin glowed clear and healthy and even though she was very much a woman now, she still exuded a gentle innocence which he found appealing. Beneath this—and if her antics at the party and reported indiscretions were indeed true—her adventurous spirit tinged with obstinacy were unchanged. Yet his admiration for her increased for her honesty and courage in admitting her guilt.

'It is not for me to decide, Marietta. Only Lady Wingrove can do that. If there is to be a scandal, then by the time you return from the north it will have died a death and the gossips will have found someone else to vilify.' He moved to stand close to her. 'Tell me. Do you miss Hong Kong?'

'Of course I do,' she answered, relieved he had turned the conversation away from the highly embarrassing fountain incident. 'It was my home for a long time. I loved it there.'

'I believe you sold your share of the business to Teddy Longford.'

'Yes. I wanted no part of it.'

'That was a sensible move.'

She glanced at him sharply. 'Why do you say that?'

'Because whomever you marry wouldn't

want to find himself the innocent party in a shady business.'

'I know,' she said quietly. 'I am ignorant as to how deep my father was implicated in the smuggling of opium—I didn't want to know, for I wanted no part of it. I haven't heard from Teddy since I left Hong Kong. Have you heard what happened to him after I left?'

Max nodded, his expression grim. 'Things became too hot for him. He had to leave Hong Kong. Where he is now I cannot tell you. Possibly mainland China—or even India. One thing you can be certain of, wherever he is he will be—comfortable.'

'Yes, I'm sure you're right. Teddy always did have a way of extricating himself from trouble.'

'For a long time he managed to hoodwink the authorities in Hong Kong into believing he had nothing to do with the smuggling of opium. It is my opinion that he should have got what he deserved. He should have received a long prison sentence.'

Marietta remained silent, not knowing how to reply to his harsh condemnation of Teddy. Perhaps he was right, but the thought of Teddy in prison made her realise that had death not claimed her father, he might very well have been arrested and imprisoned.

'I hope my granddaughter has been keeping you company, Max?'

Max glanced towards the stairs to see Lady Wingrove descending gracefully. His grim expression vanished. Smiling broadly, his pleasure on seeing her genuine, with long easy strides he went towards Lady Wingrove and held out his hand. 'Lady Wingrove, forgive me for calling at this unsociable hour. I didn't think you would mind, only there is a certain matter I wish to discuss with you.'

She smiled at him, placing her beringed fingers in his hand. 'Of course not, dear boy. How good it is to see you. You're just the man to brighten up my morning.' She looked at him askance, a knowing look in her eyes. 'And would I be correct in thinking that this matter you speak of concerns a certain parcel of land?'

Max gave her a sombre look. 'Absolutely. I will not give up on it.'

She chuckled good humouredly. 'I don't expect you to. I have a rather interesting proposition to put to you, Max. I would have spoken of it last night, but other things happened to divert me,' she said, glancing meaningfully at her granddaughter. 'I expect it will be a lengthy discussion. I'll have coffee sent in.'

'Have you not read the papers this morning either, Lady Wingrove?'

'Not yet—and I always make a point of overlooking the gossip columns.' She laughed lightly and gave a dismissive wave of her hand. 'I imagine they have gone to town about that unfortunate incident with Lady Murray, but never mind. It will all blow over in no time.' She gave Marietta a knowing smile. 'Marietta, my dear, Lord Trevellyan and I have things to discuss. We'll be in the drawing room.'

When the drawing door had closed behind them, Marietta climbed the stairs to her room. What on earth did Lord Trevellyan want with her grandmother? A parcel of land, her grandmother had said. It must be an important matter to warrant his presence just after breakfast. As for her grandmother, Marietta was curious about what she had to discuss with her visitor.

Chapter Five

Grafton le Willows was situated in the heart of the borderlands between England and Scotland. A large two-hundred-year-old manor house employing a veritable army of servants both inside and out, it was pleasantly situated in an open position with an undulating view towards bracken and heather-clothed hills and water meadows in the valley bottom, which in the dry summers provided pleasant strolling for the ladies and good hunting for the gentlemen on the higher ground.

Following a long train journey from London, after a week Marietta had begun to feel more at home, even to recapturing part of the self she had lost since losing her father and leaving Hong Kong. She was amazed at the way she was content to just drift through the days, doing nothing but getting to know her home. She not only saw the beauty all around her, but felt it—as if by some strange alchemy and independence of will and thought her body had absorbed it. She hadn't known what to expect. She had come home, to a home she had never seen, a house that had been her mother's home. Her grandmother seldom mentioned her mother, but here, in these peaceful, beautiful surroundings, she had begun talking about her.

'I do so love it here,' she told her grandmother one night at dinner. 'So did my mother. She was always telling me about Grafton when I was little.'

'Yes, she did, but she preferred London. She liked the social scene—the parties and the theatre, the shopping—as all young ladies do.'

'Yes, I do remember that about her.'

'We had such ambitions for her to make a grand marriage and were preparing to introduce her in society. But then,' she said, her expression turning grim, 'she met your father. He had her completely so that she forgot she had a mother and a father.'

'I'm sure she didn't do that.'

'You did not know her then,' her grandmother said, setting her mouth in a bitter line. 'They wanted each other rather badly. Your grandfather and I refused to allow her to marry a penniless nobody, of course, but she was determined to have him. They ran off together—eloped. Ours is an old and noble family, Marietta. But I ask you, how can a man who talks of love to a woman at the same time urge her to cruelly cast aside the natural love of her mother and father and take her away and leave her family grieving?'

'I am so sorry. I didn't know.'

'How could you? You weren't even born then. The next thing I heard was that they were living in Eastbourne. After that we heard nothing, until we received a letter from her informing us she had given birth to a child—you.'

'There were others—Mama miscarried three babies.'

Pain slashed across her grandmother's face. 'I see. I didn't know.' She sighed and appeared to crumple, as if the memory of those days was a physical weight on her shoulders. 'To his credit your father appears to have done rather well for himself. The fact that he was in trade shouldn't stop you making a splendid match— your wealth and your mother's ancestry outweighs your father's lack of birth.'

'And do you believe the Duke of Arden will see it that way?'

'I believe he will. The duke is my ideal choice.'

'But he might not be mine.'

Lady Wingrove sat forwards in her chair to drive home her point as she set about plying this wilful granddaughter with a mind of her own with her duties. 'Everything I have—the house, the estate—will all be yours when I am gone. You must marry well, Marietta,' she said forcefully. 'You are the last of the line. It is my dearest wish to see you with children to carry it on. Are you to be a spinster who rejects every man that comes courting? Marry a man of rank, a name with a lineage so pure, and your children could be powers in this country—at court. It will open doors if they have a title to aid them. No one could deny such a fine, distinguished name, nor the aristocracy of the Duke of Arden.'

'Grandmother, I am nineteen years old and do not feel in the least like a spinster. I was constantly beset by suitors from the moment we arrived in Paris.'

'And in all of them you saw flaws.'

'Because I disliked most of those who came

courting with a desire for my wealth exceeding their desire for me.'

Lady Wingrove chuckled and sat back in her seat. 'The Duke of Arden cannot be accused of that, Marietta. Our wealth—yours and mine combined—could not compare with his.'

Marietta sighed. 'Then he must be very rich.'

'And very handsome.'

'Then that's a bonus. I seem to have a difficult time coping with marriage proposals. I find all this talk of titles and rank and wealth too much. Marrying for a title has never been on my list of priorities.'

'Well then, all I can say is that if you don't want the Duke of Arden, I'll just have to concentrate on my second choice.'

'And what rank is your second choice, Grandmother?' she asked flippantly. 'A prince? A marquis, or another duke?'

Lady Wingrove raised her head loftily and when she looked at her granddaughter there was a keen twinkle in her eyes. 'A mere earl, would you believe. Unattached dukes seem to be in short supply just now.'

Marietta laughed and, leaning over, fondly kissed her wrinkled cheek. 'Then it would seem that I must consider the one that's available.

But I'm not promising anything, so don't you go reading too much into it.'

The fine weather and the arrival of the visitors her grandmother had invited up from London for some hunting and shooting during the season combined to put Marietta in an agreeable frame of mind. She stood beside her grandmother to welcome her guests, twelve all told, all middle-aged gentlemen who were happy to leave their wives behind to indulge in country sports for a weeklong affair.

There was nothing unusual in this since house parties were a regular occurrence, especially at this time of year. The guests were a jolly lot and the way her grandmother—assisted by a horde of servants to cater for them—presided over the meals and saw that everyone was taken care of would have exhausted a younger woman. She was steeped in English tradition and was secure in the belief that social conversation was the highest art of civilisation, so every evening after a hard day's shoot, dinner was a long drawn-out affair.

There was so much for Marietta to learn about the countryside, so when the last of the party had left to partake in that day's sport, she thrust her arms into the sleeves of a three-quarter-length waisted overcoat in gunmetal grey, pulled on a stout pair of boots and went exploring, eager to learn what she could about nature, the wildlife and how the land was managed. She would have ridden, since the Grafton stables housed some fine horseflesh, but had she done so her grandmother would have insisted she was accompanied by a groom and she did so want to be by herself to wander at will and take a look at her inheritance.

The day was cold, though her own brisk walking kept her warm. Often it was quite a stiff climb, scrambling up and down banks overgrown with bracken and gorse, stopping now and then to catch her breath and admire the scenery, the gently rolling, sheep-dotted hills beginning to turn to the bright-hued glory of autumn. She had to tread with care through wet patches and tangled undergrowth and brambles that lay in wait to trip up the unwary.

She'd been walking for about an hour when she finally came to a halt. Slithering down the trunk of a tree, she sat on a mound of soft green moss within the deep-set roots. The grassy hollow was concealing and secluded, but offered a perfect vista of the countryside. The canopy of leaves above her of bronze and copper and amber stirred in the breeze and the sky was pale blue with just the odd white cloud.

It was so very different from London, which she had loved, with its hustle and bustle, the cries of street vendors and the crash of horses' hooves on the cobbles. Yes, she had loved all that, but here on the Borders where everything happened at a slower, quieter pace and where a person could breathe, she loved the wonderful remoteness of it, even though she could hear the sound of guns as the shooters shot at the pheasant and grouse the beaters drove out of the bracken.

However, knowing she was so close to the shooters, she regretted coming this way today. One stray shot and her short life could be over. Standing up, she was about to go back the way she had come when a fresh volley of shots broke out over her head. Immediately she sank to her knees, aware that her actions might have put the shooters off their target. Then, hearing a single shot and feeling certain it had been aimed at her, she started shaking like a leaf and watched some young birds flap and squawk and scuttle away and become hidden in the undergrowth.

A shadow fell across her and a man suddenly appeared with a rifle in his hands. Instinct warned her that danger was near and she felt threatened. Her head shot up and she was blinded for a moment, seeing only the large, menacing shadow of a man. She was startled and, when Marietta was startled or upset, she went on the attack at once.

'Saints preserve us,' she fumed, springing to her feet. 'Don't you know better than to lurk behind trees and shoot like that? You gave me an awful fright. What are you doing?'

She couldn't believe her eyes when she recognised Max Trevellyan approaching her. Their eyes met and locked for a moment. Marietta's opened wider and wider, displaying astonishment and incredulity, before she brusquely recollected herself. He was dressed in a well-worn tweed jacket and the pale sunlight fell across him, touching his thick dark hair. His silvergrey eyes were clear and alert. For one dreadful moment she panicked, feeling an urgent desire to turn and run. For heaven's sake, she was Marietta Westwood, afraid of nothing and no one. She almost did turn and run, but the fierce resolve with which she had been born and which had developed inside her since she was a child kept her rooted to the spot.

'It's you,' she said frostily, though on a calmer note, though her heart for some bewildering reason was beating rather quickly. She hadn't seen Max since he had come to see her grandmother the morning after the party at which she had disgraced herself. What had transpired between them remained a mystery to her.

Max gazed down at her, slapping his riding crop impatiently against his leg, thinking how different she looked, with her hair all mussed up. The cold and her exertions had put red flags in her cheeks and her eyes glowed. 'Hello, Marietta. I didn't expect to find you in the fresh outdoors. I was out riding when I saw you disappear beneath the tree,' he said, indicating the fine grey stallion which cropped peacefully a few yards away. 'I came to make sure you are all right. There's no need to worry. You are quite safe with me.'

'I don't care if you're the King of England,' she snapped. 'Have you no more sense than to go around frightening people? Did you just shoot at me?'

'I'm afraid I did,' he said, leaning his rifle against a tree.

Marietta was even more outraged. 'With the intention of hitting me?'

'Don't be ridiculous. I'm not in the habit of going around shooting at young ladies—even young ladies who push other young ladies into fountains,' he uttered with a wicked gleam in his eyes, unable to resist teasing her. 'Had I been shooting at you, I would not have missed.'

Marietta stiffened. She didn't like to be reminded of the fountain incident. It had been a horrible humiliation, the second worst time of her life practically—the first being when she had kissed him—and she didn't like to think how humiliated Lady Murray must have been.

'But that is quite shocking. What if your aim had been bad?'

'My aim is never bad.'

'That is fortunate for me.'

A smile lifted the corners of his mouth. 'I did frighten you, didn't I—enough to make you come crashing out of your hideaway.'

'Yes, you did. How was I to know you were not some—some brigand with...'

He cocked a sleek black brow, a gleam of amusement in his eyes. 'What? Evil intent? Designs upon your person?'

'Exactly.' Marietta's tone was biting, telling him he should have more sense than to go around frightening people and shooting his gun at random. She raised her chin a notch to reinforce her disapproval and her thoughts circled, looking for some crack in his armour of implacable calm, some place where she could thrust the blade of her anger, but she couldn't find one.

'By your actions and after seeing those little birds escaping into the undergrowth, I have no doubt that you have spoiled the shoot.'

'So I did, which isn't such a bad thing.'

Her lips thinned into a grim line and she scowled. 'Why do you say that?'

'Because those pheasants are second-clutch birds. Visibly immature and too young to be shot,' he informed her, sitting on the ground and propping his back against a tree, his long booted legs stretched out in front of him and crossed at the ankles. 'It's very unsporting of anyone to do so.'

'I wouldn't know. There really is so very much I have to learn about living in the country. What are you doing here?' she demanded, not in the least mollified. 'Did my grandmother invite you to Grafton?'

'No. Why?'

'She has invited some people up from London for a few days' shooting and I thought you must be one of them. Do you know this area well?'

'I should. I live not far away. We are neighbours. Considering the close ties of our families, does it not seem ridiculous that we should hold ourselves in reserve?'

'Far be it from me to presume upon your for-bearance,' Marietta quipped. 'Whether or not you adhere to a strict code of gentlemanly con-duct is entirely down to your own discretion.'

Marietta's expression remained wary and an-tagonistic. He wanted to shake the stubborn-ness out of her. 'I can see I'm going to have my work cut out softening your attitude towards me, Marietta.'

For a young girl whose looks had once been so inspiring, Marietta Westwood was now no less than a rare gem. The lovely slender nose, the elegant cheekbones touched with a rosy hue, and the delicate mouth and winsome face in its entirety were admirable enough to stir the heart of many of his gender, but it was her large, silkily lashed, olive-green eyes, slanting ever so slightly upwards, that revived images of the girl she had been in Hong Kong.

As much as his heart rallied in admiration at what he saw, conversely his self-esteem suf-fered from the barbs of his erroneous judgement of the past, for it was a simple fact that Marietta was a strikingly beautiful young woman.

'When I first saw you when you stepped out on to the terrace with your grandmother, I thought your appearance had changed by such an astonishing degree that I was left in awe. I suppose I was still thinking of you as the girl I had met in Hong Kong, but that is definitely no longer the case.' His eyes twinkled. 'I never imagined you would turn into such a beautiful young woman.'

Marietta bristled in the face of his unexpected compliments. 'Then why were you so angry with me?'

'Because I was disappointed to find that, beneath all that sophisticated beauty, the girl who didn't blink an eye at dressing up as a Chinese woman and visiting an opium den in the seediest quarter of Hong Kong was still lurking in the young woman who pushed Lady Murray into the fountain.'

The vague smile that touched Marietta's lips was the best she could manage with any semblance of calm. It didn't help that moments earlier she had been forced to construct a cool reserve from the ashes of a resentment she had struggled to maintain since their parting on Hong Kong. Even after feeling as if this man had torn out her heart at that time, it was all she could do to carry on her stilted aloofness.

'Please don't feel you have to apologise,' she said stiffly.

Max arched a sleek black brow, one corner of his finely chiselled mouth quirking into something that looked suspiciously like a grin to Marietta. 'I'm not. You deserved to be chastised.'

'You're right. I did not like what Lady Murray said about my maid, but it did not merit being shoved into the fountain. If it makes you feel any better, I will tell you that my grandmother reproached me most severely. When I arrived in England, she worked hard to teach me how to show proper respect for others. I've since thought of the humiliation and the anguish my actions must have caused Lady Murray and have lamented it time and again. It all seems so petty now. What I did doesn't seem so clever any more. If we should meet in the future, I shall certainly apologise for my inappropriate behaviour and I can only look forward with the hope that I will be forgiven for the trouble I caused.'

'As to that, we shall have to wait and see. Lady Murray is noted for her formidable temper and will not be easily won over,' he said with an assuredness that gave Marietta cause to wonder how well he was acquainted with Lady Murray. He looked at her sharply. 'I imagine you hated having to leave Hong Kong when your father died.'

She averted her eyes as memories came

flooding back. 'Yes—it—was difficult, as it must have been for you when your wife died so unexpectedly.'

Max detected a note of accusation in her tone. He stood up, rage kindling in his glittering eyes. He felt as if she had just sunk her teeth into him. 'When Nadine died. Yes, it was. I was bewildered by your change of attitude and cruel remarks when I tried to offer you comfort at your father's funeral. I hope you didn't believe the gossip circulating on the island concerning the manner of her death.'

Marietta had been tormented by the memories of his callous and cruel treatment of his wife and what she had found in that hotel room in Hong Kong. They crowded in around her until she was overwhelmed by them. Finding it difficult to look at him, she averted her eyes. 'What happened to your wife is not my concern,' she said coldly. 'Do you miss her—your wife? It must be painful for you to speak of her after what happened.'

Max's whole body stiffened and his metallic eyes snapped to her face. His expression hardened into a mask of freezing rage and they glared at each other, the fragile unity they had shared a moment earlier shattered. Her words told him that what he had suspected all along was true: she believed the rumours.

'What happened? How the hell do you know what happened? You, Marietta, don't know what you are talking about and have said quite enough. You forget yourself. Whether it is painful for me to speak of Nadine or not is not your concern and I have no intention of doing so just to satisfy your curiosity.'

The raw emotion Marietta heard in his voice told her how damaged his marriage to Nadine had left him. However, his words rekindled her receding anger and her eyes sparked with chipped ice. 'You are mistaken. It is not idle curiosity. In fact, I am not in the least curious about how your wife died. As you said, it is your affair.'

'Then you will understand why I do not wish discuss it,' he said tersely, remembering how he had done his utmost to cover up the scandal that threatened to erupt over Nadine's death and returned to England. He had taken up his shattered life and carefully put it back together again before embarking on a journey to America.

'I quite understand. Now I must be getting home.'

In silence he accompanied her down the path

towards his horse. When the ground became uneven and strewn with rocks, Max offered her his hand and Marietta took it. At once she was startled by the unexpected jolt of warm pleasure that passed through her as she touched him. She paused and stared at him, and he looked back, the expression in his silver-grey eyes unreadable. She drew a sharp breath and a feeling of dizziness suddenly threatened to overwhelm her.

'Are you all right?' Max asked with sudden concern as she swayed slightly. He put out his other hand and gripped her arm, and she had the distinct impression that in another second she would fall into his arms. A volley of gunshot some distance away broke the spell.

Marietta drew back, her colour high, her eyes ablaze. 'Perfectly. I would like to go now.'

'Would you like me to walk back with you?'

'No, thank you,' she answered coolly, fixing her gaze on the path that led back to Grafton. 'I'll find my own way back.'

The party that sat down to dinner later was larger than usual. Guests from the surrounding neighbourhood were invited, including the Duke of Arden. Marietta had agreed to meet him for her grandmother's sake, although she could not deny that she was curious about him. As for her grandmother's enthusiastic hopes that the duke would countenance a marriage between them, nothing more had been said so Marietta could either assume she hadn't mentioned it to him, or she had and he had refused.

Seeking to fulfil her grandmother's request and present herself in a regal manner, she had chosen a pale blue satin gown with tiny clusters of seed pearls sewn into the skirt. Yang Ling had swept her hair back from her face and painstakingly curled it in a mass of ringlets that fell in soft tiers from the crown of her head and ended at the nape of her neck.

Standing beside her grandmother, Marietta watched the carriages deposit the guests outside the front door. It seemed as if her grandmother had invited everyone in the neighbourhood so that Marietta soon began to wonder if there would ever be an end to the formalities.

And then one face leapt out at her.

The man was Max Trevellyan.

His thick dark hair was brushed back from his forehead. His silver-grey eyes were clear and alert. Her heart for some bewildering reason was beating like a drum. Instead of showing joy at his appearance, she felt an abject despera-

tion. All she could say was, 'Lord Trevellyan!
What is *he* doing here?'

Lady Wingrove turned and looked at her, a
little smile playing on her lips. 'Who, Max? I
did tell you that not only is he a friend, but that
he is also a neighbour of ours, Marietta. Is your
memory so short that you forget?'

'No, of course not. I am surprised, that is all.
We met when I was out walking earlier.'

Lady Wingrove turned and looked at her.
'You never said.'

'I didn't consider it important.'

And then Max was standing before them,
bowing over her grandmother's hand, before
turning his head and fixing Marietta with those
penetrating grey eyes. She had to make an attempt at the right note of reserved cordiality.
'Good evening, Lord Trevellyan,' she said,
looking at him with cool disdain, her voice
tight. 'How nice to see you again.'

'And you, Miss Westwood.'

'Perhaps you would like to go inside. Not all
the guests have arrived.'

'I think you will find Max is the last, Marietta.'

'But the Duke of Arden has yet to arrive.'

'Max *is* the Duke of Arden, Marietta.'

Marietta was stunned. This revelation was so
different from what she had assumed. She stood

totally mute and disbelieving, a blaze of animosity and a shock of terror erupting through her entire body. *The Duke of Arden!* A mixture of anger and hysterical laughter threatened to bubble from her lips, for this was the man her grandmother wanted her to marry. Taking into account their past history, the very idea was madness.

Then she managed to say, 'Is this true?'

'I'm afraid it is,' Max confirmed with a grim smile.

'And you didn't think to tell me—either of you?' she said, looking accusingly at her grandmother, who didn't appear to be in the least perturbed.

'It didn't seem important,' she replied, echoing her granddaughter's earlier sentence. 'Now come along inside. The hunters are gathering. After a day in the open they'll be anticipating their dinner.'

The dinner was a jovial affair, and as the consumption of food and wine increased, the conversation became animated. Much gaiety was intertwined with the serious business of discussing the successful day's shoot. Seated next to a rotund Mr Loxley, who was louder than most of the gentlemen present, and still reeling from the shock announcement of Max Trevellyan's true identity, Marietta let most of it go over her head. Seated at the head of the table, her grandmother was enjoying herself enormously.

'You should have joined us on the shoot, Lady Wingrove,' Mr Loxley said. 'If you're as good a shot as I remember, you'd have bagged a few birds yourself and enjoyed yourself into the bargain.'

'I doubt it. I haven't fired a gun in years. If I were to do so now, I would more than likely shoot myself as a pheasant, and I don't intend to die just yet—not until I have seen my dear granddaughter wed and she has presented me with great-grandchildren. Then I will die a happy woman, knowing my beloved home is in safe hands.'

'Aye, you'll have no trouble there,' Mr Loxley said, smiling benevolently upon the young woman beside him. 'A right bonny lass she is,' he pronounced.

'Positively ravishing,' the elderly gentleman on Marietta's other side, who was well into his cups, agreed. 'By George, if I were not already quite sufficiently well provided for in my own dear wife, I do believe I might offer for her myself.'

'I've no doubt that through your grand-daughter, you'll achieve your heart's desire, Lady Wingrove,' Mr Loxley went on, 'and have Grafton ringing with the laughter of children very soon. What say you, Trevellyan? Arden Hall could do with livening up a bit. A wife and children is what you need—what every man needs.'

Max considered the remark extremely taste-less and tactless, given the fact that his wife had been dead just two years. Uncomfortable that he had been put in this position, his expres-sion hardened and lines of displeasure formed around his mouth. His reply was merely a slow nod before turning his head away in annoyance.

Regarding him from across the table, Marietta thought he seemed to recoil from the whole idea, which reinforced her belief that he did not want children of his own.

Marietta could not stop thinking about Max being the Duke of Arden and the shock of it lingered on. She was angry that they had kept it from her, angry and extremely disappointed.

It was much later before Max succeeded in waylaying an elusive Marietta on the terrace. Left more to herself, she had taken the oppor-tunity to step out of the French doors for some air. Almost in a daze, she moved to walk down the steps into the darkening garden below, and in her narrowed vision she found a hand ready to assist. It was strong, lean and well manicured. The sight of it set her heart to fluttering and she knew even before she glanced up that she would find Max standing beside her. She was right and he looked so handsome it nearly took her breath away, but she was in no mood to be nice to him.

Without preamble, Max said, 'I saw you come outside and thought you might like some company.'

'That all depends on the company, *your Grace*—and please don't touch me,' she flared, eluding his hand. Raising her head and holding up her skirts, she proceeded down the few steps.

With a mocking smile lightly curving his lips, Max followed her. 'You've made your aversion to me abundantly clear, Marietta.'

'Then what are you here for?'

'I, too, felt the need for some air.'

He accompanied her along the path and they walked slowly and in silence for several yards, until Marietta was unable to contain herself any longer.

'Why didn't you tell me who you were?' She

stopped and whirled to face him, her expression indignant and eyes hurling daggers at him. 'You could have told me when we met earlier, but you didn't.'

He shrugged and carried on walking, his hands clasped behind his back. 'A duke or a lord, what difference does it make? I am still Max Trevellyan.'

Marietta ran to keep up with him. 'It isn't just you. My grandmother also kept it from me. Why? Why do I have the distinct impression that you are concocting something between you—that I am being manipulated? And why didn't you tell her that we already knew each other? Why the secrecy?'

'It's no secret. I merely thought you would prefer to tell her yourself. What do you know of your grandmother's plans for your future, Marietta?'

'I can't see that my future is any of your concern, unless,' she said coldly, coming to a halt and turning to face him with a questioning lift to her brow, 'my grandmother has said something to you that I should know about.'

He shook his head. 'Your grandmother and I are involved in a joint business venture at present, so let us say I am an interested party.'

'I see. Well, you heard what she said over

dinner. She wants me wed, and for me to provide her with so many grandchildren that the
house will burst with them. She wants what
she wanted for her daughter before she ran off
and married my father—a penniless nobody in
those days. Now she considers me an heiress by
English standards and she wants me to marry a
title. A prince is out of the question since there
isn't one available in England, but she'll settle
for nothing less than a duke or a marquis.'

'Do you think you need money to attract a
husband?' he asked, subtly ignoring her remark
about marrying a duke. 'You are very lovely,
Marietta. Can you not attract a title by yourself alone?'

She met his eyes. There was an intense, penetrating look in their depths as he waited for
her reply. Not knowing if he was aware that
her grandmother had her eye on him as her
prospective bridegroom, from past experience
with this man she knew better than to embarrass herself by mentioning it.

'As you know, my father was a merchant—a
tradesman—which is a way of life still frowned
upon in noble circles. You are a duke—your
mother a lady as my own mother was. But I
have little interest in distinctions. I hope there
will come a day when people will be judged by

their character and achievements, rather than for their father's name and rank.'

'That is a bold hope,' he agreed. 'But to most people I will always be known as a duke.'

'While I will always be known as the daughter of a tradesman.'

Max looked her in the eye and smiled, then his face turned sombre again. 'I am certain that where marriage is concerned, your grandmother will only do what she considers is best for you.'

'Most marriages are business arrangements. Why should I imagine mine will be any different?'

'Doesn't love have something to do with it? Isn't that what all young ladies aspire to in marriage?'

She looked at him calmly. 'A man can get love, as you call it, anywhere. He doesn't have to marry for it.'

'That's true. Marriages are often made for convenience.'

'But surely a man would want to like his wife. After all, they have to spend a lifetime together.'

From under his strong, straight brows, Max gave her a quizzical look. 'The same could be said for the woman.' He had experienced the bitter dregs of a dying marriage. He had always prided himself on his control over the emotions that caused other people to make such a mess of their lives, but he had discovered through his wife's infidelities what a hollow pride it had been. 'A poor man will put up with a woman in exchange for her money. It is the law that everything a wife possesses when she marries becomes the property of her husband, to dispose of as he sees fit.'

'That doesn't seem fair. In fact, it's so unfair I am tempted to remain a spinster all my life.'

Max chuckled softly at the imperious way she thrust her chin. 'That would be a tragic waste of so much beauty, Marietta. Is it so important that you hold on to your wealth?'

'No, not at all, but I believe in equality and there's nothing equal in a wife giving everything she owns to her husband who is well within his rights to squander it at the tables or some other form of gambling if he has the fancy.'

'Since leaving Hong Kong, haven't you met anyone you wished to marry?'

'No. Oh, I had plenty of suitors in Paris, only they couldn't see me, only what I represented: the big houses, fine horses and lavish lifestyle. I enjoyed France, and in Paris I was dressed by

Worth and surrounded by luxury. Of course my looks are passable, but I knew it was my money that caused the sudden quiet whenever I entered a room. It was my money that made people look at me sideways when I approached. No one was unaffected by it. It didn't bother me, but it might have had I been interested in any one of those suitors.'

She gave him a direct look, her expression serious. 'What would you do, Max? If you were to marry me, would you take all my money? The question is a hypothetical one, naturally.'

He held her gaze for a long silent moment before he said, 'Of course, and the answer is no.' This was true. Knowing the source of Marietta's fortune, that the bulk of it had been acquired by her father smuggling opium into Hong Kong and ruining countless lives, he didn't want a penny piece of it. But to Marietta, by way of explanation, he said, 'Being a rich man in my own right, I would have no need of your money. However, if the situation was different and I was a poor man, I would take a portion of her money and make a generous settlement on my wife. Does that seem fair to you?'

She nodded her approval. 'Yes, although in real life, your dukedom gives you leave to do as you please.'

Sensing she had drawn away from him, Max sighed in vexation and looked across at the delectable beauty. 'My dear Marietta, your questions flow like silk from your lips, but like the scent of roses that clings to you, they prick like thorns into my unwary flesh, leaving me to wonder at the truth of the deep chasm that opened up between us when we parted on Hong Kong.'

Marietta's head snapped up and her eyes flew to his. 'I told you in London that I would rather not speak of it,' she replied, her voice terse. 'Not now. Not ever. Please do not mention it again. And now I think I should be getting back before my grandmother becomes worried and sends out a search party for me.'

When the guests had departed and those in residence had gone to their beds, Marietta went up to her grandmother's room.

'Marietta, come in. I hope you enjoyed yourself tonight and didn't mind too much that I kept back from you Max's true identity.'

Marietta smiled and sat on the bed, looking at her. 'No doubt it was for some mischievous reason of your own. I can't be angry with you because I haven't been entirely honest with you either. You see, Max and I met in Hong Kong. I knew him as Lord Trevellyan.'

'Oh, I see. Well, what can I say? I am most surprised. I really had no idea that the two of you were already acquainted. Why on earth didn't Max say something?'

'Because he thought I should tell you.'

'No doubt you met his wife before she died rather tragically.'

'Yes—she—she was very lovely. Tell me, Grandmother—I've been wondering how well Max knows Lady Murray. He seemed unnecessarily angry over the incident at the party— more like an irate husband, I would say.'

'Claudia Murray and Max—yes, there was a connection between them…once.'

'A connection? What do you mean?'

'She was Max's mistress before he went to America.'

The colour slowly faded from Marietta's face. 'I see. Then that explains why he was so concerned about her when she tumbled into the fountain.'

'Pushed, I think you mean,' Lady Wingrove was quick to remind her. 'You do know what it means, Marietta, for a woman to be a man's mistress?'

'I know that liaisons between men and

women married to someone else were common-place in Paris and I suppose it is the same here. Have they resumed their affair now he's back?'

'The affair had cooled before he went to America.'

'And Lady Murray's husband?'

'They have an open relationship—which is not uncommon.'

A wry, mirthless smile suddenly touched Marietta's soft lips. 'My marrying Max is quite ridiculous, you know—and I know he will agree with me absolutely. I'm afraid you are going to be terribly disappointed. Max will not countenance an alliance between us and I certainly have no wish to marry him—not for financial reasons or social aspirations. And as for pushing Lady Murray into the fountain—his aversion to me has nothing to do with that. You see, we did not get on in Hong Kong. In fact, there were times when he would happily have strangled me.'

The outburst surprised her grandmother, but it was said now and so much the better.

But Lady Wingrove was not about to give up. She mustered her forces to bring herself under control and brought as much parental inflection to her words as she could bring to bear.

'I know you are a woman who likes to feel

she has a will of her own, Marietta. Very well.
I can understand that. But we live in a world
forged and run by men and it is for women to
see their duty and understand it quite clearly
and abide by it no matter what may fall. You
are a member of a considerably wealthy family, a woman who is wealthy in her own right,
a woman destined to be a member of an even
wealthier and more powerful family, for I will
not see you throw away your life and fortune
on a penniless ne'er-do-well with a title merely
to fund his empty coffers. As such, you have
an obligation not lightly dismissed. I will not
ask you to explain your relationship with Max
since it was two years ago and people change—
including Max Trevellyan.'

'In this instance you are quite wrong,
Grandmother. Lord Trevellyan is exactly the
same as he was when I knew him in Hong
Kong—arrogant and completely absorbed with
his own self-importance. Believe me, I am the
last woman in the world he would consider taking as a wife.'

'We shall see about that.'

Marietta was a woman with a mind of her
own. Contrary to what she had told her grandmother, with cool calculation, the thought was

beginning to form in her mind that marriage to
Max might not be so terrible after all.

Max represented security and a release from
the gnawing fear and uncertainty of being
shoved into an alliance with a stranger. Despite
everything that had happened, she trusted Max,
she suddenly realised, and perhaps marriage
to a man whose feelings concerning children
were the same as her own would put an end
to her sleepless nights, when she would stare
wide-eyed into the dark, thinking and worrying about it.

But was she ready for marriage? It was all so
sudden. Was she about to give in too quickly?
Could it be? Could it work? It was, as yet, only a
whisper inside her, but it was growing, becoming more insistent. She allowed the whisper to
extend to the hope that Max might one day feel
for her what he had felt—might still feel—for
Nadine. She shouldn't have kissed him that day
in Hong Kong. It was unfortunate that he had
reacted the way he had, but she had acted in innocence and it had been kindly meant. Being
engulfed with the kind of feelings she had felt
that day, she had been unmindful of propriety
or plain good sense.

What she meant to propose was not wrong.
It was an arrangement to profit them both. She

would go and see Max tomorrow. With that motivation there was nothing for her to do now but wait out the torturous hours until tomorrow morning.

For most of the night she tossed and turned, dreaming and waking with a million things running through her mind. Though her eyes were closed and her mind drifting, his face swam dreamily into her vision. His eyes were a warm silver-grey as they locked with hers and his lips parted across his teeth. His smile was engaging as he put out a hand to her, which she took in her dreaming sleep.

She woke just as night slipped away from day and a grey mist was dispersing above the grass. She heard the first clear call of a blackbird, then the other early birds began. As soon as breakfast was over and her grandmother occupied with her guests, without her knowledge and with a cool deliberation, Marietta ordered the carriage to take her to Arden House.

Straight and prim, Yang Ling sat across from her. Her face was devoid of expression, but excitement danced behind her eyes on this her first outing with her mistress since coming to Grafton.

The arrival of a Chinese maid had disrupted

the smooth running of things at Grafton and she had been a subject of much controversy among the servants, which had concerned Marietta for a time. But, quite unfazed, Yang Ling had gone about things in her own quiet, but firm and resolute manner and things had soon settled down. To Marietta's relief, Yang Ling had now become an accepted and well-liked member of the staff.

Just a few minutes into the journey to Arden Hall Marietta's fragile serenity began to slip. Apprehension began to gnaw at the edge of her resolve as questions flew at her like bats in the night. Would Max laugh at her? Would he deny her plea with a cruel jest? She tried to calm herself as they drove through the countryside clothed in flaming shades of autumn by imagining what she would say to Max. A twinge of nervousness invaded the moment as the carriage drew ever closer to her moment of reckoning. There was only the steady drum of the horses' hooves bringing her ever closer to her destination.

The carriage eased its relentless pace and swung around a bend in the road and approached a pair of closed, tall iron gates. A gatekeeper stepped out of the gatekeeper's house and spoke to Ben, the coachman, after which the gates swung open soundlessly on well-oiled hinges. The carriage swayed on through gracious parkland dotted with trees for as far as the eye could see over the gently rolling landscape. They clattered over a humpback bridge spanning a deep-flowing stream, and finally the most magnificent house Marietta had ever seen, with immense expanses of crenulated turrets and mullioned windows, came into view.

She called to Ben to halt the carriage so she might look at it in its entirety. It was fascinating because of its overall effect, not just due to the splendour or beauty of the architecture and the rich golden-yellow stone of which it was built, but because it was enormous, ancient, powerful and beautiful. With dramatic grace it stood against a backdrop of sweeping lawns and a terraced courtyard.

She stared at it in wonder and disbelief. She had been impressed when she had first seen Grafton le Willows, but compared to this palatial estate, it would fit into one of its wings with rooms to spare. The windows looked south with a permanence of expression that emphasised her sense that she was trivial and temporary in the scheme of things. Was she doing the right thing? she asked herself. Yes, she told herself and, with more determination and vibrant with hope—I *will* see it through.

Chapter Six

As the carriage neared the house, its owner had decided to take things in hand he had neglected for too long, things that were unpleasant and evoked memories he preferred not to remember. There were several items in the house he wished to dispose of—feminine things, things which were of no use to him. Followed by footmen, he went from room to room, instructing this and that to be removed—and, no, he told a questioning footman, not to be stored in the attics but to be taken to the nearest auction rooms.

The task had put him in an unsatisfactory mood and as the morning wore on he was at his most forbidding when one of the servants announced that a carriage had drawn up in front of the house. 'Who the devil…?' he muttered.

Glancing through the open door, Max couldn't believe his eyes when he saw Marietta in the carriage, but then she did have a tendency to surprise and amaze him. He strode outside to receive her. 'Marietta,' he said, making the words more a question than a greeting. 'You always were one for surprises. What are you doing here—and without Lady Wingrove?'

Forcing herself to ignore the fluttering in her stomach, Marietta glanced at him, meeting his arrogant stare. The very air was charged with his presence. Unexpectedly, she found herself the victim of an absurd attack of shyness. A rush of familiar excitement causing her to become tongue-tied, affected strongly as she was by the force of his presence. He stood in front of her, his shadow stretching across the drive. There was a brief silence, then he was holding out his hand to assist her out of the carriage.

Studying him, she was all too aware of the strong arms where the shirt had been rolled up to the elbows, of the small area of chest exposed by the open neck of the white shirt. He looked tousled, his wavy dark hair curling into his neck and outlining his tanned cheeks and emphasising the magnetism in his silver-grey eyes. Up close, his handsomeness seemed more pronounced and the broad expanse of his chest beneath his shirt reminded her rather forcefully of how powerful his body was. Reminding herself of the purpose of her visit, the smile she gave him was entrancing while her nerves were jangling like wind chimes in a hurricane.

'You might at least seem pleased to see me,' she said, taking his hand and climbing out of the carriage.

'You have taken a scandalous chance, risked compromising your reputation, by coming here,' Max said coolly, regarding her without anger, but with a terrifying firmness and a hard gleam in his eyes.

'I know it isn't the done thing for a young lady to visit a gentleman at his home and at this hour, but I wish to speak to you and would prefer to do it in the privacy of your home, rather than in the busy confines of Grafton with Grandmother flapping her ears.'

'I see. It sounds ominous.' Marietta's outspoken humour and refusal to conform to the social mores of the day were like a breath of fresh air let into a stuffy room when the windows were opened. His cool gaze noted how the sunlight behind her highlighted her red-brown hair. 'Come inside.'

Marietta stood aside when a footman came out of the house carrying a rather dainty looking pink-upholstered lady's chair and placed it on the ground along other items of furniture. 'You're busy.'

The mocking smile that at once replaced the arrogant stare did nothing to make her feel better, although, had she known it, it was himself he was mocking, not her. She was such a refreshing sight in the circumstances that for a moment he had felt his heart lifting. Which, when he recalled her antagonistic attitude of the previous day, was ridiculous.

'Just disposing of some unnecessary household items which have been cluttering the house and should have been got rid of some time ago,' he explained, half-resenting the interruption after days of working himself up to the unpleasant task of emptying the house of items that reminded him of his dead wife.

When Marietta stepped into the great hall she took a moment to admire her surroundings. The walls were the same golden stone as the outside. Great arches were scooped into its massive walls and solid buttresses strengthened them, but under the arches were windows of delicate and lace-like tracery. It was a vast and cavernous space, with a weathered and uneven floor of ancient tiles. High above crouching wooden figures, mysteriously truncated below the knees, supported the arched timbers of the roof.

'Oh, what a beautiful house,' she murmured. 'I never imagined it would be so big.'

'Yes, I am rather proud of it. Come into the study,' Max said, his tone brusque. 'I'll order some refreshment.'

'Thank you, but there's no need.' Nothing had prepared her for the cold reception she received. 'I can see you're busy, so I won't stay long.' She looked back through the door at the carriage to indicate that Yang Ling should follow her, only to find her maid being led away by a young footman to partake of a cup of tea in the kitchen.

'It's no bother, I assure you.'

Max escorted her through the hall into his study, where he offered her a seat beside the roll-top desk, which she declined, preferring to stand. She was wearing a long-sleeved dark-green dress trimmed with black velvet. The bodice was plain with a square neckline filled with white gauze and ruffled at the throat. Perched on her silken red-brown hair was a wide-brimmed matching hat with a jaunty white plume set at an attractive angle. The overall effect was one of quiet elegance, which wasn't a word that would have occurred to Max in connection with the Marietta he had known in Hong Kong.

He wondered briefly whether she knew how seductive she was. In fact, clinically assessing her, he was forced to the conclusion that she was the most beautiful young woman he had seen. It was a pity that she was also one of the most exasperating and ill disciplined.

Perching his hip on the edge of the desk, he watched her when she moved to the wide sweep of windows and stood looking out at the rolling green hills that rose up from behind a thickly wooded area beyond the smooth lawns and shrubs.

'What a lovely situation this is,' she said, fixing her gaze on the scenery as she tried to summon some semblance of her characteristic composure. 'The view is quite spectacular.'

Max studied her stiff back for a moment longer before he spoke. 'I don't expect you came all the way here to admire the scenery.'

'No—I shouldn't be here.'

'No, you shouldn't. Well? Let me hear it.'

'Hear what?' Marietta asked nervously, turning round.

'The reason for you being here. An explanation. Yesterday I was led to believe I was your worst enemy, yet here you are this morning awash with excitement. Why?'

Marietta looked away, beginning to wish she hadn't come after all. How could she begin to tell him the reason that had brought her to his house to see him when he looked at her like that? 'Yesterday you were—disagreeable.'

'Because I kept from you that I am the Duke of Arden. I am *still* disagreeable,' he pointed out shortly. 'I haven't changed. I am not the one who is oozing goodwill this morning. What is it, Marietta? Come, you are here now. Out with it. Tell me the purpose of your visit. Something is troubling you, that is obvious. It must be something of importance to bring you to Arden to see me.'

'It is—but I am not unduly troubled, not really,' she said, turning her face back to him. Her breath caught in her throat when unwillingly she met his eyes and, seeing him here, relaxed and at home in the splendour of his house, he was every inch the aloof, elegant nobleman, the master of all he surveyed. Never had he looked more handsome. 'I've had all night to think about it…'

'Think about what?' Max prompted.

She could sense he was wary, that his guard was up and she sensed a distance between them.

He was watching her closely. He had not invited her to sit down and she knew he was deliberately keeping her on tenterhooks until he found out the full reason for her visit. She chose directness, calming herself and saying, 'My grandmother has some maggot in her head that we should marry. I know she has already broached the matter with you, so it shouldn't come as a surprise. I've come to tell you that I've thought about it and I am prepared to be your wife.'

Max couldn't remember the last time when someone had succeeded in dumbfounding him, but he gave no sign of it. Not a muscle flickered on his face. He was silent, looking at her hard, incredulously, as though she had suddenly changed before his eyes. His expression became grim and he could almost hear the funeral drum-roll of his heart.

Folding his arms across his chest, he said, 'Did I ask you?'

Marietta stared at him in sudden confusion, completely thrown by his reply. His eyes glittered with a fire that burned her raw. The words were uttered without anger, but were none the less cold and final. 'No—but—I...'

'Then wait until you are. Yes, Lady Wingrove did mention something of the sort and I did agree to give the matter my consideration. But when and if I decide to marry, I prefer to do the asking myself. I am not in the market for a wife.'

Marietta turned her face away and her heart sank. Had he exploded with fury and injured vanity she would have understood it better than this deadly quietness which frightened her.

'May I ask why you think I have any desire to marry you?'

Marietta was beginning to wish the ground would open up and swallow her. 'I—I thought… Oh, I don't know what I thought.'

'I don't know what has prompted you to come here and ask me this, but I am flattered. What man wouldn't be—to be propositioned by a beautiful woman?'

'It was presumptuous of me, I know.'

'Yes, it was,' he answered, shoving himself away from the desk and standing straight in a haughty pose, with a suggestion of arrogance which came naturally enough to him. His eyes remained fixed on her face without the trace of a smile to soften their steely expression.

Wanting to conceal her embarrassment, Marietta turned back to the window. It had all been going as she had planned. In fact, she had actually found herself thinking that she would like to be married to Max.

'Just how much has your grandmother told you, Marietta. Did she mention anything about a settlement?'

Bewildered, Marietta shook her head. 'What kind of settlement?'

'Concerning some land.'

It penetrated through the wave of alarm sweeping over her that there was something amiss in all of this, something that didn't make sense. 'What land?'

'I am eager to reclaim some land that was gifted away by my grandfather to Arthur Wingrove, Lady Wingrove's father-in-law, for saving his life when they had fought together in the Anglo-Burmese war back in the twenties. My father thought the land too insignificant to care about, but to me it is a matter of honour not to allow it to remain in another's hands.'

'But—I don't understand the significance. What has any of that to do with me?'

'Over the years I have made several offers to your grandmother to buy back the land, but she will not move an inch for less than my promise to marry you. If I agree to her terms, it would come as a portion of your dowry. It is a matter of some irritation that Lady Wingrove's proposition prevented me from choosing my own wife. Since Nadine died I have learned to be wary of marriageable young ladies who were invariably possessed by matchmaking mothers—or, in this case, grandmothers—to whom my wealth and unmarried state acted as a magnet, and I've become adept in walking away.'

'I can understand your dilemma. Was that the reason you came to see my grandmother the morning after the ball—to ask to buy back the land and she then made her proposal that you marry me?'

'Yes.'

'And what was your reply?'

'I told her I would consider it.'

Marietta stared at him through eyes huge with righteous indignation. Until that moment she wouldn't have thought she could feel more humiliated than she already did. 'So you are telling me that the two of you have discussed this—this *settlement* without consulting me— without considering my feelings?'

'Knowing how proud and stubborn you can be, I did not imagine you would accept putting more importance on a parcel of land than on you. I told her that your feelings must be taken into account. After our altercation concerning the incident of you pushing Lady Murray into the fountain, I could not imagine you would welcome the prospect of marriage to me. For that reason I took the liberty of asking if we might wait a while before discussing the matter further.'

The disappointment was too much for Marietta. 'Of all the treacherous, despicable, underhanded...' She ran out of words to express her turbulent animosity. Although her glorious eyes were glaring defiance at him, the thought was beginning to form in her mind that what he had told her could be turned to her advantage. Humiliation and hurt lay heavy on her, but she had more than enough stubborn courage to withstand it, and she was not so angry that she couldn't understand the logic of her grandmother's thinking. 'I suppose having the land returned to you would make marriage to me more palatable. I am willing to accept what my grandmother proposes if you are.'

Max's entire face instantly became hard, shuttered and aloof. His brows snapped together with brittle anger and a feral gleam appeared in his narrowed eyes as they locked on hers with angry disgust. 'Now you do insult me,' he said, his voice so controlled that Marietta felt an icy chill sweep down her spine. 'I cannot be bought, Marietta. And what makes you think you are worth a parcel of land?'

Marietta gasped. 'Now it is you who insults me,' she flared, anger rising up inside her like flames licking round a dry log, furious with herself for being stupid enough to think he might marry her.

'If you want to marry so badly, then it should not be a problem. You have plenty of money to buy yourself another husband—which shouldn't be too difficult. You have other assets to your credit besides your money,' he ground out with suave brutality, his insolent, contemptuous gaze raking over her.

Max's jibe, savage and taunting, flicked over Marietta like whiplash. Stung to anger by his harsh words, hot colour flooded her cheeks and her soft lips tightened as she exerted every ounce of her control to keep her temper and her emotions in check. 'I apologise. It would seem there has been some misunderstanding on my part.'

'Yes, there has,' he replied, his anger beginning to melt, but his voice remained hard. 'I confess the land is important to me, Marietta, but when I marry again I will do the asking. It will be on my terms and it will not be in return for a parcel of land.'

'Not even as part of my dowry?' she persisted.

'No. Be sensible. Can't you see what it would look like if I were to marry you on those terms? Would you like to think I was marrying you in order to get my hands on the land?'

'No—not really, but if it came as part of the marriage settlement, then I cannot see anything wrong with that. Lots of dowries come with similar settlements.'

Max looked at her curiously. 'Why are you so intent on marrying me? Only yesterday you were telling me you had no intention of marrying just yet. It hasn't taken you long to change your mind.'

'I know, but I've had all night to think about it.'

Her flippant reply brought a tight smile to his lips. 'Coming from anyone else that remark would have surprised me, but it is the sort of remark I have come to expect from you. Do you want to get married?'

She shrugged. 'My grandmother thinks I should—in fact, she is bent on it, but for myself...' she sighed '...I don't know.'

'Then why are you here?'

She met his gaze head-on. 'Because if I have to marry anyone, I would like it to be you.'

Deeply touched by her simple statement, Max shook his head slowly. 'Marietta, you are nineteen years old. I am merely trying to spare you what will be a very embarrassing and extremely futile ordeal in the future.'

'Futile? How dare you?' she cried, her anger quick to ignite. 'You—you arrogant—'

He cut her short by jerking her to him sharply, his dark brows pulled together. 'Careful, Marietta,' he warned, his voice deadly calm. 'Your temper is showing.'

She swallowed hard as his silver-grey eyes bore down into hers, pulling herself free.

'Shouldn't you take the opportunity to look over the other eligible suitors before you settle on me?' he suggested coldly, giving her a look that was a hundred times more deadly than his anger had been a moment before.

His tone suggested such finality that Marietta turned away. It shouldn't hurt so much, being told she wasn't wanted, she thought, but it did. She had done her best to persuade Max to marry her. She couldn't force his consent.

It was all a mistake. He didn't want her. He *wanted* her to find someone else. He was trying to get rid of her. How could she have been so unutterably gullible and blind and stupid as to believe he might actually care for her? She fought to control the wrenching anguish that was strangling her breath in her chest, tears of humiliation burning the backs of her eyes. Swallowing down the lump in her throat, she tried to recover her shattered pride. She couldn't face him and couldn't run from the room without giving her feelings away. Taking a deep breath, she ploughed on.

'You are quite right. That is an excellent idea,' she said, turning her head sideways and looking blindly at the closed door, wishing she could disappear through it without having to cross the room. When she next spoke she tried to keep her voice steady. 'Unlike my grandmother and like you, I must confess I, too, have some reservations about our suitability.'

Max heard the catch in her voice and his conscience tore at him, but he remained adamant. Moving quickly to her, he put his hands on her shoulders.

'Take your hands off me!' she hissed, jerking away out of his reach.

'Then turn around and look at me.'

Feeling utterly wretched and in danger of her control collapsing, she shook her head. She almost choked then, as the tears came to flood her throat, but she strangled them with a great effort. If she turned now, he'd see her distress and she would rather die than suffer that. Left with no recourse but to extricate herself from this awkward situation as gracefully and as quickly as possible, she walked calmly to the door. Now he was no longer close, her composure—along with a stirring of anger—began to return. Taking a deep breath, she turned and looked at him.

With a great effort she made her voice cold, implacable and determined. 'Yesterday I told you you would always be a duke, whereas I would always be the daughter of a tradesman— a rich tradesman, I grant you, but not so rich when one considers that a large part of that wealth was obtained by dishonest means. So taking that into account, how could I possibly have imagined for one moment that I am suitable for you? And I cannot imagine for the life of me how my grandmother could have thought you were suited to me. I should not have come here. I will trouble you no further.' When she saw him take a step in her direction, her hand shot out to stop him. 'All things considered, it would have been best if I had never met you. Please don't try to prevent me from leaving.'

He raked her with a contemptuous glance. 'Stop you?' he jeered. 'I'll order you the carriage.'

On that note, Marietta opened the door and

swept out, slamming it behind her, almost colliding with a servant carrying a tray of refreshments. Apologising, she walked blindly on, calling herself every kind of fool she could think of. She should have known that no one could push Max Trevellyan into any decision not of his own making, and for the first time in her life Marietta knew the real meaning of isolation and the icy coldness of its grip. From the moment she had taken it into her head to marry Max, it was as if, without warning, she had been swept off her feet by a strong current, borne along by a great, silent force over which she had no control—only to come back down to earth with a thud.

Max watched her go, trying to calm down, but the effort was futile. Why was she so hellbent on marrying him when she had shown nothing but hostility towards him since their meeting in London? The only plausible explanation for her ridiculously volatile proposal was that she might think she was in love with him. She probably thought he needed the land so badly that he would fall in with her suggestion.

Cursing under his breath, he flung open the door. He didn't need her, and he sure as hell didn't need the responsibility of a nineteen-year-old girl who didn't know the difference between sexual desire and that nebulous emotion called love. She'd be better off without him. He'd be better off, too. He'd meant it when he'd told her to find someone else.

With some half-formed notion of proving that to her, he stalked after her and, seizing her shoulders, spun her round to face him.

'Let me go,' she said fiercely, struggling within his grasp. 'Do you make a habit of behaving with so little dignity in front of the servants?'

'Then since we need to reach an understanding before you leave, we will return to the study.' His long fingers curved around her arm, then abruptly tightened like a painful vice. He marched her across the hall and back into his den. Closing the door firmly, he pressed her against it, his glittering eyes only inches from hers as he leaned over her.

'What do you think you are doing? You are despicable,' she seethed, longing to slap that arrogant, insufferable face.

'Really!' he drawled. 'Yet only a few minutes ago, you were proposing marriage to me.'

'It was a mistake. I've changed my mind. I don't want you. You are much too old for me. I realise that now.'

'Do you, indeed?' His gaze dropped meaningfully to her lips and he placed his hands on either side of her face. 'Then perhaps you need a reminder of the times you found me desirable.'

His mouth swooped down, seizing hers in a ruthless kiss that was meant to punish and subdue—twisting, bruising, rousing. Marietta struggled in furious earnest, and finally managed to twist her head aside. 'Don't,' she cried, hating the terror and plea in her voice. 'Please don't... Please let me go.'

She was pinned against the door and completely at his mercy, but there were still traces of stormy rebellion in those long-lashed eyes and the stubborn set of her chin, a courageous defiance that was gaining strength in the few moments he'd held her still. She was magnificent even in her defiance.

'Not a chance.'

Taking her in his arms, he tightened them around her and placed his lips against her neck. He trailed a light kiss over her smooth cheek before taking her mouth in a kiss, teasing her lips with his tongue, urging them to part, and then thrusting through like a brand, searing her, possessing her. Instead of sweetly offering him her mouth, she tried to turn her head away. He felt her rejection like a physical blow and, taking her chin, turned her face up to his and stared down at the tempestuous beauty in his arms, her face both delicate and vivid with her stormy olive-green eyes and soft, rosy lips. In his mind he saw her smiling up at him as she had when they had been together in Hong Kong, and his stomach clenched at the memory. He mourned the loss of that girl, of the tenderness and passion and warmth she had shown that day, when he had brutally rejected the offering of her lips.

'Please—don't…' she murmured.

'Marietta,' he whispered thickly as he purposefully held her chin firm and lowered his mouth to hers, 'kiss me back.' He smothered any objection she might make with a hungry, wildly exciting kiss, temporarily robbed of his anger that had fortified his resistance when she arrived and found him removing all trace of Nadine from the house.

Marietta couldn't free her mouth from his, so she fought him with rigid, unmoving indifference, and Max fought back, using all of the sexual expertise he'd acquired during years of dalliance with the opposite sex and his marriage to Nadine. He ruthlessly laid siege to the defences of an inexperienced, virginal nineteen-year-old until her traitorous body lost its power to struggle, and the cry of warning issued by her mind was stifled by her pounding heart and the shocking pleasure of being in his arms. His tender assault was more than Marietta could withstand. With a silent moan of despair, she yielded to his kiss, her lips parting beneath the sensual pressure and, at that moment, his tongue slid between them, invading her mouth and taking possession of her.

Lost in a stormy sea of pleasure, desire, confusion and yearning, Marietta felt his hand splay across her lower spine, forcing her closer to him, and she responded by sliding her hands over his shoulders, unwittingly moulding her melting body to the hardening contours of his. A shudder racked Max's muscular body as she fitted herself to him and his hold tightened, while one hand lifted, cupping her breast, crushing her to him, his thumb brushing back and forth across her hardened nipple beneath the fabric of her clothes.

The endless drugging kiss, the provocative firmness of his hand pressing intimately against her back, the taut strength of his legs and thighs pressing against hers, overwhelmed her, seduced her, so that she could think of nothing else.

But then it was over and he slackened his arms. Surfacing slowly from the mists of desire, she stared into his hypnotic eyes, dazedly watching their colour and mood change from the smoky darkness of his passion to their usual light silver-grey. Raising his hand, he ran his finger gently along the line of her chin.

'If you decide to consider other suitors, Marietta, now you will know how I compare.'

It was his words, not the seduction of his lips, his hands and his body, that crumbled Marietta's resistance. It was like acid on a burn. Some stubborn, protective instinct warned her that she must never let herself trust him again, never let him take advantage of her like this again. When he bent his head to claim her lips once more, reality set in and she managed to step away from him, breathing hard.

'Thank you for the demonstration, *your Grace*. I shall endeavour to grade you fairly when the time for comparison arrives.' Whirling round, she took hold of the door handle.

Feeling a stirring of admiration for this impertinent, proud, sweet and courageous girl, Max gazed at the curls in the nape of her neck. From the moment they had met in Hong Kong, some bond had sprung up between them, and nothing she'd said or done today had convinced him she wanted to break it, or that she didn't want him—quite the opposite, in fact. He placed his hand on her upper arm. 'Marietta, I did not mean to hurt you.'

Looking back at him, she glowered. 'Not for one minute will I be deceived by your pretence of tender concern. You don't want me—you told me so. And now, if you will kindly remove your hand from my person, I am going home.'

'Don't you want to listen to what I have to say?'

'I am not interested,' she burst out, blinded with wrath and humiliation, her anger in full spate—an anger she hadn't realised she was capable of. 'I'm still hurting from what you have said already. I'm glad that you refused me, glad I have been saved from marrying you. The mere thought of tying myself to you for the rest of my life is abhorrent to me.'

Thrusting him away from her, she opened the door and stalked out, holding her head high as she tried to preserve what little there was left of her dignity and pride. Max Trevellyan did not deserve that she debase herself for him. As she crossed the hall, without so much as a backward glance, she slowed her pace, refusing to give him the satisfaction of hearing her flee like a terrified rabbit.

This time there were no tears clogging her throat and her eyes were clear, her head held high as she let herself out of the house, barely resisting the wild urge to jerk the heavy oak door shut behind her with a crash. Climbing up into the carriage, she was relieved Ben was up on his perch and Yang Ling in her seat so she didn't have to go looking for her.

'Drive on, Ben,' she ordered sharply, wishing to put as much distance as possible between her and his Grace, the Duke of Arden. In a state of consuming misery, she sat back and closed her eyes. She cursed herself for her gullibility and her foolishness, and for the night past she had spent dreaming about a man who did not deserve to be called a gentleman. Her mind tormented her with images of the times in Hong Kong when she had gazed up at him like a stupid, besotted schoolgirl. How boring her inexperience must have seemed to him. Shame surged through her and she almost moaned aloud, but the mortifying recollections wouldn't cease.

Left alone with a raw ache inside him, in restless fury Max's mind was locked in furious combat with the desire to go after Marietta and the urge to forget her, but he knew the latter was impossible. As her carriage drove off, the awful, ominous silence lengthened until the air seemed to crackle with tension. He stood with his hands braced against the fireplace, staring into the fire with anger emanating from every inch of his taut, powerful frame—anger directed at Lady Wingrove for putting him in this intolerable situation in the first place, for setting down conditions that were impossible for him to agree to without hurting Marietta.

Crossing to the window, he stood gazing out, knowing that not far away Marietta was already hurting. Her proposition pounded inside his head, combining with the torment of his own harsh rejection. He realised how she had humbled herself by coming to him and just how devastated she must have been when he had shunned, scorned and humiliated her, which she had not deserved and for which he despised and reproached himself with a virulence that was unbearable.

Turning away from the window, he struck his fist into his hand in mute frustration. He had bedded other women since Nadine had died, but Marietta had dined upon his heart and very soon he would have no more heart to share. In fact, his heart had betrayed him. It had closed all exits but one that he had slammed in anger.

What emotions did she stir? Simple emotions he thought below him, for he found himself stricken by Marietta's innocence. She was intelligent, courageous, spontaneous and naturally sensual. And the surprising truth was that he enjoyed her company. From their conversations in the past he knew that Marietta liked his company, too. She'd liked talking to him—and she'd liked being in his arms.

So what was to be done? he asked himself. And as soon as the thought had entered his head he realised there was only one thing that he could do. There was only one way out of the dilemma.

Half an hour later Max was en route to Grafton.

Marietta arrived at Grafton to the sound of convivial laughter and the conversation of her grandmother's guests. Having eaten a hearty breakfast, they were about to leave for their day's sport and were in a jolly mood. She slipped into the house, planning to retreat into the solitude of her room. She headed in that direction, hoping to reach it without being apprehended by her grandmother, but it was too much to hope for. Having seen her granddaughter alight from the carriage and curious as to the purpose for her early morning drive—in particular her destination—the shrewd old lady asked her to spare her a moment.

Still angry and hurt by her visit to Arden Hall and in no mood to prevaricate, Marietta stood and faced her grandmother stony faced in her sumptuous green-and-cream drawing room.

'I have been to see Lord Trevellyan. We have talked and decided we do not suit after all. He won't have me, you see. He does not want me for his wife, nor had I any desire to be,' she stated implacably.

'What do you mean he doesn't want you?' Lady Wingrove asked in alarm. 'What has happened?'

'After I left you last night I did a lot of thinking. I decided that if I am to marry anybody then I would like it to be Max. I went to see him to tell him I would agree to be his wife, but it appears he cannot agree to the terms you set. That's about it. There's nothing else to talk about.'

To her surprise, her grandmother did not stiffen in affront or chastise her for going to Arden without her knowledge or her permission. As a stickler for propriety, she would normally have been shocked at the thought of an unwed young woman visiting a gentleman at his house. It really was most inappropriate. 'I disagree,' she said with a stubborn expression. 'I think there is a great deal to talk about.'

Fully expecting some sort of reprimand for her discourtesy, Marietta shook her head, her eyes holding a deep sense of sadness. 'Whichever way you look at it, the conditions are not to his liking or mine. Think about it, Grandmother. The land he has coveted for so long cannot be his without taking me with it. It is abhorrent to him and humiliating and degrading for me.'

'Oh dear,' Lady Wingrove uttered softly, sinking into a chair. 'It would seem that instead of doing what I thought was right, I have done the opposite.'

'Like you said, you were only doing what you thought was right.'

In the space of seconds, Lady Wingrove considered Marietta's denial of Max, noted the total absence of her normal warmth and correctly assumed her granddaughter's current attitude of proud indifference was a façade to conceal some sort of deep hurt. Since Max was the only one who had the power to truly hurt her that meant he was the likely cause of the problem. She was prepared to go to great lengths to undo whatever damage her ill-thought-out ploy to bring two people she sincerely believed were meant to be together had done.

'You have no idea just how badly I hoped the two of you would marry.'

'And I suppose you are not going to try to convince me that Max Trevellyan is as eager to marry me as you are for us to marry.'

'I couldn't say what I don't know, Marietta. Tell me what he said to you this morning that made you think he does not desire to marry you?'

Marietta hesitated, searching her grandmother's face for some sign of censure, and saw only earnestness and concern. 'I suppose it can't do any harm—except to my pride,' she said with a weak attempt at a smile. In a relatively unemotional voice, she managed to recount what had happened that morning at Arden Hall and what Max had suggested in an attempt to nip any romantic plans she might have for him in the proverbial bud.

'And Max actually suggested that you should take the opportunity to consider other eligible suitors?'

'Yes. Nothing could have told me better than that that he didn't want to marry me.' She wondered what her grandmother would say if she were to tell her that after that Max had the audacity, the arrogance, to kiss her. Oh, yes, she had tried to stop him—but then she hadn't wanted to, so he had won. 'I was so angry and confused and over-emotional I could cheerfully have hit him. He must be feeling very proud of himself.'

'Knowing Max as well as I do, I very much doubt that.' Hearing a clattering of horses' hooves on the gravel drive, Lady Wingrove got up and looked out of the window. 'We have a visitor. He hasn't wasted much time.'

'Who is it?'

'Max, and he looks to be in the foulest temper. For a man who wishes to reject a betrothal between the two of you, he is definitely not in a happy frame of mind.'

Somewhat cheered by that, Marietta smiled, then her smile faded and she shook her head. 'I wonder why he has come—what he wants? I thought everything there was to say had been said.'

'Apparently not.' She glanced at her granddaughter's pale face. 'Are you all right, Marietta?' she asked worriedly.

'Perfectly,' she replied, taking a deep, fortifying breath. 'Although the prospect of actively trying to engage Max in verbal combat so soon after our last encounter fills me with dread. He must think I'm the gauchest female alive.'

'Nonsense. Despite what passed between

you, I am certain Max will think you are as brave and quite wonderful as I do.'

'I don't think he will. If I keep my head and try not antagonise him more than I already have, I may be able to make him decide to go away.'

'Worry not, Marietta.' Lady Wingrove chuckled softly. 'I'll stand by you—as I have ever since your father placed you in my charge. Have I not the white hairs to prove it?'

The time it took for Max to enter the house, for her to come face to face with him once more, played on Marietta's lacerated nerves and she existed in a state of jarring tension. Her grandmother saw her stricken expression and went to her. She flashed a sympathetic, encouraging look at her and then carefully placed herself so that she was standing a little in front of her, almost blocking her from Max's view to give her time to compose herself.

Curled into a tight ball of suspended anguish, Marietta silently counted the seconds until the butler admitted an irate Max Trevellyan into their presence. She shot a sharp look at his inscrutable features. Her grandmother's hand suddenly came to rest over hers and she gave her fingers a brief, encouraging squeeze in a tightly gentle gesture that clearly said, *Stay and see it through.*

His broad shoulders squared, his jaw set with implacable determination, to Marietta Max seemed to emanate the restrained power and unyielding authority she had always sensed in him. His expression was hardly contrite. She tried to temper the pleasure she took on seeing him with the coolness appropriate to his behaviour.

Feeling his scorching gaze on her, she found it impossible to greet him with any degree of casualness after the harsh words they had exchanged just a short while ago. She now realised that her earlier recklessness which had sent her to Arden Hall had been deluded, for how could she have believed that by telling this man she would marry him he would fall at her feet in gratitude? He was no silly romantic youth to be persuaded with a warm smile or even a kiss. Not once since she had met him had she ever emerged the victor in any conflict with him.

Lady Wingrove took the initiative. 'What a pleasant surprise. It's kind of you to finally join us, Max. Marietta has explained what transpired between the two of you earlier and I have to say I am both surprised and more than a little disappointed.'

Twenty-nine years of strict adherence to certain rules of etiquette could not be completely disregarded and Max managed, albeit with anger and frustration, to acknowledge the woman who was addressing him. There was just time for him to look astonished and then his tall frame went rigid when he shifted his gaze. All his attention was riveted on Marietta. 'Marietta told you *everything*?'

'*Almost* everything. I am certain there are some things she prefers to keep to herself.' Pretending not to see the sharp look Max threw at Marietta and the ominous narrowing of his eyes, Lady Wingrove smiled imperturbably and gestured a chair. 'Won't you sit down, Max?'

'Thank you, but I prefer to stand.'

Lady Wingrove's gaze skittered away from his steely eyes. 'Very well. I trust you won't mind if I do. My legs aren't as young as yours.' She quirked a brow at her granddaughter. 'Marietta?'

'No—I, too, prefer to stand,' she replied, feeling disadvantaged enough with Max towering over them like a dark, threatening thundercloud without having to look up at him.

Max bore purposefully down on Marietta, who unconsciously took a step back. 'I am

happy to see you arrived home with no ill effects, Marietta.'

'Yes—as you see,' she replied coldly. 'Although I am amazed that you have followed
me—and so soon. I thought you might have
been relieved to see the last of me.'

'Not at all. I behaved abominably and I've
come to apologise.'

'And so you should—although I deeply regret having called on you in the first place. I
should have known better—but then, my father
was always accusing me of being impulsive and
spontaneous. You will be interested—and more
than a little relieved, I shouldn't doubt—to learn
that I have decided I don't want an arranged
marriage—which I am sure can be difficult to
adjust to, particularly when the chosen gentleman is imperious and arbitrary about a possible betrothal—and of the evil-tempered sort.'

'How distressing for you, my dear,' Lady
Wingrove said, giving her granddaughter a
sham sympathetic look of understanding. 'I
had no idea.'

'Then perhaps you didn't know *his Grace*
nearly as well as you thought you did,
Grandmother.' Marietta cocked a glance at the
glowering Duke of Arden. *Please love me*, she
implored him silently. *Don't put me through*

this. 'Do you not agree, Max?' she asked, turning her head away so he would not see the softening in her eyes.

'Indeed,' he replied blandly, glancing pointedly at Lady Wingrove. 'Would you mind leaving us, Lady Wingrove? I want to speak privately with Marietta.'

'Very well. Maybe it is time for me to withdraw and leave you two young people alone.'

'I have also decided the land deal is off. The price you ask is too high.'

'I am surprised. It would appear I have made quite a mess of things. What can I say— except that when I presented you with my proposition, Max, I was only doing what I thought was right?'

'I'm sure you were, but that isn't the way I work.'

'No, I'm beginning to realise that.' Regarding him a moment longer down the full length of her aristocratic nose, she swept out of the room.

Chapter Seven

Marietta watched her grandmother leave. Max strode across the room to the window and shoved his hands into his pockets. The silence scraped against her raw nerves as he stared rigidly out across the lawns, his profile harsh, forbidding. She knew he was about to tell her that he wanted nothing to do with marriage to her, that she was going to go the same way as the land he had so coveted, and she also knew that beneath that tautly controlled façade of his he was still very angry.

She watched as he lifted one hand and massaged the taut muscles in his neck, his expression becoming darker and more ominous as each second ticked by.

'I don't know what you hope to achieve by

coming here, Max,' she said coldly. 'I think everything has been said between us, and I must thank you for being so frank with me.'

He turned so abruptly that Marietta took an automatic step backwards. She stood perfectly still as he came closer. There was an aura of calm authority about him. His expression was now blank and impervious, and he looked unbearably handsome. The sight of his chiselled features and bold silver-grey eyes never failed to stir her heart.

Max stood gazing down at her, looking deep into her eyes. 'Don't look so scared, Marietta. I haven't come here to argue. Please listen to what I have to say.'

A deadly calm settled over Marietta, banishing everything but her hurt and disappointment. Her small chin lifted, her spine stiffened, and before his eyes Max saw her put up a valiant fight for control—a fight she won. She stood before him looking like a proud young queen, her eyes sparking like twin jewels.

'Very well, but if I decide to leave don't you dare try to restrain me. I'm still hurting from the last time. And please don't think that just because you kissed me you have to commit yourself to anything.'

'No. Life isn't like that. I have kissed many

women I have been attracted to, but that doesn't mean to say that I wanted to marry any of them.'

Marietta was conscious of a sudden surge of anger, realising just how stupid and naïve she had been. How dare he treat what had happened between them casually, as if the kiss was insignificant and meant nothing at all? But perhaps this was nothing out of the ordinary and he was used to kissing ladies all over the place. And perhaps ladies took his kisses in their stride. After all, she thought bitterly, how would she know? Gripping her hands tightly by her sides, she regarded him coldly.

Mortified and humiliated, she nevertheless managed to lift her chin a notch and look at him directly. 'I do not have your experience. Apart from yourself, no other man has kissed me,' she told him with simple honesty, giving Max further insight into just how truly innocent she was. Turning from him, she moved to stand by the hearth, staring down into the fire. 'Please say what you have to say, Max, and then leave.'

The coolness faded from Max's face, replaced by an expression so intense, so profoundly gentle, that it would have had Lady Wingrove positively purring. He went to stand close to Marietta, who still had her back turned to him. Time after time when he had been in Hong Kong and he had seen her, he had been drawn to her, either driven to angry distraction by her antics or laughing silently at some of the set downs she had given him.

Since leaving Hong Kong he had avoided further contact with her, then he had stood in Lady Wingrove's garden in London and there she was. Even when he had been reproaching her for tipping Lady Murray into the fountain he'd fought down the insane impulse to bend his head and slowly, endlessly, kiss her down-turned lips, to carry her into the darkness and make love to her right there.

Marietta was a natural temptress, alluring and provocative, warm and witty and as elusive as a butterfly, with the voluptuous body of a goddess and the smile of an angel. She also had a sense of humour and irreverent contempt for the absurd that matched his own. He had given up trying to understand the reasons why he wanted her. He did, and that was reason enough.

He was seized by a passionate longing to protect and revere this lovely young woman who had crept into his heart. He ached to treat her as she should be treated, to tread with the hesitant steps of courtship and woo her as she deserved.

He saw that she was looking at him frankly, openly, and with a dispassion so chilling that he was intensely moved by it, yet he sensed that beneath it all was a heartbreaking dejection.

'I haven't handled things particularly well have I, Marietta? I wasn't considering your feelings.'

'No, you were not. As for you being a duke,' she scoffed turning to face him, unaware of his change of attitude, 'if you were the King of England, I wouldn't want you. Therefore your present title—which my grandmother deems so important—is scarcely an inducement.'

'I quite agree. In fact, I regard it as a likely hindrance to marital harmony. The same can be said of the land,' he added quietly.

Marietta looked up at him, sensing the change in him. 'Is it true what you said? You are really serious about withdrawing your offer for the land?'

'Yes. Despite my desire and effort to buy back all the land my father sold to pay off debts in his time, and having mostly succeeded, that piece of land eludes me because of your grandmother's determination to hang on to it. That said, I do realise there was good reason for my grandfather to make a gift of it to your grandfather—it adjoins both estates and is good fertile land. However, I've decided to leave things as they are. As I said,' he murmured, cupping her face with his hand, 'the price is too high.'

'Do you mean me?' she asked in a whisper, hoping beyond hope that was so.

'I do.'

'And you would do this for me?' He nodded, calmly watching her. Touched by this gently spoken indication that he had done this noble thing to please her, Marietta felt she could not meet his gaze. Lowering her eyes, she stared at the buttons on his coat, but she could not ignore the warmth she felt. 'I'm so ashamed that I went to Arden Hall earlier. I should have waited for you to come to me. How pathetic I must seem to you—'

'Don't say that,' he cut in, his voice raw. 'Please don't say that. It isn't true.'

Tilting her head back, she looked up at him. 'Then why did you reject me?'

'I wasn't rejecting you, Marietta. Your grandmother made the situation virtually impossible for me to ask you to be my wife.' He cupped her face between his hands. 'She wants us to marry and my own parents would have approved of the match wholeheartedly. But *we* have to decide what *we* want. Are you ready to settle down?'

'I never thought I would be. But now I think I am. What about you?'

'I do want to marry you—you adorable little fool.'

'Why?' she whispered. 'Tell me why, Max?'

'Because I am attracted to you—surely you know that. I want to give you my name and everything a woman wants—everything a woman *really* wants—and the only way I can do that is to settle the issue of the land.'

When he placed his hands on her upper arms, Marietta felt herself being drawn relentlessly closer to his chest. He had told her he wanted to give her everything, everything a woman could want—everything but love. She was unable to fathom that cynical remark, because his firmly chiselled lips began a slow, deliberate descent towards hers.

'I'll give you riches beyond anything you've ever dreamed of,' he murmured, his free hand cupping the back of her head and tilting her face up for his kiss. 'In return, all you have to give me is yourself.'

Strangely, Marietta thought he was selling himself too cheaply, asking so little of her when he was prepared to give her so much—surely he had a right to expect more from her than this? At that moment her mind went blank as his mouth seized possession of hers in an endless, drugging kiss that suddenly intensified to such demanding insistence it left her trembling. He touched his tongue to her lips, coaxing them apart, then kissing her to dizzying heights and sending shock waves jolting through her. She moaned and pressed herself against his hard length as his protective arms tightened around her, his kiss a wildly erotic seduction.

By the time he finally lifted his head, Marietta felt dazed and warm.

Max scanned the lovely face for signs that she regretted her capitulation to his kiss, but there was a melting softness in her eyes that told him she didn't. Unable to help himself, he caught her into his arms once more, crushing her to him and burying his face in the fresh fragrance of her hair.

'My God,' he whispered hoarsely, 'how will I ever wait the length of a courtship to make you mine?' Raising his head, he gazed down at her. 'It was not my intention to cause you pain, Marietta. I owe you an apology. It was wrong of me to speak to you so harshly. I apologise for my boorish behaviour. I said things to you of which I am deeply ashamed. You're trembling,' he whispered, putting his hand beneath her chin and tipping it up. 'You're not afraid of me, are you, Marietta?'

Regardless of all the raw emotions quivering through her, Marietta gave him a wobbly smile and shook her head. She wasn't afraid of him—she was suddenly inexplicably afraid of herself. 'No, I'm not afraid of you, Max.'

A smile curved his lips. 'Good, because you've no reason to be.'

'I'm just not used to being kissed—twice in one day.'

'You must expect to be kissed more than that when you are my wife.'

'I can't believe you really do want to marry me?'

He laid his hand against her heated face, slowly running it back and forth. 'Yes, and you mean far more to me than any parcel of land. I don't need an excuse to marry you. It shouldn't be an issue, but your grandmother made it so. If we marry under her conditions, then there will always be some doubt in your mind about my reason for marrying you.'

'But—if you want to marry me, then it shouldn't be an issue.'

'But it is—for me. Can't you see that? You would resent me for that reason.'

'No, I wouldn't.'

'I can't take that chance. There will always be doubt in your mind. You are far too precious, too important, to be part of a bargain. It's sordid and not how I work.'

Marietta bit back a teary smile, afraid to believe him, to trust him—to love him. 'I would have talked to my grandmother, although my influence over her is very little to say the least. She is a very determined lady—and she must realise that when she is no longer with us and I have inherited Grafton, all that I have will be yours.'

'Ours, Marietta, and you are right, but that's for the future.'

'What she did was wrong. I'm sure she sees that now.'

'Had that wily old lady had any notion of what my feelings were where you are concerned, my love, she would never have made it so difficult for herself—and for me. May I at least have your answer? Will you marry me, Marietta?'

She kissed him then. That was her answer. 'I hope I can make you happy. I think I can, you know.' She could feel her heart beating, her face warm. She had spoken before she had chance to think and yet she knew this was what she wanted.

Max raised her hand to his lips and kissed the soft white skin of her wrist. 'I have no doubts about that. What do you think? Are we compatible?'

Taking his hand, Marietta drew him down on to the sofa, sitting sideways so they were facing each other. 'That all depends on when you were born and in what year.'

Lifting her hand, he kissed her fingers and laughed. 'Now would I be right in thinking you are about to quote some Chinese customs at me?'

'Oh, absolutely. They have to be taken into account. It's very important. I lived in Hong Kong for a long time and the Chinese New Year is a reflection on how people behave and what they believe in most.'

'Very well, Miss Westwood.' Max laughed, continuing to hold her hand. 'Fire away, if you must—but one thing I must ask you. When we marry will you behave as the Chinese do at their New Year and clean my house to sweep away all ill fortunes in the hope of making way for good incoming luck?'

'But of course—although I do believe it is now the custom for the bridegroom to completely furnish the house in which the newly married couple intend to live. There are exceptions to every rule and sometimes the bride's father gives the whole of the furniture, but this is only when the bride is an heiress who marries a comparatively poor man. So you see, since I have no father and you are a rich man, it doesn't count.'

'That's a relief, although as for clearing the house, I was doing precisely that when you turned up out of the blue earlier.'

'So long as you replace everything. You have yet to meet Yang Ling, so you have no idea what you are going to be up against. By the time she has finished with her *feng shui* and other Chinese customs, she will have turned your house upside down and inside out and have every one of your servants running for cover. She will have every door and window decorated with coloured-paper cut-outs and couplets with popular themes of happiness, wealth and longevity and like the Chinese New Year tradition, our marriage will be about reconciliation and peace and happiness for everyone—although, as I said, we have to consider if we are compatible.'

'If it helps, I was born in '53, which I believe was the year of the Ox.'

'That makes you sweet and loyal—though with a lack of humour—which I have to say on occasion is true,' she teased, a sharp twinkle lighting her eyes.

'Ah, but I am also supposed to be a realist—which is what I am. What sign were you born under?'

'I was born in '63—which, I am afraid to say, for I know you will laugh,' she said wrinkling her nose, 'was the year of the Rat. It's not very flattering and not something I tell everybody.'

'I will smile,' he said, doing just that, 'but I will not laugh. Anyone born under the sign of the Rat has some wonderful attributes.'

'Such as?'

'Intelligence, humour, gifted—and money comes to you alone and you will never lack anything.'

Tilting her head to one side, Marietta considered him with a thoughtful look on her lovely face. 'You are very knowledgeable about these things, Max. I am surprised.'

'Before I went to Hong Kong I made a point of learning what I could about the Chinese and their customs that might prove beneficial to me. I also learnt that anyone born during the year of the Rat is faithful in love and that their sign is compatible not only to someone born in the year of the Tiger and the Monkey, but also in the year of the Ox. So you see, Marietta, according to Chinese tradition and the experts, we are an ideal marriage combination, so I am sure your Yang Ling will approve of me.'

'When she finally meets you, how can she not?' Marietta murmured softly.

When Lady Wingrove came back into the room after kicking her heels in her room until she considered it the right time to return to the drawing room, she was rewarded by the sight of Marietta blushing as Max held both her hands by the window. As they gave her the news, she looked from one to the other. 'I will not pretend that this is not my dearest wish since I've made that blatantly obvious, but I hope you've not agreed to do so because it is the wish of a dying woman.'

To both ladies' astonishment, Max threw back his head and burst out laughing. 'Lady Wingrove,' he said when he could speak calmly, 'you are definitely *not* a dying woman, but a woman with as much cunning as a fox, can outwit the Devil himself and will outlive us all.' He sat beside Marietta and, defying all the proprieties with his usual careless elegance, he put his arm around her shoulders, drawing her close. He cast a smiling, meaningful look at Lady

Wingrove. 'Be happy that Marietta and I have at last got around to the business of marriage.'

Lady Wingrove eyed him narrowly. 'Not without my help.' Her lips twitched into a reluctant smile. 'I could cheerfully murder you, Max Trevellyan.'

'Why, what a thing to say,' Max teased, laughing. 'Be satisfied and enjoy the result of all your scheming.'

'I intend to.' Her expression became one of mock severity. 'I am entrusting my granddaughter into your keeping, Max, and I shall hold you personally responsible for her happiness, is that clear?'

'Quite clear,' he said in a solemn voice, but he eyed the elderly woman who was issuing vague threats to him with thinly veiled amusement.

Lady Wingrove scrutinised his handsome, tranquil features sharply, then nodded. 'Good. As long as we understand one another. It goes without saying that her dowry will be generous.'

'Everything that came to Marietta from her father remains her own. I repudiate my legal right to her assets.'

Lady Wingrove was surprised. 'That is unusual and highly irregular, Max. When a young lady marries all that she has is transferred to her husband.'

'Not in this case, Lady Wingrove. It may seem unusual to you, but that's the way I want it.'

Recalling their conversation of the night before about making a generous settlement on his wife, Marietta smiled. 'Now why doesn't that surprise me?'

'It shouldn't. I meant what I said. Your wealth is your own, Marietta.' Given time, perhaps she would come to realise why he had an aversion to her money—that it was tainted with opium, and he wanted no part of it.

'We shall arrange the wedding to take place as soon as possible,' Lady Wingrove said. 'Here, I think, at Grafton. I trust that suits you both.'

'Perfectly,' Max replied.

'And going back to the conversation at dinner last night and my impatience for a great-grandchild and the fact that I cannot live for ever—despite your eagerness to differ—I shall not countenance any delays on your part.'

'You have my word that as soon as Marietta and I are wed, I shall give the matter my prompt attention,' Max said, straight-faced, but with laughter lurking in his silver-grey eyes.

'And there will be no showing a lack of decisiveness on your part either, Marietta,' Lady Wingrove warned her suddenly ashen-faced granddaughter, whose body had gone rigid with fear at the realisation that her grandmother and everyone else would expect her to bear a child not long into her marriage to Max. Patting her hand, Lady Wingrove added rather wistfully, 'I shall miss you when you are no longer here with me, but Arden Hall is only a short distance from Grafton, so we will visit each other most days.'

Marietta felt that this had all happened very quickly, but then everything Max did seemed to take her by surprise. Her grandmother spoke of a short engagement, but surely there must be more of a courtship, a period of mutual discovery and sweet anticipation? She wondered if she was giving in too quickly. Yet their kisses were too urgent to be contained for long. And by marrying Max, at least she and her grandmother would agree about her future, and she would at once dispatch any possible marriage to someone else who would not share Max's aversion to children.

As Max rode back to Arden Hall, now that he had admitted to himself and to Marietta his desire to marry her, he wanted her with an urgency that was almost irrational. The desire she ignited in him every time they met was eating at him like a fire licking at his insides. He wanted her so badly that he ached with it. His growing need for her made him feel vulnerable and uneasy, for he knew from past experience how vicious, how treacherous, the female sex could be. Despite this, he could not stop himself from wanting her and his firm hope was that they could make each other happy.

Everything—the extensive preparations for the wedding and the wedding itself went without a hitch. Invitations were sent out the length and breadth of England and Scotland, the news that the Duke of Arden was to marry Miss Marietta Westwood, the granddaughter of Lady Wingrove, striking the Borders with the force of a hurricane.

Marietta was so feverishly busy she had little time to think, but unfortunately by the time the wedding was little more than a week away, her practical attitude had deserted her entirely, and her dread about the wedding night itself and what Max would expect of her was steadily mounting. Even her cream wedding gown, which was hanging in the dressing room, sent a shiver of fear up her spine every time she looked at it, for it was a bold reminder of

what was to come. She had no fear of what Max
would do to her—in fact, whenever he took her
in his arms and kissed her she almost melted
with desire for him. No, it was what would happen as a result of the passion they would share,
of the child she might conceive. She could not
expect him not to impose his desires on her, for
once they were married she would see an entirely different side of him to the one she knew.

To add to her misery, her agitated mind
began tormenting her with constant visions of
those terrible times her mother had tried to give
birth, and then again of Max's first wife. It all
came back to haunt her, magnifying her memories until she was a mass of fear and trepidation.

It was a bright blue morning, the sun warming wherever it touched as Max took Marietta
on a guided tour of the vast, well-manicured,
formal gardens at Arden Hall. At the back of
the house there were glasshouses and walled
gardens, which grew vegetables and herbs, and
an orchard with regimental lines of fruit trees.
The gardeners and groundsmen were raking
up leaves ready to burn and took little notice
of the couple as they strolled along the paths.

The grounds gave way to woodland and a
magnificent lake on which ducks floated se-

renely. Birdsong coloured the air and the warm
sun drew them on as, arm in arm, they made
their way towards it. A small pillared pavil-
ion stood on its banks and they sat inside for
a while, surrounded by cushions, looking out
over the water where lily pads spread across the
surface rippled by a gentle breeze. It was a paradise for swans and a wide variety of water fowl.
A pair of moorhens waddled flatly by before
sailing forth on the water. Max and Marietta
came out to continue the tour.

Max put his arm about Marietta's shoulders
and drew her close, sensing the tension in her
body, and when she looked at him he saw something in her eyes that was akin to fear. He regarded her attentively, his suspicions beginning
to work overtime as he wondered if she might
be having second thoughts about marrying him
and, if so, why.

Aware of his scrutiny, Marietta ran a nervous
hand over the back of her neck, tucking non-
existent strands of hair beneath her bonnet.
'Why are you looking at me like that?' she
whispered.

'It is difficult not to look at you, Marietta.
You are very beautiful. And very frightened.'

He said it so coolly, so unemotionally, that it
was a long moment before Marietta was certain

she'd heard him correctly. By then it was too late for her to react. Max was already walking on. Then abruptly he stopped and faced her, blocking her path. 'Why?' he demanded in a terse, frustrated voice. 'Why are you frightened?'

'I—I'm not,' Marietta denied, startled.

'Yes,' he said harshly, 'you are.'

Marietta stared at him. Despite his harsh tone, there was a gentleness in his eyes and calm strength in his features. 'I think it's because everything seems to be happening so quickly,' she said with partial honesty.

His brows drew together in a frown. 'Is it only the haste that worries you? We could delay the wedding if you prefer.'

Marietta hesitated. She could not explain the source of her fear to him. She didn't entirely understand it herself. 'There is so much to be done and so little time to do it in,' she prevaricated.

He sighed with relief as his hands slid up her arms, drawing her close to his heart. 'Marietta, try not to worry. You grandmother is handling all the necessary arrangements perfectly. Everything will be ready on the day.'

His velvety voice, his breath stirring her hair, the musky scent of his body, were all combining to work their magic on Marietta. 'I am sure you're right and I'm worrying needlessly,' she breathed, her attention absorbed in the sensuous masculine lips slowly coming nearer and nearer to hers. Desire was beginning to flow through her veins, sweeping aside her doubts and fears.

'We have to meet with Canon Unwin later. You will find time for that?'

'Do we have to? We know the procedure.'

Max chuckled low in his chest. 'Canon Unwin is a stickler for doing everything right. We have to convince him of our suitability.'

'It is you I have to convince, not Canon Unwin.'

A lazy smile touched Max's lips and he curved a hand behind her head. 'So, convince me,' he murmured, bringing his mouth ever closer.

Marietta's hand slid inside his coat and glided up his chest in a devastatingly tantalising caress that made his muscles tense and his breath catch in his throat.

'How long do you think it will take me to do that?'

'About two seconds.'

Capturing her lips, he proceeded to kiss her long and deep, leaving her breathless. She melted against him, the fire in her response igniting the flames deep within him. When he raised his head, he placed his arm around her shoulders in an intimate embrace and together they stood gazing wistfully across the lake to the distant hills. She felt the peace of the countryside. A sudden explosion of starlings lifted across the sky. The rain of the day before had left a freshness, a sweetness, a sparkle to the vista spread out before her, and the essence of it settled on her heart, finding a place there which she knew it would never leave.

'Did the kiss cure you of your problems?'

Marietta's long curly lashes fluttered up and eyes like deep olive-green pools of languid wonder gazed into his. 'Not really,' she replied lightly, 'but I suppose that's to be expected when one is marrying a duke in a week from now. But—I am reminded of another kiss. At the risk of making you angry, if you don't mind I would like to explain.'

His eyes darkened and his jaw tightened. 'I remember.'

'You should. You were furious as I recall. But—when I kissed you—I wanted to thank you, to show my gratitude. You were so kind to me at that time...'

'And I misunderstood.' His expression began to relax.

'Yes, you did. I wanted to explain then, but I was upset and you were so angry with me.'

Smiling softly, he tilted her face to his. 'I'm sorry, Marietta. Truly, but what you have just told me does little for my ego. It's the first time a woman wanted to kiss me out of kindness.'

'Then *I'm* sorry,' she teased, relieved that he understood her reasons for the kiss at last. 'Heaven forbid I should do anything to damage your ego, but—well, that's how it was.'

Max smiled at her and Marietta could not help but smile back at him, that curiously attractive smile which lit her eyes to a brilliance. Her lips, which in repose were rosy pink, parted over her even teeth and the flush deepened in the soft curve of her cheek. He let his mind drift back to their meeting in Hong Kong when she had been so full of fun and daring. She had captivated him, dazzled him—baffled him. Marietta had something in her that he could not get hold of—a brilliance, a magical something that had made him unable to look away.

There was also a strength of character in her he admired, an alertness which he had never seen before in a female. The ladies he knew were concerned with little more than fashion, marriage, children, the running of their households and their submission to their husbands.

They lived in a world where they must conform to the strict code of conduct laid down by their mothers, but Marietta was different. Her mother had died when as a young girl she had needed her most, and she had been raised without guidance by a father who had been too wrapped up in his own nefarious affairs to concern himself overmuch with a growing daughter.

'Do you hear from your friends, Marietta? Those who came to England?'

'Yes. Oliver and Julian are at the university at Oxford—and Emma is in Switzerland. We correspond now and then. She's due to return to Hong Kong very soon.'

Max saw a wistful, faraway look enter her eyes as she scanned the horizon that hinted at her sense of loss. 'Would you like to go back to the island?'

'Yes—some time. I do miss it.' On a sigh, with shining eyes she looked around her. 'But this really is a beautiful place. I can't believe it's to be my home.'

'You'd better believe it. I haven't seen much of you. I've missed you.'

'I'm sorry. I've been so busy.' Her cheek nestled against his shoulder, her hand drifting over his chest in a gentle caress.

'Just over a week from now it will be all

over.' He tilted her chin up. 'Now you're here
and I have you to myself at last, show me how
much you've been missing me.'

Marietta knew he was going to kiss her
again. Eagerly, she lifted her face and met him
halfway. His mouth covered hers and caressed
hers in a long, tender, undemanding kiss, and
within moments Marietta felt all her pent-up
tension begin to melt away in the heat of his
passion. Even when the kiss deepened and her
lips were being sensually shaped and moulded
to his, she knew he would let her pull away
if she tried. Instead her hands crept up his
chest, twining round his neck, and everything
changed.

As he removed her hat, his fingers slid into
her hair, loosening the pins and tangling in the
luxuriant tresses. They tumbled over her shoulders in a glorious mass the colour of burnished
copper beneath the sun's rays, framing a face
of heartbreaking beauty.

Tenderly cupping her face between both his
hands, Max gazed down into her melting green
eyes. 'My God, you are so sweet,' he whispered.

Marietta's heart skipped a beat, then began
to hammer as he slowly, deliberately covered
her lips once more. He kissed her long and lingeringly slow, compelling kisses that made her

head swim. He groaned and crushed her tighter
to his chest, his mouth leaving hers and tracing
its way across her cheek to explore her ear before returning to her lips again. She was jerked
back to reality when she felt his hand cup her
breast.

'Don't—Max, please... We mustn't,' she
choked.

'Why not?' he said hoarsely, his long fingers sliding downwards and curving around
her neck while his mesmerising silver-grey eyes
gazed deeply into hers. As if the confessions
were being tortured out of him, he said, 'I've
tried a thousand times to stay away from you
until our wedding night, but having you here
with me now makes it impossible.'

While Marietta was reeling from that incredible statement, he again took her lips in an
endless drugging kiss that stole her breath and
stunned her into immobility. His lips moved
against hers with tender, hungry yearning, tast-
ing and fitting them to his own. Something
deep and primitive within Marietta responded
to it. Her lips softened and melted against his
as jolt after jolt of wild sensations shot through
her.

Subtly increasing the pressure on her nape,
he was inexorably drawing her down on to a

seat. But in a sensual haze from his tongue teasing, exploring, Marietta had scarcely noticed the shift in position. Her senses swam. His kisses were deep, assaulting, yet soft, and he whispered gentle endearments against her lips. His fingers probed at the tiny buttons on her gown, deftly unfastening them, his hand slipping through, and before Marietta could react his long fingers had crept beneath her chemise and were leisurely exploring and caressing until his fingertip was deep in the hollow between her breasts. It stayed there, moving up and down, stroking the sides of her breasts, while tiny flames began shooting through Marietta's body, making her breathing shallow and rapid.

'Now tell me you don't want me to touch you,' he invited softly, his eyes holding hers imprisoned, his fingers teasing her hardening nipple. 'Tell me what you feel, Marietta,' he murmured against the sweet flesh of her cheek. 'Does it feel good to you? Do you like my hands on your breast?'

'Yes—yes, I do.' Her voice was shy. 'I—I had no idea it could feel so...'

'What?'

'Nice.' Marietta felt her breast swelling to fill his hand, turning her head aside and staring fixedly at the lake, absolutely amazed at her inability to control her own treacherous body.

'I'm glad I please you, but there is more, my love.'

It was through these words that Marietta was brought back to reality. Pulling away from him, she struggled to sit up, forcing him to withdraw his hand from her breast. 'Max, please don't do this.'

Startled by her reaction, Max started to reach for her again, but she sprang to her feet and shot off, halting by the edge of the lake, her face red, her breathing rapid, her fingers trembling as they hastily fastened the buttons on her bodice. Her blood thrummed warm beneath her cheeks, the skin stretched taut beneath her breasts where his fingers had been. Her pulse beat faster than a small bird's heart. She heard Max come up behind her. He didn't touch her, but she could feel the heat of his presence, and when he spoke his voice was cold.

'I don't know what you're thinking, Marietta, but you act as if you're frightened to death. Nothing is different from how it was before when I kissed you and I don't recall you objecting then. What is it—offended modesty? If so, I will tell you now that as my wife, kissing me is something you will have to get used to.'

Marietta slowly turned to face him. He watched her as she started to speak, changed her mind and bit on her lip. 'What is it?' he prompted, gentling his voice.

In her nervousness she hastily gathered her hair together and shoved the pins back in before replacing her hat. Looking up, she caught Max's eye as he watched her. There was a strange expression on his face, sad, she thought, brooding, as though he were looking at another woman whose passing had left a hole in his life that had never been filled. Why did he never speak of Nadine? Was the pain he felt still too raw? He must have loved her very much if he couldn't bear to speak of her. Swamped with a terrible hurt that he would never be able to love her as much as he had loved his first wife, her eyes were large and luminous as they worriedly searched his face. She drew a long, unsteady breath.

Pride and courage showed in every feature of her face, from her high cheekbones and stubborn little nose, to her small chin. And yet her mouth was vulnerable and soft, as soft as her breasts, which he had so recently touched. Max frowned with worry over the tension and anxiety he saw in her eyes.

'It isn't that. I like it when you kiss me—

very much. It—I—there is something, Max, something I want to ask you. Only— Oh, it's so embarrassing. I don't know how to begin. It—it's about…'

At last it dawned on Max what might be troubling her. 'Our wedding night.'

Relief flooded her eyes. 'Oh, yes. I was hoping you would understand. Because, you see,' she said, very simply and without embarrassment, 'I do love you.'

His smile faded. 'Oh, I see.'

'Don't look so surprised. It's quite natural for a woman to fall in love with the man she is going to marry. I—'

He pressed a finger to her lips, silencing her, and shook his head. 'Don't say it again,' he said with quiet, implacable firmness. 'Don't give me more than you already have, Marietta.'

Marietta averted her head and said nothing, but his rejection hurt her more than she imagined possible. But he *must* love her a little bit. She couldn't believe he didn't. She could feel it in the tenderness of his hands when he touched her and the fierce hunger of his lips.

'You don't even know me—not the real me,' Max said.

'I think I know you better than you realise,' she said, knowing that whatever she said now would determine their future. 'Why do you never talk about your wife?' she blurted out, despising herself as she did so, because she hadn't wanted to ask, hoping he would tell her. 'You never speak of her.'

Max didn't meet her eyes. His reply was brusque. 'No, I don't.'

Marietta was overcome with a desire to hit out at him. She didn't, of course, adopting instead a casual tone, less precipitate than before, almost light, and saying, 'It doesn't matter. I understand perfectly if it upsets you to talk about her. But—why didn't you have children?' she dared to ask.

His attitude suddenly changed and Marietta's breath caught in her throat as she noticed the ominous glitter in those silver-grey eyes and the muscle leaping in his hard jaw. Behind that sardonic façade of his, there was a terrible burning anger, she realised. Despite the civilised elegance of his superbly tailored tweed suit, he had never looked more dangerous, more overpowering than he did at that moment.

Max stared at her, his eyes hard and ice-cold. He remembered how shattered and enraged he had felt when he first discovered Nadine's perfidy. 'It didn't happen. Neither of us wanted children.'

'But—the rumours.'

'Ah—the rumours. And there were plenty of those when Nadine was found in our hotel room dead from a haemorrhage.'

'Yes—yes, there were,' Marietta said, emboldened. 'Were they true?'

'Damn it, Marietta. Yes—my wife died of a miscarriage. There, I've said it. Are you satisfied now?'

'I see,' she said quietly. How could she argue without divulging her presence in Max's hotel room on the night Nadine died? *She had to do it*, Nadine had told her. Do what? Get rid of her baby because Max didn't want children?

'I—I know you didn't want children with Nadine…' She quailed when his eyes sliced into her. 'Teddy told me,' she whispered, hoping and praying he would never discover the lie. She averted her gaze so he wouldn't read what was in their depths, for she was not a liar and she did not cope well with subterfuge.

Rage blazed in his eyes for a moment. Hearing that man's name—that liar, braggart and seducer of other men's wives—made him want to lash out. But Marietta was disillusioned enough about the corrupt dealings of her father and his business partner without him making matters worse for her. He shrugged resignedly. 'He had no right to tell you that.'

'No—but is it true?'

It was a question subtly asked, but Max left it too long to reply. Marietta took his silence as assent. She sought something else to say, but there was too much and too little and Max, who was standing waiting for something further, must have realised that it wasn't coming because he took her arm and said, 'We should be getting back. I promised your grandmother I wouldn't keep you too long.'

On the point of walking back the way they had come, she paused and looked at him. 'I'm sorry if what I said made you angry, Max. I didn't mean to.'

'Marietta, are you afraid of our wedding night—about what will happen between us?'

'Yes,' she told him flatly. 'I'm sorry. I can't help it…' She was as pink as a rose when she trailed into pathetic silence.

Placing his finger beneath her chin, he tilted her face up to his. 'Then don't be. I promise you, Marietta, your worries are needless. I'm aware of your fears and I do understand.'

Relief flooded over her. Along with many other things to do with the opposite sex, Yang Ling had explained there were certain things

men could do to prevent children being born.
Marietta could only imagine what these certain
things might be for matters of a sexual nature
were never discussed openly with a young unmarried woman, but she believed Yang Ling
implicitly. Thankfully Max knew what she was
saying and understood her fears. She was confident he would take care of everything.

'Please don't be despondent,' he murmured,
his lips against her hair. 'Especially not now.
We are to be married in one week. It's a time
for happiness, Marietta, a time to look forward
for us both.'

Lifting her head, she laughed in an attempt to
dispel her fears. 'You're right as always, Max.
I'm so sorry if my questions upset you. I don't
care about Nadine. I don't care how much you
loved her, if only you can find it in your heart
to feel for me a fraction of what you felt for her.'

'What I feel for you goes way beyond anything I believed possible, my love. Do you know
how beautiful you are?' he said hoarsely. Lifting his hand, he laid his palm against her soft
cheek, his fingers softly tracing the delicate
bones of her face. 'You have nothing to fear
from me, Marietta. I promise you.'

Completely captivated by the intimate look
in his eyes and the compelling gentleness in

his voice, Marietta swallowed hard and said, 'I know. I do believe you, Max.' His hypnotic gaze held hers as his hand continued its seductive stroking. She was mesmerised by his voice and the sweetness of his words. She smiled and took his hand. 'Come along. Take me home—back to Grafton le Willows. Just think, it won't be that for much longer and when I ask you to take me home, it will be to Arden.'

Chapter Eight

The morning of the wedding was warm and sunny, which, a sighing Yang Ling proclaimed as she helped Marietta into her costly wedding dress, was a good omen. The dress had been designed in the latest fashion, with a high neckline and long sleeves, tiny waist and flowing skirt. The fabric was cream duchesse satin set with tiny pearls and Brussels lace on the bodice. There was no other adornment or frills or flounces. The train spread about her feet like a puddle of cream.

Lady Wingrove came bustling into the room, her eyes suspiciously damp. 'I must say you do me credit, Marietta. You look radiant. Your dear mother would be so proud of you. If you are quite ready, Lord Russell has arrived.'

Lord Russell was Lady Wingrove's oldest and closest friend and since Marietta had no close male relative to give her away, he had been delighted and honoured to oblige.

'The bridesmaids are about to leave for Arden. Your maid should go with them so that she will be on hand at the chapel to tidy you up when you get out of the carriage.' She moved to stand close to her granddaughter. 'There is just one thing, Marietta, before you go down.' She paused and her voice became flustered. 'My dear, I feel I might have neglected my duty somewhat, and it's a little late in the day to be thinking of it now. But—it—it's—are you prepared to do your duty by Max?'

Without warning Marietta's stomach suddenly clenched into knots. She felt as if she were being torn to pieces. Her mind pulled her one way and her heart tugged another. Fear coiled in her chest, desire pulsed through her veins, and her love for Max burned like a steady, glowing fire in the centre of it all. And she did love him. She loved him very much. Aware of what her grandmother was referring to, she smiled inwardly. 'Please don't concern yourself, Grandmother. Yang Ling instructed me long ago in what comes later. In Hong Kong, it was all part of a young girl's education.'

Lady Wingrove's eyebrows crept steadily up her forehead, clearly scandalised by this revelation. 'Really? Gracious me! Then since you don't need any advice from me, we will leave directly.'

Marietta smiled when she had gone. *Advice* was a strange word to ascribe to the consummation of love between a man and a woman on their wedding night.

The open carriage that was to take her and Lord Russell to Arden Hall was festooned with flowers and ribbons and drawn by a pair of greys, which were considered indispensable, for it was usual to have grey horses. The fact was that because of the importance of the occasion—since it wasn't every day a duke married a commoner, despite the bride being an heiress and Lady Wingrove on intimate terms with certain members of the royal family—a smart pair of greys attracted a desirable crowd along the way. As if to prove the point, the road was well lined with crowds of people waiting for a glimpse of the bride.

When they arrived at the chapel, which was a part of the great house, servants from Grafton and Arden Hall, farm labourers, the tenant farmers and so many people from the surrounding villages were milling about outside, wide-eyed at the bridal vision about to become the Duchess of Arden. Everyone agreed she was the most beautiful bride any of them had ever seen. Her eyes shone and her cheeks were flushed with rose.

The inside of the chapel was reserved for the gentry. It was small and perfectly proportioned. A gallery ran around the top and the ceiling was domed and beautifully painted with saints, angels and cherubs.

Yang Ling fussed around her, arranging her train and adjusting the tiara on her head before drawing the translucent veil over her face and handing her a bouquet of gardenias. Lady Wingrove awaited her arrival inside the chapel misty eyed. Marietta knew beyond any doubt that the emotion she saw in her grandmother's eyes was love—love and a profound and terrible regret that she had missed out on her own daughter's wedding.

Marietta took Lord Russell's arm with her free hand and, to the sound of music from the small choir, she entered through the carved doors flanked by two pillars and climbed the four steps into the sanctified building, the pool of cream satin drawn behind her. Slowly she walked down the short aisle to where Max was

waiting at the altar. Dressed in an immaculate
dark-grey frockcoat and a light-grey waistcoat,
he made the most handsome groom. As she
reached his side, he looked through her veil
deep into her eyes and smiled. His hand closed
over hers and he leaned towards her.

'You look absolutely lovely, my darling,' he
murmured. Sensing her nervousness, he said,
'It's all right. From now on I am here to cherish you. Be assured that I will always take care
of you, Marietta.'

And love. The unbidden word came into
Marietta's head. *What about love?* Would he
ever be able to love her as much as he had loved
Nadine—and more?

Then the minister began intoning the words
that would bind her to Max for ever and she
heard him repeat them in that rich, deep voice
she loved. Then she felt the coldness of the gold
ring on her finger as Max slid it gently over
her knuckle. He held her hand tightly as she
made her own low responses with great clarity.
Finding the moment one of such emotion, that
it was all a dream, she was unable to stop her
voice from quavering. Max was watching her
and suddenly she found it difficult to breathe.
Even as she uttered the solemn words to love,
honour and obey this man she was giving her-

self to, a small part of her remained detached, wondering which words she'd use if asked to describe the way she felt that was making her lungs constrict.

And then the minister pronounced them man and wife in the eyes of God and the assembled company. Max lifted the veil from her face to kiss her lips as a seal of the marriage. His mouth was soft and gentle on hers as befitted the occasion. The time for passion would come later.

At the back of the chapel, Yang Ling wept with happiness, for she was certain her young mistress could not be in better hands. The register was signed and, placing her hand on Max's arm, Marietta and her husband left the chapel. She stole a glance at him and, immaculately attired in his wedding finery, Max Trevellyan was the stuff that dreams were made of. She marvelled at the strength and pride carved into every feature on that starkly handsome face. With that lazy, intimate smile of his and those silver-grey, penetrating eyes, she thought he must have been making female hearts flutter all over the world for years, and they must have found him as completely irresistible as she did.

The wedding breakfast was held at Grafton le Willows, an extravagant and splendid affair presided over by Lady Wingrove and crowded with friends and acquaintances, all of them telling one another as they drank champagne that Max was a lucky man in his choice of wife. Max kept Marietta close by his side, and Marietta was so very aware of him, watching her, admiring her, even if he didn't yet truly love her.

Congratulations were offered and glasses raised to toast the happy couple and soon they were leaving to return to Arden to begin married life and shortly to leave for their honeymoon in Paris.

The bedroom, she had been told considerately and diplomatically by Max, had been his mother's room and had not been slept in since her death and therefore had not been shared by himself and Nadine. It was a beautiful room, light and airy and tastefully furnished with glowing satinwood and velvet chairs and a sofa drawn up to the fireplace, the overall colours pastel shades of green and soft beige. The bed was an enormous tester draped in green damask.

But it was not the elegance of the room that Marietta—Lady Trevellyan, the Duchess of Arden now—was concerned with as her new husband emerged from the dressing room and crossed to stand beside the bed they were to share—the bridal bed. He wore a long, rich, brocade robe tied about his lean hips with a loosely knotted sash. His hair was neatly brushed and his eyes were as dark a grey as the evening sky just before night falls.

Marietta was sitting up in bed in a modest nightgown. It was plain and sensible and covered her beneath the bedclothes from her neck to her toes, but there the severity ended. Yang Ling had removed the pins from her hair and brushed it until it snapped and the red-brown tresses curled about the bristles. Now it lay like a lion's mane about her shoulders, a living, shining brilliance, transforming her into a breathtaking picture Max could not quite believe.

She was watching him warily, her eyes deep, apprehensive pools of dark green. She was pale, her hands folded tightly on the top of the covers, her lips clamped together to stop them from trembling.

'You look like the girl I met in Hong Kong in that nightgown.' Max smiled, his eyes shadowed with some emotion. 'And your hair is magnificent.' Moving closer to the bed, he saw the fear and confusion in her eyes when she gazed at him. Sitting on the bed beside her, he

gently enfolded her in his arms, trying to ignore the incredible feel of her soft body crushed
against his robe. He wanted to kiss her, but,
sensing her tension, he just held her and stroked
her lustrous hair. Eventually her tension eased
and she kept very still, her breathing light and
rapid.

'As we are now man and wife, Marietta,
would you object if I kissed you?' he ventured
softly, aware of her innocent sensibilities and
knowing that if he charged ahead and started
to make love to her he would never have her
confidence and trust again.

She leaned back a little and looked up at him,
her face so lovely and vulnerable that Max's
heart wrenched at the thought of hurting her—
for there would be a moment when he would,
but he hoped it would be fleeting and forgotten
in the aftermath of the lovemaking.

'I have no objections,' she said.

'And you would have no objections if I get
into bed beside you?'

'No, in fact I would be terribly upset if you
didn't. I don't want to spend our wedding night
lying all alone in this great bed.'

Turning to face her, Max brushed her hair
back and placed his hands on her shoulders. He
laid his lips on the pulse which beat frantically

beneath the curve of her jaw, then let his mouth drift to her cheek. He could feel her tension, but something told him it was not the strain of rejection but a wondering, a curiosity, a wanting to move on and make some sense of what she was feeling.

He kissed her neck, then with unhurried fingers untied the ribbons at her throat and breast and tenderly eased the gown aside, relieved that she didn't try to stop him. Her ivory shoulders and full, rosy-topped breasts gleamed in the light from the lamps.

'My God, you are so beautiful,' he breathed, and felt her body quiver when his hands slid down her arms.

He took her soft lips in a long, sweet kiss, then, releasing her, he divested himself of his robe and swept the satin coverlet back and slipped his naked body into the bed beside her. Relieving her of her nightgown, so that she wouldn't be overly conscious of their nakedness and the jaunty size of his erection, he drew the sheet over them and gathered her close. When their bodies came into contact a small gasp escaped her lips and he felt her hesitate.

Burying his fingers in her hair, he stared for a long, long moment into her eyes. 'What is about to happen between us is nothing to be afraid of, Marietta. It will be an act of giving and taking for us both. Initially you will feel pain, but it will be brief. I will be as gentle as I can be. Do you understand what is to happen?'

She nodded. 'Yes, and I do not fear it, Max.'

Tilting her face up to his, she offered him her lips. Very slowly he began to kiss her, long and lingeringly, with all the aching tenderness in his heart and she, after a few moments of tense passivity, began to kiss him back. Her soft lips parted with only the slightest urging from his probing tongue. Her slender arms went around his neck and she pressed herself to the full length of his hard, unyielding contours. Max groaned, his mouth opening passionately over hers, and when he shifted her on to her back and leaned over her, what Marietta was feeling was drugging, delirious and quite wonderful.

She looked up at him, her eyes enormous and unblinking in her small flushed face, and her mouth was rosy, as though waiting for further instructions on how to proceed, as if she wanted to take a more active part in this pleasant pastime, but was not sure how to go about it. Tentatively she moved her fingers over the furring of dark hair on his chest and felt the slight increase in the steady thudding of his heart, the rippling of his powerful chest muscles when she slid her hand a little lower.

Max felt it as a flame racing uncontrollably through his veins. Careful not to unnerve her, with gentle, skilful hands he slowly caressed her slender form, her waist and belly, and he could feel her flesh ripple in the aftermath of his warm, strong hand. Her back arched like that of a cat in a shaft of bright sunshine, lifting itself to meet his touch, and when his hand very gently cupped her breast she gasped and her nipple hardened against his palm. He lifted his head and she looked up at him with drowning, feverishly bright eyes.

'What is it?' he murmured. 'Would you like me to stop?'

'Oh, no... Please don't stop...'

And he didn't—in fact, he doubted very much that he would be able to if he tried, for her arms had crept around his neck once more and she was pulling him down on to her.

'Tell me what you feel, Marietta,' he murmured, since he believed that humans should give and take love with words as well as actions. 'Does what I am doing please you?'

'Yes—yes, it does, Max. I really had no idea I could feel like this.'

'I'm glad, but there is more, much more, my love.'

It was as though these two words unlocked Marietta's heart and all the love she was capable of feeling for this man came pouring out of her. *My love*, he had called her and she wanted to be nothing else. She could sense the need in him, the need he had of her and her body, and she gloried in it, and when his fingers reached that part of her that was totally private she could hear herself begin to moan in the back of her throat. The sensations were utterly exquisite, burning her flesh to a compelling, melting, quivering need, to go on until the very core of her ignited and inflamed every part of her body.

Leaning on his forearms, Max gazed down at her lovely face. 'I want you,' he whispered against her parted lips, his voice hoarse with tenderness. 'I want you so very badly, Marietta. I ache for you.'

Suddenly there was pain as his hard shaft pushed its way quickly inside her, breaking through her barrier, and she gasped and bit her lip, then the pain was gone, leaving only pleasure. A fierce exhilaration swept through her, filling every vein with liquid fire. She wrapped her arms around him, lost in incoherent yearnings. With his lips devouring hers, more eloquent, more demanding than before, he moved inside her. Some essential part of her Marietta had not been aware of until now awoke and she ceased to think at all. She felt something unfold inside her, spreading and filling her with warmth, with colour and light and reaching every nerve in her body. The volcano that had been threatening to erupt suddenly exploded with a force that shocked her, tearing a low moan from her throat. Max stifled it with his mouth and with one deep thrust, he poured his shuddering warmth into her.

After a moment when their bodies ceased to tremble, Max rolled on to his side, taking her with him, cradling her in his arms. With her face resting in the curve beneath his jaw, Marietta experienced a joyous contentment, a languorous peace. It was unlike anything she had ever known. The room had become a magical place—their own private heaven. Sighing now, she settled against him, their naked bodies, despite the difference in their height, fitting together in sweet perfection. Marietta could smell him now she had her senses back, smell his skin, the scent of his cologne and a musky odour she could not identify, not an unpleasant odour—an odour of sensuality, one

which she knew she would always associate
with this moment.

They lay for a while, not speaking, and then
Max raised his head and gazed down at her,
half-expecting her to have fallen to sleep. 'What
a truly amazing creature you are, Marietta. You
were made for loving.'

Tilting her head back, sated and happy, she
smiled up at him, her heart almost bursting with
love of him. 'And you would know that.'

'Naturally. You know very well there have
been others—'

She stopped his words with her lips when an
image of Lady Murray sprang up unbidden into
her mind. 'Don't,' she whispered. 'I don't want
to know about the others—not now. This is my
time—our special time. Please don't spoil it.'

'I'm sorry, Marietta, that was insensitive of
me.' On a sigh he laid his head back on the pillows, holding her close. 'However, I now realise
my wife is no prim miss, but a lusty woman
with an appetite to equal my own.'

Rolling on to her belly, Marietta leaned on
her elbows and began tracing a line of tantalising kisses over his chest. 'I am a married
woman now so I can be as lusty as I like.' She
grinned up at him puckishly. 'Are you complaining by any chance, your Grace?'

Taking her arms, he drew her up so she hovered over his face. 'Not a bit of it, my lovely new duchess. I want you to be as lusty as I could wish for. You were a delight.'

'And I'm delighted to hear it.'

His eyes darkened as he looked at her. 'Do you realise just how desirable you are?'

'Am I?' she said curiously. 'I'm amazed you can say that, for I never thought you felt anything for me beyond irritation—at least that's the impression you gave me in Hong Kong.'

He laughed. 'Was I that bad? I suppose you were irritating at times.'

'There you are. You were positively dreadful to me—in Happy Valley—and then again when you found me in China Town.'

'Call it self-defence,' he chuckled softly.

Laughing delightedly, she wriggled away from him and stretched her body for him to inspect. 'I don't think I care for that remark. I think I'm going to have to punish you.'

'And how do you propose to do that?' he asked, devouring her with his eyes, his fingers tweaking a lock of her hair.

'By insisting that you make love to me again.'

'You call that punishment? I call it pleasure, my love.'

And to prove his point, leaning over her he

took her hands and held them above her while he carefully inspected her breasts, her waist, the curve of her hips. He knew her now, every part of her, knowing the true nature of her. The thrill reverberated throughout Marietta's whole body with an intensity that would have told him everything he needed to know about her—if he had not already known it. His senses were alive to every inch of her form languorously stretched out before him and, desire pouring like boiling lava through his veins, he kissed and nuzzled and caressed her until she felt the heat return to the pit of her belly and she sighed with absolute delight as he took her again with a lovely languor consumed in a passion infinitely more powerful than before.

It was in the early hours when Max finally unlocked their bodies with a slow, supple deliberation calculated to cause Marietta every last ounce of exquisite pleasure, torture and rapture. Lying exhausted in her husband's arms, she fell into a deep slumber.

The morning was well on the way when Marietta opened her eyes to the knowledge of her husband's lovemaking, and during the nights that followed the desire, the anticipation, the excitement drew them to their bedroom. It would begin in the lamplight, an incandescence which turned their bodies to a honeyed glow. Here they made love with increasing ardour and satisfaction. This was where Marietta was most truly happy. In their bed Max was hers, hers alone, his body—which was to Marietta a miracle of male beauty lovingly put together with long graceful bones and flat muscles— rousing hers with a male rapture and delight she found utterly satisfying.

But although Max made love to her in the way she liked, the way she responded to, he didn't succeed in soothing away her fears of pregnancy.

Seated in the drawing room at Arden amidst exquisite furnishings, with some discarded correspondence on the occasional table beside him, Max looked up at the gilt-framed portraits of his ancestors that lined the walls. Above the mantel his great-grandfather, the first Duke of Arden, looked down at him, a couple stag hounds at his feet. By his side were his eldest son, Max's grandfather, and a lovely fair-haired girl. He was holding her hand and she was looking up at him with a look of adoration on her young face.

Bored with studying his ancestor, Max turned his head slightly and indulged in the more pleasurable occupation of studying his wife who was seated across from him, reading a recent magazine. This woman in such a short time had brought him peace, a peace of mind he had not dreamed of and delight to their bed which he had never before experienced, not even with Nadine in the first passionate weeks of their marriage. And she asked nothing of him. She gave, which was her nature, he knew that now. Mentally he bent his head and kissed her lips, his hand caressing her silken flesh and cupping her breast. He was about to deepen his kiss when he realised she was watching him with an amused and knowing look.

She let her magazine fall into her lap and smiled across at him. 'What are you thinking that makes you look at me like that?'

His grin was almost salacious. 'I cannot tell you that without offending your sensitive ears, my love. But I was thinking how very lovely you are and that our offspring—if we are blessed with a daughter—will look exactly like you.'

Marietta felt the blood drain from her face and her heart began to race. 'A daughter?' The word began to howl like a banshee in her brain. 'But—what are you saying?'

296 When Marrying a Duke...

'That if we have a daughter, I would like her to have your hair—your eyes…'

Marietta's mind registered disbelief. It started to shout denials—even while something inside her slowly cracked and began to crumble. 'But Max—I—I thought you understood.'

'Understood? Understood what?'

'I don't want children,' she burst out, her voice almost unrecognisable, brittle and frantic. 'I thought you didn't either.'

Max's eyes narrowed. 'Have I given you reason to think that?'

'Yes—I mean…'

'What?'

'That day in the garden, you said you understood.'

'What I understood was that you were afraid about what would happen between us on our wedding night. Are you telling me it was something else?'

Marietta took one look at the anger kindling in his glittering eyes and hastily stood up, wringing her hands in front of her. 'Yes.'

'Marietta, why were you so certain I didn't want children?'

'Because I—I saw Nadine,' she uttered wretchedly, unable to keep the truth from him any longer. 'She told me you…' She trailed off at the sight of the murderous look on Max's face.

Gripped by something unexplainable, he felt his body stiffen and his eyes were hard and probing when they looked at his wife. '*When* did you see Nadine? And why would she say something like that to a seventeen-year-old girl she hardly knew?'

'I was there—at the hotel when she…'

He shot forwards in his chair, his hands gripping the arms. 'You what? Are you telling me that you saw her before she died?'

Marietta nodded. 'Yes,' she whispered.

'And you didn't think to tell me?'

'I couldn't,' she replied without realising she was moving towards him, wanting to make him listen, her words tumbling over themselves. 'Max, please listen. I went to return her fan— you remember. I told you I found it on the night of the ball. When I got to the hotel she was in bed. I knew she was ill—and she—she told me she was pregnant and that you didn't want her baby, which was why she…' She stared at him, her eyes mirroring the horror of what she had seen and the pain she still felt. 'She had lost so much blood, Max—so much blood. I knew she had done something—I didn't know what, but… Oh, Max, why did you make her do it if you wanted children?'

'The child wasn't mine,' he told her brutally. 'I would not accept another man's child—not even the man who sired it wanted it. What Nadine did she did of her own volition. I found her after you left.'

'I didn't leave,' Marietta confessed quietly. 'I was in the dressing room. I saw you come in—I was too shocked, too afraid, to let you see me.'

'And did you not think that Nadine might need assistance?'

Marietta shook her head and tried to swallow the lump that had risen in her throat. 'She wouldn't let me—and afterwards, when you left—I knew I had to get out. I felt numb with nothing in my head to get a grip on and think about. I was seventeen years old and had no sense of what was really happening or what I should do next, but at the same time I was conscious of the swirl of disorientated thoughts which were flying round and round inside my head like a flock of starlings. I knew I was in deep shock. The enormity of what I had seen I could scarcely grasp.'

That was the moment Max understood. It was as if a veil had been lifted. This explained Marietta's hostile behaviour towards him at her father's funeral. It had nothing to do with the brutal words he had flung at her following her kiss. Having seen Nadine's lost fan on her bedside table and Marietta having told him she had found it and would return it, it was a wonder he hadn't figured out how it had got there straight away—it was so plain now that he knew.

With hard eyes he looked down at her. 'And you blamed me, didn't you?'

She nodded, gulping down the tears that threatened. 'At the time, yes, I did. I didn't know she had been unfaithful—I didn't know— truly, I never thought… How dreadful for you.'

'Which was why you spoke to me as you did when I approached you at your father's funeral to offer you my support. And yet despite this, you were prepared to put aside the grievances you harboured against me and marry me.' His eyes turned to shards of ice and the muscles of his face clenched so tight a nerve in his cheek began to pulse. 'Your desperation not to bear a child must be very strong indeed for you to do that.'

'I know it must seem like that to you, but it wasn't like that.'

'All this has been brought on because I failed to understand the true reason why you feared our wedding night.'

'But I thought you knew that my fear was that I would become...'

'What? Pregnant?' She nodded. 'Marietta, we have made love every night since our marriage and you have shown no fear of pregnancy.'

Her anger melted away and she flushed, embarrassed. 'I—I thought you would... I mean, I know there are things that can be done...'

'Why didn't you tell me this? There are precautions that can be taken, but there is only one sure way to prevent the conceiving of a child, which is abstinence,' he told her coldly.

'No,' she cried, suddenly distraught, her fear and her emotions running high as she wrapped her arms about her waist in a protective manner. 'There are other ways. There has to be. I will not allow myself to be dragged down to the status of a breeding animal subject to the whims and fancies of any man. I do not want children,' she cried, quite distraught. 'I will not have them.'

'I think I get the picture,' Max said in an awful, silky voice. 'So what is to be done? Separate beds, separate rooms? Is that what you want?'

She shook her head. All she wanted to do was fling herself on his chest, to beg him to help her, to make things right for her. But she couldn't. 'Of course it isn't. I don't know the answer. But if that is the way it has to be, then there is no other way.'

'Damn it to hell, Marietta!' he said, his voice low and ice-cold. 'I cannot live like that. I'm human—a man with needs. I want to make love to my wife. I'll tell you true it isn't easy keeping my hands off you. But I will not play the monk. That tender scene in the garden when you told me you loved me was an act, wasn't it? You played it because you didn't want children and believed I was of like mind.' Although he had expected her to be fearful of her wedding night, he had not expected anything of this magnitude. 'I'm sorry you look at it like that. You see, I do want children, Marietta. I want an heir to inherit Arden after me. Don't you like children?'

'Yes, I happen to like them very much.'

'Yet you don't want children of your own.'

'No,' she replied brokenly.

'You do realise I could divorce you for this.'

Her eyes flew to his in alarm. 'Max, you wouldn't.'

'Admit it, Marietta. You married me believing I didn't want children. You were wrong. So, believing this, that made me an ideal candidate for a husband,' he said bitterly. 'Am I right?'

She opened her mouth to deny this, but found

no words would come. She blinked and was astonished to feel a wave of warm tears threatening to spill.

'Answer me,' he demanded when she remained silent.

Mentally recoiling from the blinding violence flashing in his eyes, she whispered, 'Yes. But I also fell in love with you. That was no act. I am sorry,' she whispered achingly, reaching her hand out to him.

Max jerked away from her touch, his brows snapping together over biting silver-grey eyes. 'You're sorry?' he mocked scathingly. 'Sorry for what? For marrying me?'

'No, Max—not that. Never that.'

His gaze held hers. 'Then what do you expect me to do? What do you want from me?'

She opened her mouth to speak and couldn't. Her mouth went dry and her heart began to beat in heavy, terrifying dread as she sensed that Max had withdrawn from her, as if the closeness, the tenderness and laughter they'd shared had never existed. She tried to say something, but the words wouldn't come because of the hideous memories that continued to torment her. With a low anguished moan she went to him and wrapped her arms around his neck and began kissing him in a frenzy of desperation while every muscle in his body was tensing to reject her.

Pain tore through Max like a hot, jagged knife. She didn't love him or she would not be doing this. Damn her!

'I can't help it,' she wept brokenly, clinging tightly to him, her body moulded to his. 'I can't do what you want. I can't.'

Max stared at her, hating her and hating himself for loving her—because he did love her, so much he could feel the pain of it. Reaching up, he started to pull her arms from round his neck, but Marietta wildly shook her head, tightening her hold, pressing even closer to him. Tears rushed from her beautiful eyes, sparkling on her long lashes, wetting her smooth cheeks.

'Please don't turn against me,' she said fiercely, 'just because I don't want to bear a child.'

'Marietta, don't do this,' he said harshly. Her soft lips trembled at the cold rejection in his voice, and he gripped her shoulders and freed himself. His face was turned away from her, his profile a hard, chiselled mask, devoid of all compassion or understanding. He was furious with her, angry and unforgiving. Fear of what he might do jarred her nerves, adding more tension to her already overburdened emotions. She wondered frantically if she had created a breach between them that would never heal.

Drying her eyes with the back of her hand, she pulled herself up straight. 'I'm sorry for getting everything wrong. When Nadine told me about the baby and that its father didn't want it, I assumed that because you were her husband she meant you.'

'You assumed wrong,' he bit back.

'I know that now. I can imagine how hurt you must have been.'

'You can have no idea,' he bit back coldly.

Despite his attitude of sarcastic anger, Marietta had heard the clipped terseness in his voice when he referred to her being sorry for marrying him and her heart sank. Evidently that bothered him very much.

'Clearly you consider this marriage the greatest mistake of your life.'

'No, Max—but I really do not want a child— I cannot…' The mere thought of it made her shudder.

Seeing it, Max backed away. 'Enough,' he said, turning from her and striding to the door. 'I have heard enough. I will not listen to any more of what you have to say on that subject.'

Marietta watched him go, knowing nothing she could say would change his mind when he was in this mood.

* * *

He did not have supper with her and that night she slept alone—and the next. In fact, he went out of his way to completely avoid her. He rode out early each morning and when he returned he worked in his study with his secretary and met with businessmen who came up from London to discuss all manner of unfathomable business transactions. If he encountered her at all, he greeted her brusquely and without familiarity as if she were a stranger. When he was finished working he went upstairs to change his clothes and went out. She wondered what he did when he was away from her—probably spent his time at the houses of his friends gambling and drinking the night away.

Marietta spent most of her time paying and receiving calls. She avoided going to Grafton. Her grandmother would be sure to suspect all was not well between her and Max and Marietta couldn't face the questions. Her fear was silent, too painful to talk about. Yang Ling knew all was not well between her mistress and her husband. Apart from offering her quiet support, she held her tongue.

But no matter how busy Marietta kept herself, she missed Max. She missed him at mealtimes, eating slowly in the hope that he would come rushing in, flushed and vital after his ride and apologetic. She missed their conversations and his teasing, but most of all she missed him in her bed and the wonder and magic of when he had been a considerate and tender lover—when he had called her his love and praised her ability to please him and she had expected—what? Not protestations of love, since he did not love her and was honest enough not to lie about it. Not his constant presence nor his attention even, which he had given her since she had become his wife, but a little of his time, of the discussions, the laughter, the interests they seemed to find agreeable to them both, all leading to that magical time at the end of the day and the joy they shared. Now he was purposely and effectively keeping her at arm's length. He had locked her out of his heart and mind as if she didn't exist.

Her mind dwelt constantly on what he had told her about Nadine and the hurt and pain she must have caused him. How he must have suffered. Her heart wept for this man who had known nothing but pain and humiliation and betrayal at her hands. If he felt bitter and disillusioned by her betrayal, he could not be blamed.

Max wanted to understand why Marietta was adamant about not wanting a child. He would have given anything to understand, but he had no idea where he should begin to try to break down the barrier she had erected around herself. The strain on him was acute and because the mere sight of his wife made him want her, he began staying away from home more often. Eventually, when the separation became unbearable, he decided to leave for London and ordered his valet to pack his bags.

Returning to Arden after visiting a neighbour, on her way to her room to change, Marietta was passing her husband's room when his valet walked out, carrying a valise. Her heart hammering wildly, she moved to stand in the doorway, pausing to gather her wits before he turned and saw her. He was thrusting his arms into his tweed jacket, and with a pang of remorse she saw his face was lined with tension. She tried to think how to begin and because she was so overwhelmed with emotion she tackled the obvious.

'Max—where are you rushing off to?'

She saw his shoulders stiffen at the sound of her voice, and when he turned and looked at her, she could almost feel the effort he was exerting to keep his rage under control. 'London,' he replied in a calm and authoritative voice. Picking up some documents, he shoved them into his briefcase and then consulted his watch. 'I have to catch the train for York to be in time for the connection to London and I haven't a moment to spare.'

In silent, helpless protest she shook her head and started slowly across the carpet, dimly aware that this was worse, much worse, than she had imagined.

'I wouldn't come any closer if I were you,' he warned softly.

She stopped cold, her mind registering the physical threat in his voice, her gaze searching his granite features. 'London? But—were you going to leave without telling me?'

'You were out. I've left you a note.'

'A note. But surely I deserve more than a note. And what about me?'

'What about you?'

'You can't just go like this.'

'Why not?' he asked with cold politeness. His head twisted towards her and he fixed his metallic eyes on her, and for the first time Marietta actually saw the savage, scorching fury that was emanating from her husband. 'Will you miss me, Marietta?'

Her eyes ached and her throat burned. 'I—I…'

His twisted smile was scornful. 'You can do as you damn well please.'

'Max,' she began, stretching her hand out in a gesture of mute appeal, then letting it fall to her side when her beseeching move got nothing but a blast of contempt from his eyes. The tension between them was so thick she could barely stand to breathe as she pleaded and hoped. 'I don't want you to go. I don't like the way things are between us and I know the fault is mine...'

Hearing the pain and desperation in her voice, he gave her an odd, searching look. 'You do admit it, then?'

She nodded. 'I realise that you must despise me for what I've done.'

'I don't despise you, I just wish I understood. I *want* to understand.'

'I know,' she went on bravely, speaking more quickly now, driven by panic and an awful sense of foreboding that nothing she could do or say would ever make him soften. 'I would like to put things right—if I could.'

He turned away with a half-laugh that had no humour in it. 'If you could? Oh, Marietta— you could if you wanted to.'

'But we have been married less than two weeks. How will it look if you leave me here alone so soon?' she cried on a note of desperation. 'We are supposed to be going to Paris next month.'

'Forget it. It's no use. It was to be our honeymoon. Little point in that now, don't you think? I must go. I have urgent business to attend to in London—and I also think it would be best if we are apart for a while.'

Marietta flinched. 'Going away won't solve anything.'

'For me it will. I have to do something to quench the fury of not being able to make love to my wife,' he retaliated coldly. He was going away because, having become hopelessly entangled in his desire, he couldn't help himself. He was weaker than he thought, for she had bewitched him, and if he didn't put some distance between them he was afraid of what he might do.

'How long will you be gone?'

'I can't say.'

Suddenly an image of the beautiful Lady Murray paraded before her eyes and her stomach clenched at the thought that he might be going to her. She moved further into the room and, fighting to control the mistiness that suddenly affected her vision, she drew a shaking breath. 'Max, are you leaving me?' she asked quietly, overwhelmed with emotions and the fear that this might be so.

Picking up his briefcase, he crossed to the door and loomed over her. 'As yet I haven't decided what I will do. When I do you will be the first to know. I don't think you realise what this enforced abstinence is doing to me, Marietta. It is both intolerable and unacceptable.'

'And in London I suppose your needs will be catered for by someone else—by another man's wife. How excruciatingly naïve and stupid you must find me, Max.'

It had been a vain attempt on her part to hit back, an irrational expression of anger, misery and hurt. And then she saw that her remark had drawn blood.

Max's eyes were like ice as he fixed her with a piercing stare and every muscle in his face and body was like a spring, coiled to snapping point. 'Are you referring to anyone in particular?'

'Lady Murray,' she burst out, unable to keep the knowledge of his liaison to herself any longer. 'My grandmother told me she was your mistress.'

'Your grandmother was correct. However, the affair ended when I went to America. Are you accusing me of seeking my pleasure else-where?'

'What else am I to think?'

'Don't try to put the blame for any of this on me, Marietta. It is your doing, not mine. What I have to do right now is put some distance be-tween us so that I can try to make some sense out of it. And, yes,' he said with a deep cold savagery, with a desire to hurt her as much as she was hurting him, 'there are numerous beds in London with willing occupants and Claudia is still available to me should I still desire her, so you would do well to consider that during my absence. Am I not being driven to it by my own wife?'

Marietta's cheeks burned from the cruelty of his remark and she was swamped with guilt. He was dismissing her as someone he considered unworthy to be his wife. He wanted to leave her—to be rid of her. She could feel it. And why shouldn't he, something inside her cried accusingly, when he had saddled himself with a wife who refused to bear his children?

Max strode out of the room. Marietta watched him go, her heart crumbling even as the door closed, leaving her heartbroken and bereft, the tears springing to her eyes.

* * *

Not until Max was on the train heading south did he allow his thoughts to drift to his wife and her last heartbreaking words and how his enforced separation would be hurting her. To have implied that he would take another woman to his bed was contemptible, and to take Claudia as his mistress again was out of the question. The gossip created by a renewed liaison between the two of them would be endless, and the humiliation Marietta would suffer as a result of it would be immeasurable.

But he had to put some distance between them. He could not go on living with her as his wife and being unable to touch her, to make love to her, but to divorce her was not to be thought of. Despite his threat, which he knew had hurt her deeply and was not what he had intended, he could not contemplate doing something so cruel to either of them. The grounds of her refusal of conjugal rights in order to prevent the conception of a child would be sufficient to grant him a divorce, but he was damned if he was going to stand up in court and tell the world that his wife refused to share a bed with him.

Why was she doing this? That was an agonising thought and an infuriating one. But only for a minute, for in the purple light of deepening dusk, he couldn't actually believe that a young woman as tender and gentle as she was wouldn't want a child of her own without good reason.

Was she afraid of bearing a child and, if so, why? Or did she genuinely not wish to be a mother? He'd been so wrapped up in his own need, misery and anger that he hadn't even bothered to ask, to get to the bottom of it. It might have been the lulling motion of the train that had this mellowing effect on him, but it seemed to him somehow that for whatever reason she had married him, she had come to care for him deeply. He thought of the short time they had been together as man and wife before the subject of children had driven them apart, of the way they had passed their days in quiet talk and laughter and unbridled passion. No woman alive could have tried to give him as much pleasure as he was giving her if she didn't care for him.

The countryside had changed in the weeks since Marietta's marriage to Max. Autumn had given way to winter and dried leaves carpeted the ground, and as Marietta slipped deeper into the world of Arden, she began to notice the changes in herself, in her own body. At first she couldn't bear to contemplate that her worst nightmare had been realised, that she might be pregnant, but with each new day, each morning when the sickness had her scrambling from her bed and reaching for a bowl, she knew it had to be faced.

She missed Max dreadfully and now wanted him more than ever. His leaving had hurt her deeply. She ached for the warmth and strength of him. Her world was collapsing about her in some horrible, inexplicable way. Max had taken with him all the vitality, all the colour from her life, and there was nothing but emptiness and this new fear in her heart. She was also sick with dread that he might have returned to the arms of his former mistress—and that she had sent him there. She tried to tell herself that he would not do that to her, but her tormented imaginings almost drove her mad.

Everything had gone wrong between them because there had been so many misunderstandings on her part about him and his relationship with Nadine, and because she hadn't been capable of making him understand her irrational, physical fears about bearing a child. Perhaps she would have tried, had she been able to understand them fully herself. What was to be done? All she had was her own fallible strength.

Battered with a torrent of conflicting emotions and self-condemnation, and aware that, having trampled his pride, Max would not come near her unless she made the first move, she realised that to make things right between them her pride was going to have to suffer now. She would not let her fear ruin her life and destroy her chance to have a warm and happy marriage. She would have to go to him and try to explain the best she could her fear of childbirth. Not only that, the mere thought of him enjoying the delights of another woman—especially those of Claudia Murray—was beyond bearing.

With that motivation, she told Yang Ling to pack her bags and arrange for the carriage to take them to the station first thing the following morning. She then wrote her grandmother a letter, informing her that she was to join Max in London.

Chapter Nine

Darkness had settled over London and the lamplighter was making his way down Curzon Street when Marietta finally arrived at the door of Trevellyan House near Regent's Park. Mason, the elderly butler who opened the door, regarded her with courteous enquiry and Marietta immediately made it known who she was. She was suitably impressed with the enormous central hall and colonnaded gallery.

'Is my husband at home, Mason?'

'No, your Grace. The duke is attending a musical evening at Lady Dunaway's residence in Kensington. I don't expect he will be late home since he is leaving early in the morning to spend the day with an old friend in Surrey.'

He handed her a gold-embossed card that

had been delivered two weeks earlier. Marietta turned it over in her hand, seeing the invitation was addressed to the Duke and Duchess of Arden. 'I see. Well, my decision to come to London was a spur-of-the-moment decision. Still...' She bit her lip thoughtfully. After coming all this way, she was impatient to see Max. 'A musical evening, you said, Mason. What a pleasant way to relax following a long and tedious journey. Have someone show me to my rooms and have the carriage brought round.'

'To take you to Kensington, your Grace?'

'Yes,' she replied with a confident smile. 'Since my husband is out enjoying himself I think I shall surprise him.' Which Marietta did the moment she entered Lady Dunaway's elegant mansion, where, contrary to what she had said, Max was not enjoying himself.

Max was seated with a hundred other guests in Lady Dunaway's salon, with his legs crossed and a bland expression on his face. After listening to music by Chopin and Bach for over an hour, he was bored out of his mind and somewhat irritated.

It was during the interval when the musicians and guests paused for refreshments, to stretch their legs and to mingle and indulge in polite conversation, that, with wine glass in hand, Max suddenly found himself confronted by a grinning Lord Toby Basildon and his former mistress, Lady Claudia Murray. Max had it on good authority that Basildon was Claudia's present lover.

'Max, it's good to see you.' Lord Basildon's mocking voice cut through the conversation going on around them. He drew Claudia forwards. 'I'm sure that no introductions are necessary between the two of you.'

Max turned to Claudia and inclined his head slightly. 'Claudia? I trust you are well.'

'Never better,' she replied coolly, not having forgiven him for marrying Marietta Westwood. The humiliation she had suffered at that woman's hands had not gone away.

'Your wife is not with you? Is it not unusual for two people who are so recently married to be at opposite ends of the country?'

'You are at liberty to think so if you wish, Claudia,' Max replied coldly.

At that moment his attention was diverted to a latecomer who had just arrived. She was surrendering her coat to the maid at the door and being greeted by Lady Dunaway, who engaged her in quiet conversation. The glass in Max's hand stopped en route to his mouth when he recognised his wife. Attired in a dress of gold satin with a flat-fronted skirt and drawn over a soft bustle at the back in a complex drapery of pleats and flounces forming a small train and clutching a small gold-silk reticule, she was the most radiant creature present.

After weeks of missing her, seeing her now gave him the most piercing joy of his life to find her here. Leaving her had almost torn him apart. With single-minded determination he had thrown himself into the task of not thinking of her. He'd immersed himself in work, spending hours each day poring over business investments and reports in his study and meeting with business managers and bankers. He worked until it was time to go to bed, where he would stare into the darkness, knowing that close by there were buildings with rooms where many a warm bed waited, and his hunger would grow, but it was not for the ladies who occupied those beds. It was for the memory and the gentle dream of Marietta, his wife. So stricken was he with the innocence of her, that he could not rouse himself to seek relief in someone else's bed.

His thoughts would grow tender as he remembered the golden candlelight upon creamy, silken flesh, still moist from making love, her soft curling hair flowing across a pillow as she slept, and his thoughts brought memories to mind of how those sweet and gentle arms had felt about his neck, and how those full, pink lips had pressed against his and how her warm young body had cleaved to his. She had served his pleasure well, more than any woman before, and from that first moment he had clutched her to him, she had held his every thought so tightly that even in his sleep he could dream of nothing else but her.

As these thoughts beset his mind he would turn over and strike his fist into his pillow in mute frustration. My God! he thought. My wife denies me and my very soul crumbles. She had closed all doors to him but one, and that he had slammed in anger when he had left for London. But in his heart he knew he could not keep away from her much longer. Already he was contemplating his return and what he might do to win her back. I'll bide my time carefully, he had mused, play the suitor all over again and court her tenderly, and then perhaps she would turn to him. It had been late when he fell to sleep with the realisation of his love and new resolve.

And now, what the hell was she playing at, coming to London without notifying him? But then he shouldn't be all that surprised. She had the passion, the intelligence and the courage to dare to do anything.

'My wife has been unavoidably detained,' he said in reply to Claudia's question. 'But she is here now. Excuse me.'

Putting his glass down, Max strode out of the salon to join Marietta. After exchanging a few pleasantries, Lady Dunaway melted away. Max stepped in front of Marietta, neatly isolating them from view of those in the salon and to all appearances he looked like a relaxed gentleman in intimate conversation with his wife.

'Marietta,' he said in an ominously calm tone that belied the leaping fury in his eyes. 'What are you doing here?'

Marietta stared at him. When he had strode through the door, the hall seemed to shrink. He was so tall that she thought he must surely have grown since she had seen him last, but otherwise he was unchanged. There was still the same masterful face, the same silver-grey eyes, the same thick, well-groomed black hair. In formal evening dress—dark tailcoat and trousers, a dove-grey waistcoat, white bow tie and shirt with a winged collar—he was devastatingly handsome. Marietta gazed at him wonderingly, forgetting for a moment all that she had suffered because of his absence.

'When I arrived at the house and Mason told me you were attending a musical evening, since the invitation included us both, I didn't think you would mind if I came.'

'Why should I if Lady Dunaway doesn't? Come into the salon, the music will be starting shortly.'

Placing her hand on his arm for him to escort her into the salon where everyone was craning their necks in curiosity to see them, for it was the first time the Duke and Duchess of Arden had been seen together, they looked in accord, Max just a step behind his wife. Max would have to be blind not to notice the open admiration in the eyes of every male in the room as they settled on his wife. Sheer, unadulterated jealousy tore through him. She was the loveliest woman here, drawing men's attention to her like bees to a flower. She was glorious and his own adoration and need of her was barely under control. He wanted to drag her into his arms and kiss her until she, and he, were breathless. Instead he said, 'I see, Marietta, that you only have to walk into a room to bring the entire male population to their knees.'

A sparkle twinkled in Marietta's eyes as

she glanced at him sideways, a tantalising little smile playing on her soft lips. 'Not quite the entire population, Max,' she said meaningfully. 'But then I would be astonished to find you in such a silly position as on your knees.'

Suddenly Marietta saw Lady Murray standing a little away. Her arms and legs began to tremble from the moment she saw Max's former mistress, in the very same house as Max. Was it coincidence or had they arranged it so? Lady Murray was alone, her partner having disappeared to get her a glass of wine. In sick dread, Marietta felt tears burning the backs of her eyes as Lady Murray fixed her cold eyes on her. Why, she thought, did Lady Claudia Murray have to be so provocatively beautiful, and why did Max have to look so devastatingly handsome tonight, so utterly desirable? Marietta felt the muscles in Max's forearm tense into rigidity and he would have steered her in another direction, but Marietta carried on walking towards the woman who was eyeing her coldly.

The two women regarded each other for a moment with open hostility, the unpleasant events of their previous encounter on both their minds. However, despite Lady Murray's previous relationship with Max, Marietta had said that when they next met she would apologise for her unacceptable behaviour and she had meant it.

'This is my wife, Marietta,' Max said. 'I believe the two of you are already acquainted.'

Every pair of eyes swivelled to them, surprised that the two women were speaking to each other given Lady Murray's previous friendship with the duke.

'Yes, we are,' Claudia said tightly. 'Introductions are not necessary.'

In a state of angry, humiliated pain, though making a concerted effort not to show it, Marietta met Claudia Murray's assessing gaze with quiet composure. 'Lady Murray, I feel an apology is in order.'

'So you admit it, then. You did push me into the fountain.'

'I—might have—brushed against you,' Marietta prevaricated. Despite having quietly admitted the fact to Lady Murray at the time, she was determined not to let the other woman have the upper hand. 'Anyway, however your tumble into the fountain came about; I would like to offer my apologies for any discomfort it may have caused you.'

'What *you* did was most uncalled for,' Claudia protested as Max was about to guide Marietta away.

Marietta fixed her with a level stare. 'I recall you were saying unkind things about my maid. Your malicious comments took me off guard. Because you despised her and because you laughed at her, you paid for it.'

'That Chinese woman is your *maid.*'

'She is also a human being and my friend, but I do not expect you to understand that. You took me off guard that night. I could not help myself.'

'Then you should practise self-control.'

'I couldn't agree more. Unfortunately, I've always been an impulsive and often difficult person of an unpredictable disposition and the despair of all my governesses and my late father.'

A slow, sensual smile curved Claudia's lips as she glanced provocatively at Max. 'I appreciated your support that night, Max. I found it such a relief to have you there.' Her tone of voice carried the implications home.

'I was glad to be of help, Claudia—as any gentleman would,' Max replied coolly, hoping to bypass the storm.

As he turned away, leaning forwards and glaring at him, Claudia hissed, 'You are not forgiven either, Max Trevellyan. You left me to twiddle my thumbs while you sailed off to America.'

Pausing, Max looked at her, his expression hard. 'It was over then, Claudia. I told you. Excuse us. There are people waiting to meet Marietta.'

Minutes later everyone took their seats as the musicians began to play. Max did not leave Marietta's side, but neither did he say much to her or so much as glance at her. He was with her, though, and Marietta clung to that fact as if it were the beginning of the reconciliation she wanted so very badly. She had been tempted to tell him about the pregnancy before the music began, but because of her lingering irritation over Lady Murray she decided this was neither the time nor the place. She would not divulge her childbearing state to her husband until there was more accord between them.

Not until they were in the coach heading for home did he speak.

'Are you going to explain what you are doing here, Marietta?'

'There's nothing to explain,' she replied. 'I simply grew tired of rattling about the house on my own. I thought it was about time I came to savour the delights of London—as you have been doing for the past month.'

'I've spent most of my time working. Parliament is in session at present and I have taken up my seat in the Lords, which keeps me busy.'

'I imagine it does, but you must have had plenty of time to socialise—take this evening, for instance—and I was amazed to find you attending an event with your mistress present.'

Max glanced at her sharply. 'My what?'

'Lover?' Marietta said, her voice hoarse at the indelicacy of asking such a question. She wished she hadn't spoken, except that the hurt was spreading through her like an ache that wouldn't stop hurting. 'Can you promise me that I am the only woman in your life, which is what a wife has every right to expect?'

'There are no other lovers,' Max said impatiently, turning his head and glancing out of the window.

'And you can assure me of that, can you, Max? I am aware it is fashionable for men, even those in high places, to take mistresses, and for wives to turn a blind eye while they do their saintly duty and produce heirs for family continuity.'

Max jerked his head round. 'Heirs? I am surprised to hear that word on your lips, Marietta, since your refusal to give me an heir is part of the reason why I left Arden. If I took a mistress to provide what you deny, then you should not complain.'

'So you do not have a mistress?'

He gave a short laugh. 'I will not answer that. If you can't take my word for it, then you can surmise all you wish. I will not be browbeaten by a chit of a girl to swear on oath. I did that when I married you.'

The carriage drew up outside the house and they went inside.

Max looked at her. 'I've arranged to spend tomorrow with an old friend of mine in Surrey—Sir William Hopkirk—we were at university together. I intend to leave early. I'm sure you will find plenty to occupy your time in my absence. Sleep well.' He stood and watched her walk towards the stairs. Something about her—perhaps it was the slight droop to her shoulders or the way she walked… Whatever it was, on a softer note he called her name. 'Marietta, wait.'

With her hand resting on the newel post she turned and looked at him, waiting for him to speak.

'I hope the time we have been apart has given you time to think things over—as I have—and

Claudia Murray was not in my range—which I gather was what you were trying to ask me in the coach.'

'She wasn't?'

'No.'

She smiled tremulously. 'Thank you, Max,' she whispered simply, and turned and went on up the stairs.

The following morning Marietta ate alone in the breakfast room. Max had left as he had said he would for Surrey. Early afternoon found her accompanied by Yang Ling walking in Regent's Park.

She was distracted when a man suddenly stepped in front of her, a tall, thin, rumpled gentleman in a felt hat.

'Good gracious!' Marietta exclaimed with genuine surprise when she recognised her father's business partner. 'Teddy! What are you doing in London?'

Removing his hat, he inclined his head. His hair was thinning now and the red hue turning white. The year of enforced exile from Hong Kong and heavy drinking and opium smoking in some of the meanest hovels in India had not dealt kindly with Teddy Longford. His health was not good, and the poor condition of his liver often reflected itself in fierce, quicksilver changes of mood. He suffered black depressions of discontent and remorse that laid him low for days at a time, followed by long periods of oblivion when he smoked the opium. He lived mainly by his social wits and his skills at the gaming tables. There was little trace of the irresistible charm, the twinkling golden-brown eyes had faded, and the lopsided smile, ever capable of melting even the chilliest female heart, was more like a leer. It hurt Marietta to see it.

'Walk with me a while, Teddy.'

They fell into step, Yang Ling holding back. The conversation was stilted as they talked about inconsequential things, mainly London and the English climate, and Teddy congratulated her on her marriage to the Duke of Arden, jokingly remarking that out of respect for her title he really should address her as 'your Grace'.

Marietta gave a gurgle of laughter, surprised that after the strains and stresses of the last few weeks she could still laugh. 'Don't you dare, Teddy. Being a duchess makes me feel old and ancient and to be addressed as your Grace by someone who has known me almost all my life is intolerable to me. Tell me what you have been doing since I left Hong Kong.'

'Things became—difficult for me,' Teddy said after a moment.

'How are you, Teddy?'

'In dire straits, I'm afraid. Things haven't been going too well for me since I bought your share of the business. I plan on starting again—in India. There's still a large demand for luxury goods from Europe—and China has developed a strong demand for silver, a commodity your father found difficult to obtain.'

'I hope you aren't looking for sympathy, Teddy, because if so you have come to the wrong person.'

'It wasn't sympathy I had in mind,' he said quietly.

'What, then?'

'A loan, Marietta. I have no difficulty in supplying the necessary commodities, but I'm suffering from a shortage of funds at present. I need some capital. After inheriting the money your father accumulated before we met and the money you got when I bought your share of the business, I was hoping you'd help me out—for old times' sake, you understand.'

'I understand perfectly. So you really came to England to see me.'

'Yes. You're the only person I know who can help me.'

'The only person foolish enough, you mean. If you are short of money now, then you have only yourself to blame. I was shocked when I heard what you had been up to and that you were in serious trouble with the Chinese authorities.'

'I managed to get out of Hong Kong before I could be questioned—but my misdemeanours were no more serious than those of the other traders out there, hoping to make money the best they could.'

Marietta was secretly pleased that he'd avoided trouble and that he hadn't had too rough a time of it. He did look dreadful, his tan having faded to a yellow hue from which all other colour had fled. The lines around his eyes and mouth were chalk white. Prison would have finished him.

'Do you have access to money, Marietta, or is your every penny controlled by your husband?'

'I have my own money, Teddy, but I'm not sure I want to loan you any of it. I doubt very much I would see a return.'

Looking down at his feet, he shook his head with weary dejection. 'Then I am finished. Without money and without reputation, a man is better off dead.'

Marietta stopped and looked at him. Teddy's

financial situation wasn't her problem or her concern. It was his own shady dealings in opium that had got him into this mess. But she couldn't turn away from him. Besides, she had given a great deal of thought to the money she had inherited from her father—a large amount having been obtained by corrupt means. Why, even Max wouldn't touch it. She intended putting some of it to some use, something that would benefit others. She had a project in mind, which was something she would discuss with Max when he was in a more agreeable mood.

'Please don't say that.' She became thoughtful, thinking of her father. What would he have done? What would he want her to do? Would he have refused and sent Teddy on his way after all their years of friendship? He set great store by friendship and Marietta knew he would have given him the money.

'Very well, Teddy,' she said, setting aside her own monumental concerns for the moment, but she loathed giving in to him. She hated the idea of paying him off to make him go away. She loathed herself for the doubt growing inside her about his intention to pay back the loan. 'I will loan you the money—as you said, for old times' sake. Come back to the house with me and I will write you a bank draft. But I am doing it for my father—not for you.'

Teddy's expression didn't alter, but relief flooded his jaundiced eyes. 'I shall be eternally grateful to you, Marietta. Your husband...'

'Is out of town. He's not expected back until this evening.'

On reaching the house Marietta went to her room to write Teddy a bank draft, leaving him in the drawing room. With a strange feeling that Teddy's presence in this house was unwelcome and wanting him gone, she did not offer him refreshment. On the point of handing the bank draft over, she stood perfectly still, her gaze suddenly riveted beyond Teddy to the open doorway.

Feeling cold shock run through her, she saw who stood there. It was Max. His tall, broad-shouldered figure blocked out the light and seemed to fill the whole room. He had appeared too suddenly for her to prepare herself, so the heady surge of pleasure she experienced on seeing him again was clearly evident, stamped like an unbidden confession on her lovely face. But then she sensed his fury and her features closed like a book.

Teddy looked at her with impatience, think-

ing she was about to withdraw her offer of the
loan. Her face was stricken, her eyes fearful as
she stared at the doorway. Teddy turned slowly,
his expression freezing.

'What the hell is going on? I didn't realise my
wife had invited a guest. What are you doing
in my house, Longford?'

Marietta shrank away from Teddy, her eyes
never leaving her husband's brilliant silver-grey
eyes, wide and savagely furious. He was wearing riding clothes and his hair was dishevelled,
as if he had been riding hard. Her first reaction
was cold, numbing fright at the terrible, utter
rage on his face. All that had ever been good-
humoured, teasing and attractive had given way
to hot fury and positive revulsion as he looked
at Teddy.

Completely bewildered by Max's hostility towards Teddy and sensing there was something
between them she knew nothing about, Marietta
tried to soothe over the situation. 'I—I met
Teddy when I was walking in the park, Max.
He—I—had something to give him. He was
about to leave.'

Max's gaze sliced to her. The lightness of his
eyes seemed sheathed in ice, anger fixed his
mouth into a straight line, his temples pulsed
with the rapid beat of his heart. 'Have you any

idea what you have done? This worthless excuse for a man was Nadine's lover. She shamelessly flaunted their affair in front of me. She was a great favourite among the men on the island of Hong Kong—Longford was just one of many.'

'Max—what are you saying?'

'That Nadine spent her life going from bed to bed after we were married. The more the merrier, it would seem.'

Marietta backed away then, deadened with shock at what he had said. 'I'm so sorry, Max. It is plain that your memories of your former marriage are still raw.'

'Small wonder,' he said tightly. He looked again at Teddy, who stood rooted to the spot. 'By God's eyes, Longford,' he said in a voice so low it was a deadly whisper, 'you made a cuckold of me once. Are you now trying to ingratiate yourself with my second wife?'

Marietta gasped. 'Max—that was a terrible thing to say. But Teddy—and Nadine?' She looked at Teddy. 'Is this true, Teddy?'

Teddy nodded, a grim smile twisting his lips. He was eyeing the tall, powerful man warily, bitter hatred in his eyes. 'Like your husband said, Marietta, I was just one of many where Nadine was concerned. She was the most beautiful, corrupt woman I have ever met.'

Marietta remained stricken. 'And the baby?'

Max's expression was one of absolute contempt. 'I didn't know Nadine was pregnant until
the day she lost it. The child wasn't mine. Our
marriage was over. I no longer cared what she
did. At the time she died you were her lover,
Longford, so I imagine the child was yours.'

Marietta moved towards Teddy and looked
at him hard, remembering Nadine's pain. 'The
child was yours, wasn't it, Teddy?' He nodded
ever so slightly, reluctant to admit his guilt,
finding it hard to look into her accusing eyes.
'And when she told you you said you didn't
want it. Which was why she—she… Oh, Teddy,
how could you do that? I remember seeing the
two of you together on several occasions, but I
never imagined you were lovers.' Her eyes were
burning. 'I saw her before she died. She was in
agony, Teddy.' He glared at her. 'You may well
look horrified! It was your doing.'

Marietta was still holding the bank draft.
Teddy looked at it and, afraid that she might
withdraw her offer of the loan, reached out and
slipped it out of her hand. He was relieved when
she didn't try to take it back.

Max's suspicious ice-grey eyes saw, assessed
and understood the transaction. 'What is that?'

'A loan. Teddy needs capital to start again. I agreed to give it to him.'

Max sneered. 'If you want to squander your money on a lame duck, then go ahead. But don't hold your breath for any return. Now get out, Longford. You have finished here.'

'No, don't go yet, Teddy,' Marietta said quickly. 'My husband may have finished with you, but I haven't. There are things I have to ask you, things I must know, things I have a *right* to know—about my father.'

Max stepped forwards, deeply concerned about what Longford was about to divulge and anxious about how it would affect Marietta. 'Are you sure you want to know?'

Marietta looked at him. His anger was so intense that she felt the blood rush to her cheeks and then drain away completely as her own anger came to the fore. 'No, I am not sure, but my father has made it so, so I must. I'm older now and can judge people for myself, but back then I could hardly go around asking people if they happened to know whether my father was respectable or not. I loved him dearly, but I always knew he was no saint. I really don't know anything and I have to know. I *need* to know.'

Max could imagine the ice spreading through her veins, her nerves being stripped raw. He knew her brain would refuse to accept it at first, but she had to know everything, no matter how distasteful it would be.

Marietta fixed her gaze on Teddy, her eyes hard and unrelenting. 'Teddy, I will have the truth. Tell me. I know you traded in opium and that you only avoided going to prison by the skin of your teeth. How involved was my father? He was involved, wasn't he?'

Teddy met her punishing gaze and then looked away. He couldn't bear to look at her, and she would not let him go until she had wrung the truth out of him. 'Monty was involved up to his neck. He took to trading in opium when times were bad—we both did. He enjoyed it. Danger and beating the customs men seemed to excite him.'

'Even though it meant social ostracism if he was found out?'

'Even then. His ability to charm was his stock-in-trade, but when it was leaked before he died, you must have noticed how invitations to this and that began to dwindle. His social life was ruined.'

'Yes, I do remember,' Marietta said quietly. 'Had he lived it would eventually have killed him. Although once opium had him in its grip, he would never have escaped that. Oh, I know he smoked it—perhaps not until after he died, but I remember the signs—the unpredictable moods, eyes with pinpoint pupils, the way he picked at his food.'

Teddy nodded and said absently, 'That and…'

Marietta glanced at him sharply. 'And what, Teddy? Tell me. I am no longer the ignorant, prudish young girl you knew in Hong Kong. I am a married woman now and not as naïve as you think.'

'His—illness…'

'His heart?' she prompted. 'Is that what you mean?'

He shook his head. 'Your father—he enjoyed…'

'Other women—even while my mother was alive.' She moved closer to him, her eyes cold and unrelenting. 'He was unfaithful, wasn't he? Is that what you are trying to tell me, Teddy?'

He nodded. 'He was faithful for a while—but your mother's health forced him to seek… He was clean for a time…'

'*Forced*? There is such a word as abstinence, Teddy. And clean? Will you kindly explain what you mean by that?'

Embarrassed to be speaking of so delicate a matter to Marietta, he looked away.

'Marietta, are you sure you want to know

this?' Max said. 'Your father is dead. It is no longer important how he behaved in private.'

Marietta turned her burning eyes on her husband. 'But it is to me, Max. What I am hearing is significant to my future—to *our* future, and may well go some way to resolving—or at least allowing me to understand my fear of...' She fell silent. His eyes locked on to hers, understanding exactly what she was getting at.

Max looked at Teddy. 'Go on,' he said coldly. 'Tell her.'

'Almost half of the men who go to Hong Kong catch—something.'

'Contagious? I get your meaning, Teddy. Yang Ling has been my maid and confidant for a good many years. She has taught me a great deal about the goings-on in the poor quarters of Hong Kong, about what men get up to away from their wives, and the terrible diseases that are endemic and do not discriminate between men, women and children. What you are saying is that my father went to brothels—visited the flower girls?—who are just prostitutes when all is said and done.' She saw Max go rigid at her use of the word, but she ignored him. This was too important for her to think of phrasing her words to suit him now. Teddy nodded. 'Even though he loved my mother?'

'The brothels are full of men who love their wives. Monty—suffered three bouts and took the cure.'

It was much as Marietta had expected and her heart went out to her mother. Had Marietta known any of this she would have screamed out her fear and misery and horror. As it was, she stared at Teddy's taut, watchful face and said, 'What was it, Teddy? I know it was more serious than a common cold or consumption of the lungs. Yang Ling has told me all about gonorrhoea and syphilis and how they can affect an unborn child. Was it one of those that killed him, or some other disease which contaminates a man in a brothel? Whichever disease he contracted would have made little difference to my mother. They are both disgusting and dangerous—and fatal. He infected her, didn't he? And through her their children. Did she know?'

He nodded. 'She knew. It was—syphilis.'

The brief statement, so bluntly spoken, struck Marietta like a hammer blow. Her body seemed to sag, robbing her of her physical substance, a stricken expression on her face. 'Syphilis,' she echoed in a small voice.

'A common enough affliction,' Teddy said.

She glared at him. 'For some, perhaps. Not for a gently reared woman like my mother. My father handed her a death sentence. It was fortunate the babies were born dead—but not so fortunate for my mother.' She didn't look at Max, but she would have seen he was listening intently as he began to piece together what troubled her, and with it at last there came understanding. 'Before I left Hong Kong I went with Yang Ling to visit an orphanage in the poor quarter, where there are children born as a result of syphilis and cast out by their parents as freaks. Some of them are quite mad, others horribly deformed, and some so sick they will die of it. It's a terrible affliction to give a child.'

'Monty would not like to hear you speaking like this. Whatever happened, it was not intentionally done.'

Marietta stared at him, hating him now. 'How can you say that? Of course it was. He wasn't dragged kicking and screaming into a brothel.' She made a dismissive gesture with her hand. 'Get out, Teddy. I don't want to see you again—and from the look of you I don't think I shall.'

Teddy was chastened when he left, still clutching the bank draft, but Marietta didn't believe for one moment that it would last. As soon as he reached India he would head for the nearest brothel and opium den. Getting up, she went to the hearth and gazed down into the glowing embers of the fire. Her salvation was in her own hands. Only she could cure herself of what had become a virtual obsession.

The silence inside the room was profound now that Teddy had gone. Marietta looked at Max. His granite features were an impenetrable mask, and she was too nervous to notice anything about his mood except that he was tensed.

'When are you going to tell me the real reason that has brought you to London?' he asked quietly.

'I came to see you.'

'So, is it just a visit? Do you intend returning to Arden, or are you here to stay for the time I am here?'

Marietta drew a tortured breath, trying not to show her trepidation. 'It is not a visit, Max, I have come to stay. I would have thought the purpose was obvious.'

'Not to me.'

'I've come to explain why I behaved as I did as best I can—which I am finding extremely difficult in the light of what Teddy has just told me, and I sincerely hope you will not make it more so. You came back from seeing your friend earlier than I expected.'

'It was fortunate that I did. Would you have

told me about Longford coming here if I hadn't?'

'Since I was completely oblivious to the fact that there was any kind of hostility between the two of you and that he was Nadine's lover then, yes, I would,' she replied truthfully.

'And what are your feelings now you know?'

'Shock. I really had no idea that Teddy and your wife...' Her words trailed off into silence, for she could understand if he didn't wish to speak of something that caused him pain. What he told her next shocked her to the core.

'How could you?' he said, thrusting his hands deep into his pockets and staring down into the hearth in which a warming fire burned. 'I didn't know Nadine was pregnant. The child wasn't mine. She spent her life going from bed to bed after we were married. I didn't realise how much pressure her family had put on her to marry me. She wanted to marry someone else, someone her parents didn't approve of. As a result she resented me as well as her parents. Our marriage was over before we went to Hong Kong. I no longer cared what she did.'

Marietta stared at him in disbelief. 'But—I thought you loved her.'

Max's face became taut, his eyes hard and when he spoke his voice was brittle. 'Loved her? Dear God, I never hated anyone the way I hated her.'

'Then why did you marry her?'

'I was dazzled by her looks and in her case the saying is true that beauty is only skin deep. It didn't take me long to find that out. In the beginning she gave me her body for everything she could wheedle out of me—money, jewels that would please a queen. She took everything I gave her and repaid me by bestowing her body on any man who invited her into his bed. Yes, I hated her and I've felt the guilt and the shame of it ever since she died. I wished it on her a thousand times and yet when she died I tried to be sorry for her, but I couldn't.'

Marietta became still, like a statue of marble. Any colour left in her face drained away. She was totally, utterly disorientated. She put up a trembling hand to her mouth and felt her body shiver.

Turning his head and observing her reaction and the extreme shock of his disclosure mirrored in her eyes, at any other time Max would have gone to her and swept her into his arms, but now he could only stand and look at her. 'Did you think I actually loved her?' She nodded dumbly. 'Then I must have been a better actor than I thought,' he uttered bitterly.

If anything could have brought life back to Marietta's body that did. She wanted to hit him, to deal him a blow that would make him feel like she had felt all these weeks. Without a pang of remorse her anger sprang, fully roused, to the surface and she was glad of it, since it swept away the memories of their nights of love. It swamped the hurtful love which seemed to multiply with every heartbeat, gripping her in its painful, unwanted embrace. There was nothing more agonising than a love unreturned.

'How could you,' she cried. 'You've let me believe all this time that you were pining for your first wife. That you still loved her even though she was mouldering in her grave and all the while...'

It was Max's turn to be disorientated now. He was shocked by her verbal attack on him and bewildered by the ferocity of her anger. Her back had stiffened as though her spine had been turned to steel and her eyes, which had been a soft shade of green, flashed to a glittering, burning of a wild animal Max had once had in his gun sights in India. His own anger erupted, emotions were high, charged with some power which captured them both and his reaction was instinctive.

'Where the hell did you get that idea from?'

'From you. How many times have you refused to mention her name, and if I did I would see you gazing soulfully into the distance…'

'In the name of God, Marietta, if I gazed anywhere it was not soulful—never that, not when I thought of Nadine.'

'How else was I to see it?' Marietta's face was scarlet now and her eyes flashed with fury.

His voice was ragged with rage that was hazardous, but when he took a step towards her she did not flinch. 'You foolish woman, you must have known—could you not see how it was with me when I married you, what you meant to me?'

'How could I? I'm not a mind reader, Max. I thought you loved her, that I would always be second-best to you. How could you make me feel that way?'

'You exaggerate, Marietta…'

'Liar,' she cried. She was becoming hysterical and her hysteria suddenly brought Max at last to the realisation of what was happening between them, the words they had thrown at each other and their meaning.

'If I gave you reason to believe I loved Nadine, then I apologise,' he said stiffly. 'But what of you, Marietta? When I married you my feelings for you went way beyond anything

I had ever felt for Nadine. But those feelings meant sharing, and that, it would appear, is where everything began to go so dreadfully wrong. You shut me out and I was unable to understand why. Are you ready to explain?'

Marietta swallowed and nodded. 'I will try—but you must bear with me. You see the only knowledge I have of childbearing is of pain and blood. I was there when my mother suffered three miscarriages. I was young—too young to understand what was happening. After the last time, when she died, I swore I would never have children if I had to suffer like that to bring them into the world. I know that some illnesses are inherited from one's parents and I truly believed I had inherited my mother's inability to bear children.'

'Your mother gave birth to you, Marietta—a perfectly healthy girl.'

'Yes, I know, which confused me as I grew up. I thought if she could have me, then why not another healthy child? How could I possibly have known then that it was my father who had contaminated her?'

'And now you do know.'

She nodded, swallowing down the tears that threatened. 'How could he? How could he do that to my mother? She was such a gentle, caring, loving woman. He must have known, he must have. How could he not? But all he did was take his pleasure where he found it in his own warm, amiable and unthinking way.' She turned and looked at Max. 'My grandmother knows nothing of this and I would like to keep it that way. It would break her heart.'

'Of course. I understand.'

'Thank you. I now realise it was through no fault of my mother's that she failed to produce another healthy child. More than anything I wanted to have a baby to love and cherish, but the fear was constant. The long agony of the birth of my mother's babies merged insensibly with the tortured memories of Nadine's loss. It was something I could not put into words. My mind and brain recoiled from it. My mother suffered her first miscarriage when she was barely into her sixth month. When she went into labour the second time it was blessedly short, but it almost killed her. The last time— there was so much blood—she was in so much pain—I didn't know what to do. Her health was always delicate—but that alone did not kill her. I realise now after what Teddy told me that she had syphilis.'

'I'm sorry, Marietta, but it does appear so.' Max realised she was terrified, that the memory of her mother's miscarriages followed by Nadine's abortion had taken possession of her mind—the fear in the act of begetting and the tragedy of its end, for she fully believed that, like her mother, she too would miscarry. 'If only you had told me this at the beginning I would have made things easier for you, been considerate and understanding of your fears. I would never have left you. I have enough experience with life—and women—to be able to handle any problem of that sort.'

'I couldn't tell you. I was too ashamed. I didn't know how to. It's not the kind of thing a woman discusses with her husband. As young as I was, the memories and the fear left their mark, I'm afraid. The fear of having to suffer what my mother did has tortured me for so long I could not think of marriage without feeling horror at getting with child. Which was partly the reason why marriage to you seemed like the answer to my prayers.'

Max leaned his shoulder against the mantelshelf, hands in pockets, looking across the room at her. 'And now?'

After a brief, faintly smiling silence, Marietta swept away once and for all the trouble that for so many weeks had divided them, the trouble that Max had found himself still fearing to mention. Slowly she walked towards him, her eyes never leaving his as she stood in front of him. They were soft and warm and full of all the love she carried in her heart for this man.

'Despite everything, I've missed you so much. I've been so miserable without you. Even if I hadn't already reached the conclusion that my fears weighed very lightly in the balance against love, Teddy's disclosure would have settled it. I was never afraid of love, only of its consequences. I love you, Max. There are no reservations.'

'What about regrets?'

'No regrets, Max. And I shall be very happy to prove it. So would you please hold me now?'

Max's arms closed around her with stunning force. 'God help me if you don't mean it,' he warned fiercely, 'because I'll never let you go or be parted from you again. At this moment, I can't possibly imagine how I could love you more than I do right now, or, for that matter, have loved you since you fell off that damned horse at my feet.' Holding her from him, he touched her chin, turning her face up to his. 'First and foremost it is you I want, Marietta. A child would be a bonus.'

Marietta searched his face, her eyes wide and uncertain, then she smiled as she laid a hand upon her stomach and for the first time her lips spoke of the matter which had haunted her of late, but no longer. 'I think you will have your bonus fairly soon, Max,' she whispered, 'in approximately seven months' time, in fact.'

Max stared at her in stunned disbelief, an array of fleeting, conflicting emotions crossing his face. His concern for her was sharp, and then he pulled her into his arms once more. 'My God, Marietta!' he said, his voice sharp with dawning alarm. 'This is just what you didn't want. How do you feel about it? Are you displeased?'

Marietta closed her eyes and shook her head, feeling his warm breath on her face. 'No. It pleases me, Max. Truly. I have suffered enough because of my memories. I have to put my fears behind me now.'

Max was quietly jubilant with her condition—in fact, he was euphoric, believing that with the birth would finally come the curtailing of her fears about bearing a child. When he took her in his arms his mouth was dry and his hands shook and all his senses were completely occupied with her, as though she were a little girl in need of someone to care for her.

'I need you, Max,' she whispered against his chest. 'I don't think I can manage this on my own.'

Her confession wrenched his heart and his

arms tightened around her, but then he held her from him. He stared at her for a moment in wonder at the emotion he saw and then his face flickered with amusement. 'I think you under-estimate yourself, Marietta. I think you will manage very well. But worry not, my love,' he murmured, lovingly cupping her face between his hands. 'I have no intention of going any-where. You will have the finest doctors money can buy, and I shall be with you every step of the way. Have you any preference as to the gen-der of the child?' he asked tentatively.

'It would be nice if we had a boy to continue the Trevellyan dynasty,' Marietta explained. 'After that, whether girl or boy, I'll be grateful for whatever will be born to us. As long as they are healthy, that is all that matters.'

The tinkling chimes of the clock on the man-tel stirred Marietta from the depths of sleep. Lying in the curve of Max's long body, she lis-tened to the delicate notes until finally the fifth note heralded the dawn. Hoping for at least an-other three hours before having to leave this warm bed, she nestled more closely against her husband, placing soft kisses on his chest and his sheltering arm under which she lay. As was Max's preference, she was naked, as was he.

A smile curved her lips as her fingers slowly plied the firmness of his flesh and moved over the furring of dark hair on his chest and felt the slight increase in the steady beat of his heart, the rippling of his powerful chest muscles when she slid her hand a little lower.

Max felt it as a flame racing uncontrollably through his veins. He half-laughed, half-groaned as he stirred beneath her questing fingers. Propping himself on his elbow, he met her tender gaze as he peered down into her face. There was a devilish gleam in his eyes. 'How does it feel to know you can make my body respond to your slightest touch? You can take pride in having such power over me. I can find a reason for joy in it.'

Reaching up, Marietta threaded her arms around his neck, pressing herself to the full length of his hard, unyielding contours and kissed his lips, feeling the warm smoothness of them. Max groaned, his mouth opening passionately over hers, kissing and caressing her with gentle, skilful hands. Marietta had a feeling of pride, drugging, delirious and quite wonderful.

'I want you,' he whispered against her parted lips. 'I want you quite badly, my love.'

Sensitive to her pregnancy, Max's lovemaking had taken on a whole new dimension to before their separation. He roused her until she was delirious with wanting him, and then he loved her with painstaking gentleness, pleasurably and unbearably prolonging the moment of joyous release, providing Marietta with the reassurance that such a tender invasion of her body could not hurt the child growing inside her.

Epilogue

Marietta's child was born at Arden Hall. Max, who had been a pillar of strength for her during pregnancy, paced the room next door like a caged animal while Lady Wingrove sat and calmly waited for her great-grandchild to come into the world. She was quietly confident that all would go well despite Marietta's mother, her dear daughter, having died in childbirth. Why it had happened was a mystery to her, but it was not unusual. Her daughter's health had always been fragile and women died in childbirth far too often.

Her confidence paid off. With the doctor present and assisted by Yang Ling, Marietta's son was born following a brief labour and a relatively easy birth—far less painful than

Marietta had imagined and dispelling any remaining fears regarding the terrors of childbirth. After all the years of recoiling from it, of rejecting it, when her infant son was placed in her arms, she could scarcely bear to be parted from him.

Max was as besotted as she was by the little mite whose official name was James Alexander Trevellyan. Marietta watched her husband as he strolled around the room, the plump, milky baby in his arms. He was distracted for a moment from his doting contemplation of the tiny fascinating little creature who was not yet an hour old when he looked at his wife in her nest of pillows, her eyes deep and tired in her pale face and his own softened with love.

'I'm so happy I gave you a son,' she said, smiling sleepily.

Max placed the sleeping infant on the bed beside her and, swallowing audibly, he smoothed her tousled curls off her cheek. 'Thank you, my love,' he said helplessly, his voice still raw from the terror he had lived through when her pains had started. He leaned down and covered her mouth with his own, his tender kiss eloquent of love and profound relief that she was well.

'He's so beautiful,' she said when he finally lifted his lips from hers.

Reaching down, Max touched the tiny hand with his finger, then he glanced at Marietta. 'He seems so tiny.'

She laughed lightly. 'Not for long. Babies grow so quickly. He'll be a little man before you know it.' Taking his hand, she looked up at him. 'Have you given any thought to what we talked about—about using some of my money to open an orphanage in Hong Kong? You said as soon as the birth was over we would discuss it.'

His smile became a puzzled frown. Marietta was right. They had talked about it, but he had insisted they wait until their child was born. 'What? Now? Can it not wait until you are up on your feet?'

'No, Max. I want to set things in motion as soon as possible. I do so want to put that money to some good and there are so many children in need. Besides, it will be nice for Yang Ling to visit her family. She can talk of nothing else.'

Max took her hand and held it. 'As a matter of fact I've given the matter a great deal of thought. I know how much you want this. Would it help if we went out to Hong Kong— on an extended visit—on the understanding that we wait until our son is a few months old, of course?'

Marietta's grateful green eyes crinkled responsively before her eyelids began to droop sleepily. 'Of course. That would be perfect. Thank you, Max. I knew you would understand which is why I love you so much.'

Marietta drifted into a contented slumber, her long lashes forming two crescent shadows on her cheeks. Max stared at her sleeping in his arms. He observed the shifting shadows in the room, knowing the special kind of peace that only a loving woman could give her husband.

* * * * *

So you think you can write?

It's your turn!

Mills & Boon® and Harlequin® have joined forces in a global search for new authors and now it's time for YOU to vote on the best stories.

It is our biggest contest ever—the prize is to be published by the world's leader in romance fiction.

And the most important judge of what makes a great new story?

YOU—our reader.

Read first chapters and story synopses for all our entries at
www.soyouthinkyoucanwrite.com

**Vote now at
www.soyouthinkyoucanwrite.com!**

Have Your Say

You've just finished your book.
So what did you think?

We'd love to hear your thoughts on our
'Have your say' online panel
www.millsandboon.co.uk/haveyoursay

- 🌹 Easy to use
- 🌹 Short questionnaire
- 🌹 Chance to win Mills & Boon® goodies